YAROOH!

A Feast of Frank Richards

PRESENTED BY GYLES BRANDRETH

EYRE METHUEN
LONDON

This collection
First published in 1976 by Eyre Methuen Ltd
11 New Fetter Lane, London EC4
Introductory essays: 'I say you fellows' and
'Oh Crikey!'
Copyright © 1976 Gyles Brandreth
Stories and poems by Charles Hamilton © 1976 Una
Hamilton-Wright

Filmset and printed in Great Britain
by BAS Printers Limited, Wallop, Hampshire
ISBN 0 413 34410 X

Books By Gyles Brandreth

ALADDIN
CINDERELLA
MOTHER GOOSE
DISCOVERING PANTOMIME
I SCREAM FOR ICE CREAM
BRANDRETH'S PARTY GAMES
BRANDRETH'S BEDROOM BOOK
BRANDRETH'S CHRISTMAS BOOK
BRANDRETH'S BOOK OF WAITING GAMES
COMPLETE BOOK OF HOME ENTERTAINMENT
GAMES FOR TRAINS, PLANES & WET DAYS
THE GENERATION QUIZ BOOK
SCRAMBLED EXITS
KNIGHT BOOK OF PARTY GAMES
KNIGHT BOOK OF SCRABBLE
KNIGHT BOOK OF CHRISTMAS FUN
KNIGHT BOOK OF EASTER FUN
KNIGHT BOOK OF HOLIDAY FUN & GAMES
KNIGHT BOOK OF HOSPITAL FUN & GAMES
KNIGHT BOOK OF FUN & GAMES FOR A RAINY DAY
KNIGHT BOOK OF FUN & GAMES FOR JOURNEYS
KNIGHT BOOK OF MAZES
DOMINO GAMES & PUZZLES
NUMBER GAMES & PUZZLES
PAPER & PENCIL GAMES & PUZZLES
GAMES & PUZZLES FOR COINS & MATCHES
THE ROYAL QUIZ BOOK
HOTCHPOTCH
CREATED IN CAPTIVITY

CONTENTS

I SAY YOU FELLOWS!

— BY GYLES BRANDRETH —

Frank Richards was probably the most prolific writer the world has ever known. In a career that lasted longer than the reign of Queen Victoria, the undisputed Master of the schoolboy saga wrote over 7,000 stories under twenty-eight different pen-names for several dozen different papers and magazines. From Latin verses to cowboy adventures, from melodramas to romances, from thrillers to television scripts, his total output was in excess of 72,000,000 words—and that's according to the *conservative* estimate of the *Guinness Book of Records*. At the age of thirty he was writing the equivalent of a novel a week. At the age of eighty he was still producing a quarter of a million words a year. The outputfulness was terrific!

Frank Richards' real name was Charles Harold St John Hamilton. He was born at 15 Oak Street, Ealing, Middlesex, on 8th August 1876, the sixth child in a family of five brothers and three sisters. The household seems to have been solid and respectable, belonging to the impoverished middle-class. We know that Frank Richards thought a lot of his mother, but very little of his father ('he was mostly a decorative ornament who never did much work'[1]), a journalist and one-time stationer and bookseller who died when Richards was only seven. Apart from that, we know almost nothing of the Hamilton household. In later years, Frank Richards always rebuffed, and gave the impression that he rather resented, any inquiries about his background. Questions about his schooling he found particularly distasteful: 'We can wash that one out'[2] was his stock response when the subject was mooted. His reticence is explained, of course, by the fact that he didn't go to the sort of Public School he depicted in all his most famous stories. He was educated privately to be sure (apparently at Thorn House, 'a school for young gentlemen' in Ealing, and elsewhere), but not, very definitely not, at an old foundation like Greyfriars.

Frank Richards' formal education ceased and his writing career began in 1893, when he was just seventeen. Once launched (and he was paid the handsome fee of five guineas for his first published story) he never looked back. For sixty-eight years he sat at his typewriter (and for forty of those years it was the *same* typewriter), churning out story after story. He almost never worked from a draft and very rarely needed to correct anything he had written. Out it poured, ream upon ream of closely typed foolscap, almost always effortless, almost always entertaining.

In the first decade of his life as a professional author, adventure stories—with a *penchant* for the piratical—were his speciality. They appeared in a variety of papers, most notably in the many comics published by George Trapps and George Holmes. Frank Richards cut his teeth in the pages of *Picture Fun*, *Smiles*, *Vanguard*, *World's Comic* and *Funny Cuts*, but he found fame (and a fortune of sorts) in the pages of *The Gem* and *The Magnet*.

The Amalgamated Press launched *The Gem* in March 1907 and *The Magnet* in February 1908. They were destined to

become the best-loved and best-known of all the boys weeklies. And Frank Richards was destined to be their principal (and practically their only) contributor. *The Gem* featured St Jim's (a school created for *Pluck* in 1906) and the endless adventures of Tom Merry & Co. *The Magnet* featured Greyfriars (a school that first appeared in *Smiles* in 1907) and the doings of Harry Wharton & Co.—to say nothing of that fat, frabjous, froozling fraud, Billy Bunter, who began life as a minor walk-on, but ended up swamping the stage.

Although he created many other schools (Rookwood in the *Boys' Friend* and Cliff House for girls in the *Schoolfriend*, for example) and invented many other characters (the Rio Kid in the *Popular* and Ken King of the Islands in *Modern Boy*, for example), nothing else that Frank Richards ever did managed to equal the popularity of his work for *The Gem* and *The Magnet*. Both papers ran for thirty-two years (with Frank Richards writing the bulk of almost every issue) and would perhaps have run on forever if the Second World War hadn't intervened. In the issue of 18th May 1940 *The Magnet* boasted: 'The jolly old *Magnet* will still play an important part in the country by appearing every week with its high-class stories which have done so much to kill the black-out blues.' Brave words, but they had a dying fall. The paper shortage, which had already killed *The Gem*, now despatched *The Magnet*. The issue of 18th May 1940 was the last.

Frank Richards was daunted, but not defeated. The war years were certainly his leanest, but once they were over he found himself, to his own amazement and delight, on the brink of a Richards boom. The boys' weeklies might be dead and buried, but there were now fresh fields to conquer, new schools to invent, old ones to revive. Frank Richards started writing books. He wrote books about old friends (Tom Merry & Co., Jimmy Silver & Co.), he wrote books about new friends (Jack of All Trades, the fellows of Felgate), above all he wrote books about Bunter. During the last fifteen years of his life Frank Richards wrote thirty-eight books about Billy Bunter and looked on, incredulously, as the Fat Owl of the Remove became a star of stage and screen. There were Bunter annuals and Bunter cartoon strips, there was Bunter on record, Bunter on the radio, Bunter on TV, even Bunter 'live on stage' in the West End. It was extraordinary and exciting and it ensured that when Bunter's creator, who was by now something of a celebrity, passed away on Christmas Eve in 1961, he died a happy man.

His career was highly successful. It was also fairly straightforward. It had its ups and downs, of course, but none of them were over-dramatic. He was often tempted to tell his editors to go to hell, but he only succumbed to the temptation once. On the whole, he viewed his employers with suspicion (the offices and staff of the Amalgamated Press were known as 'the menagerie') and regarded them with downright contempt whenever they engaged a substitute writer to pen a story under one of his pseudonyms. Since there was a limit even to his output and he was often abroad and occasionally unwell, it was something that had to be done, although something he could never forgive them for doing.* He felt plagued by these hapless substitute writers right up to the end. In 1954 he wrote to a friend:

'Have you come across Gilbert Harding's latest: a dull and prosy book called *Treasury of Insult*. The good man evidently thinks he can cash in on his reputation as the most disagreeable crank in the country. It has pleased him to put in what he alleges to be a quote from a Bunter story. This was NOT written by me, and I am asking for an explanation. It is possible, I suppose, that it was written by some plagiarist: it must have been, if ever it appeared in print at all: but I am at least going to make the malicious rat prove that it did appear in print.'[3]

Curiously, Richards was not much more charitable in his attitude to the many artists who illustrated his work, although he did reserve a special spot of affection for C. H. Chapman, the best-known of all the Bunter artists. He didn't feel illustrations enhanced his work a bit and he was even a little jealous of his illustrators. When Leonard Shields, one of the best of *The Magnet* artists, died in 1949, the report of his death in the *Sunday Express* carried the headline 'Bunter Artist Leaves £67,902', which prompted this churlish letter to the Editor from Frank Richards:

'Mr Leonard Shields, who left £67,902, did not create Billy Bunter, even as an artist. He was the creator, as artist, of my other character, Bessie Bunter. The character of Billy Bunter in *The Magnet* was created by me as author and by Arthur Clarke as artist.** Whether Mr Shields was one of the many artists who drew Billy Bunter after Arthur Clarke's death I do not know ... It is good news that the artist was able to save 'thousands'. He had better luck than the author, who is still under the necessity of kicking for a livelihood at getting on for eighty.'

Frank Richards was still 'kicking for a livelihood' at eighty-five, but not because he had been poorly paid for his labours in the past. Before the war he had been earning not less than £5,000 a year and probably a good deal more. In one of his letters to George Foster he reveals that he was paid £200 for the last four of *The Magnet* stories, and a fee of £50 per story, given his incredible output, suggests a very acceptable income indeed.

Frank Richards undoubtedly earned a lot of money, but he was never a rich man because he always spent as much as he had, and often a little bit more besides. 'Monte Carlo was my spiritual home ... I loved the casinos.'[1] And no doubt they loved him too, 'for seldom had Frank so much as a five

---

*Frank Richards actually wrote about 1,380 of the total 1,683 Greyfriars stories in *The Magnet*. He wrote roughly two-thirds of the St Jim's stories in *The Gem*. In all some 35 substitute writers were used.

** His petulance got the better of him. In fact, Hutton Mitchell was the first Bunter artist and C. H. Chapman drew the first Bessie Bunter.

franc piece left when he quitted the Rooms'.[4]

Gambling was his only vice. He was not a heavy drinker, though he enjoyed brandy, whisky and wine, especially Moselle. He was not a heavy smoker, though he loved his pipe, especially towards the end of his life. And he was most emphatically not a womanizer, though reading between the lines of his austere and unrevealing autobiography one gets the impression there was once a little American miss who genuinely caught his eye. He coyly called her 'Miss N.Y.', but their brief encounter hardly counts as a *grande passion*. 'No "inexpressive she" ever fell in love with Frank, so far as he knows. Certainly Miss N.Y. didn't.'[4]

On the whole, he was not at ease with women. He wasn't that much more relaxed in the company of men. Children and elderly spinsters he never minded! He had his eccentricities (the dressing gown, the carpet slippers, the unconvincing toupée*) and he had his depressions (when he was turned down for service in the Great War on grounds of health; when he became convinced that his head was too big for his body and agonized over his 'deformity'; when he had kidney trouble and had to cut down his work-load by a third); but he was far from being the unhappy schizophrenic some suppose. Certainly he preferred the persona and the name of Frank Richards to the background and the name of Charles Hamilton, but since the former had looked after him so well for so long it's hardly surprising.

Throughout his life Frank Richards was sustained by a fundamental optimism and a fundamental faith. With the gambler's conviction that his luck's about to turn, he was forever hopeful. Even at the outbreak of the Second World War, when *The Magnet* and *The Gem* folded, the value of his shares dropped from 30/- to 3/6d, and he was forced to leave his house in Kent with the evacuation of the coastal zone, he managed to keep going. 'It was rather hard to be left

---

* Later replaced by a much more becoming velvet skull-cap.

stranded at that age. I took a house in Hampstead Garden Suburb, and all those six years I used to go to my desk each morning and write. I did a lot of hard work, but there was very little published. I was rather on the rocks, but I kept going. However, I have always been lucky, most of all in having a natural buoyancy. I did not let the situation affect my spirits much.'

After the war, both his spirits and his finances took a turn for the better, thanks, in large measure, to the revival of interest in the most glorious of all his creations, William George Bunter. The Fat Owl, who was technically 76 by the time his creator died, made his first (and uncharacteristically modest) appearance in *The Magnet* of 15th February 1908, but he was conceived some years before that. The story of his genesis is an intriguing one:

'Billy Bunter was invented—if you can call it invented— as far back as 1899. I had to see an editor then and I took him several sketches. Among them was Bunter. And he looked them all over and chose something else, so I slipped Bunter back into my coat pocket and that was that. And he remained in cold storage for nearly nine years. And then one day the *Magnet* editor called me up to the office and told me he was starting a new paper and I was to write for it. And I said I would and did. And then when I was doing the first number, I remembered my old Bunter, so I just inserted him in the first story—but he was a very minor character to begin with . . .

'Bunter is a combination of three persons. His circumference was borrowed from an editor: he overflowed the arms of his armchair and how he ever got into that chair and out again I never knew! But his circumference struck me very strongly and I handed it on to Bunter. One was a relative of mine who used to peer at me through spectacles like an owl. That is where he got his specs. And another was another relative who was always expecting a cheque that never arrived, and in the mean time was anxious to borrow a pound.

Top left: Frank Richards' favourite armchair and his library of 'classics' at Rose Lawn his house in Kingsgate, near Broadstairs in Kent.

Top right: A middle-aged Frank Richards, without toupée or skull cap.

Bottom left: 'The Old Remington', the typewriter Frank Richards used for forty years.

Bottom right: Frank Richards in his eighties, complete with skull cap, pipe and chess set.

That became Bunter's postal order . . .

'Bunter is short, plump, plump cheeks, ruddy cheeks, big pair of spectacles, round spectacles with little round eyes behind them, and he rolls instead of walking. His fingers are always sticky, and he often gropes in sticky pockets with sticky fingers for a coin which he thinks he may have forgotten, but which isn't there. He is not very fond of washing. He *does* wash, but the other boys often describe it as a "catlick". He thinks he is a very bold fellow, and occasionally he does show pluck. He has, occasionally, done quite doughty deeds. He doesn't go seeking danger, but once or twice has faced up to it quite boldly . . .

'Bunter is certainly the stupidest boy in the Remove, but he has rather a gift of cunning. He is simple, but at the same time a little sly. Bunter wanders from the truth without realising what he is doing. He doesn't realise that he is a liar. He is very indignant if his word is doubted, very indignant indeed. He *thinks* he is a very fine fellow. In fact, he thinks that he is really the only decent fellow at Greyfriars, and all the rest are more or less beasts!'[2]

The world of Greyfriars, totally unreal and utterly unlike any Public School that ever existed, was the world Frank Richards liked best. 'It is a life of innocence. It's as things *should* be. It is no good saying that they are exactly like that because we know they are not, but it's as things should be and *might* be.'[2]

Frank Richards wasn't very modern—why on earth should he have been: he was born in the year of Custer's Last Stand! He couldn't see how a school could be run without the use of the cane. He didn't like women who wore make-up. He really did think that Shaw and Ibsen and Chekhov were 'duds'. He spent a lot of time moaning and groaning about the 'new dispensation' and the fact that 'Jack's as good as his master now'. It was little wonder that he and George Orwell couldn't see eye to eye.*

'Clean, wholesome literature' was The *Magnet*'s motto. And clean, wholesome literature is what Frank Richards endeavoured to provide. But there was more to his writing than that. His style may have been uneconomical, repetitious and quaint, but it was also consistent, unambiguous, stangely hypnotic and quite unique. His characters may have been cartoon figures overfond of the melodramatic, the sentimental and the slapstick, but they were also delightfully larger than life, entertainingly outrageous and, again, quite unique.

'Everything, good or bad, comes to an end. Except Billy Bunter.'[1] Who would be peevish enough to deny that the Fat Owl is immortal? Frank Richards may be dead, but Bunter will be scoffing tuck and shirking prep for the rest of time!

A few weeks before his death, Frank Richards made a record and the making of it prompted some amused intimations of immortality. They make a fitting epitaph:

'An odd thought came to me, that now I shall be able to say with Horace "non omnis moriar"! Records last longer than the makers thereof, especially when the latter have counted eighty-five birthdays! "Vox Ricardi" will still, like the voice of the turtle, be heard in the land. Somewhat like the Cheshire Cat in Wonderland, who vanished leaving only his grin behind!'[3]

Notes

1. From a conversation with Kenneth Allsop conducted in 1960 and published in *Scan* by Kenneth Allsop (Hodder & Stoughton, 1966).

2. From a conversation with Denzil Batchelor, John Chandos and Denis Preston recorded in 1961. Extracts from the recording were included in the E.M.I. record *Floreat Greyfriars!* issued in 1965 and in *The Myth of Greyfriars*, a programme broadcast on BBC radio in September 1966.

3. From the unpublished letters of Frank Richards to George Foster, October 1947–October 1961.

4. From *The Autobiography of Frank Richards* (Charles Skilton, 1952).

*See page 168.

Charles H. Chapman [signature]

Top left: Charles Chapman, not the first and far from the only Bunter illustrator, he became the best known and the one that Frank Richards admired most. Richards and Chapman first met in 1912 and they remained friends until the former died in 1961.

Top right: A sketch by C. H. Chapman of C. H. Chapman working at a sketch of Billy Bunter.

Below: A selection of the *Greyfriars Holiday Annuals* now on display at the Charles Hamilton Museum in Maidstone, Kent.

OH CRIKEY!

BY GYLES BRANDRETH

This book represents less than 0·1 per cent of Frank Richards' writing! I know it's a ridiculously small proportion of his output, but I am hoping it may be just enough to give an entertaining (and fair) impression of the range and flavour of this remarkable writer's work over six decades. Naturally, I have done my best to include all the ingredients Frank Richards fans would expect to find in a collection of his gems, but since two-thirds of the material I've selected has never been seen in print before, I am also hoping readers will find a few surprises as well as old favourites in the pages that follow.

Of all the schools Frank Richards created, the best known is, of course, the best represented. I have included two complete Greyfriars stories and two of the scripts that Richards wrote in the 'fifties when Billy Bunter eventually reached radio and TV. I have also been lucky enough to be able to include something of a 'scoop'. When *The Magnet* folded in May 1940, Frank Richards had already delivered to the Amalgamated Press the next four Greyfriars stories. These stories—*The Battle of the Beaks, Bandy Bunter, What Happened to Hacker* and *The Hidden Hand*—were never published and the manuscripts have since been lost. However, there was a fifth story, intended for *The Magnet* Number 1688, that Richards had not yet delivered to his publishers because he had not yet completed it. That story now appears in print for the first time. It is unfinished, but connoisseurs of *The Magnet* will have no difficulty in conjuring up an imaginary ending for *Exit Bunter!*

Had space allowed, I should also have liked to include one of Frank Richards' Greyfriars sagas in Latin: 'Quelchius magister supercilium contrahebat. Et disciplebat aliquid. Oculi ejus ad Bunterum nitebant. Discipuli Quelchii in classe sedebant. Whartonus, Nugentius, Cerasus, et ceteri, praecepta magistri attendebant—sed non Bunterus!' However, suspecting (possibly incorrectly) that only a handful of readers would honestly appreciate page after page of Bunter in Latin, I have confined my representation of classical Richards to his Latin version of *Waltzing Matilda!*

Apart from the schoolboy sagas, I have tried to feature Frank Richards in more romantic and melodramatic mood. I have included a Wild West adventure, a murder mystery and one of the celebrated cases of the spoof sleuth, Herlock Sholmes of Shaker Street. There are also a number of poems (including a rather bitter verse inspired by the threatened teachers' strike in the autumn of 1961), a number of songs (including some satire at the expense of Mrs Simpson in 1936) and a brief extract from an unpublished, unperformed and unfinished musical comedy.

Altogether it's a bit of a hotchpotch and you may well cavil at my selection because I haven't included *your* favourite yarn from *The Gem*. No doubt in the remaining 99·9 per cent of the great man's *opus* there are some pearls I've overlooked, but all the same I hope you'll find enough to feast on in the pages that follow. To find out, just turn the page and tuck in!

Who would not love to wander
  With Keats in realms of gold,
With Wordsworth muse and ponder
  Upon the lonesome wold?

With Milton at the portals
  Of Heav'n itself to sing,
To soar above all mortals
  On Shakespeare's mighty wing?

But these are dreams of glory,
  That never can come true,
To tell a simple story
  Is all that I can do.

And if my tale give pleasure
  And ease the daily task,
And charm an hour of leisure,
  Then what more need I ask?

THE LATEST & BEST!

THE **Magnet** 1d.
½

No. 18. LIBRARY Vol. 1.

By
FRANK
RICHARDS

ROUGHING IT!

COMPLETE
STORY
FOR ALL.

BILLY BUNTER COOKS THE DINNER.

Top left: Hutton Mitchell's cover for a 1908 issue of *The Magnet*. He illustrated the first thirty-seven issues and was succeeded by Arthur Clark, who was also the original illustrator of *The Gem*.

Top right and bottom right: Two of Arthur Clark's drawings of Billy Bunter in action. It was C. H. Chapman, who was brought in after Arthur Clark's death, who gave Bunter his famous checked trousers.

Hard Lines!

By
Frank Richards

CHAPTER ONE

SKINNER THE LEG-PULLER

"YOU will go on Bunter."

"Oh, lor!"

"What? What did you say, Bunter?"

"Oh! Nothing, sir."

"Go on at once!" snapped Mr Quelch.

"Yes, sir! Certainly, sir!" stammered Billy Bunter.

Bunter unluckily, was not prepared to "go on". Never, indeed, had he been more completely unprepared.

The Remove were in form. Latin was the order of the day. Every fellow in Quelch's form was—or should have been—giving attention to the proceedings of the pius Aeneas. But quite a number of them were thinking of quite other things. It was the day before the big Soccer event of the term—the match with St Jim's. Harry Wharton and Co. and other fellows, just couldn't keep Soccer quite out of their thoughts, even under Quelch's gimlet-eye in form. Six or seven juniors had already received lines for inattention or faulty construe, and Mr Quelch's temper was growing sharp. His voice had a snap in it when he called on Bunter to —"go on".

Bunter, certainly, was not thinking of Soccer. Billy Bunter was most likely to be found in an armchair before the fire in the Rag, while other fellows were playing football. But Bunter had his own food for thought. Having given prep a miss the previous evening, his fat mind was a perfect blank on the passage in the Aeneid with which the Greyfriars Remove were dealing that morning. He was in dread of being called upon for "con". His eyes, and his spectacles, were fixed anxiously on Mr Quelch in terror of the gimlet-eye singling him out.

So far he had escaped the gimlet-eye. Harry Wharton, Bob Cherry, Frank Nugent, Johnny Bull, Vernon-Smith, Skinner, and several other fellows, had taken their turn. Billy Bunter's fat heart palpitated with mingled hope and dread. And then—!

The Quelch called on him to "go on".

Willingly Billy Bunter would have "gone on", had he known how. But his little round eyes, and his big round spectacles, fixed dismally and hopelessly on a page of Latin that meant absolutely nothing to him.

17

"I said go on, Bunter!" came a snap from Quelch.

"Oh! Yes, sir! I—I—I—I've lost the place, sir!" stammered Bunter.

"Go on at Line 305," snapped Mr Quelch."

"Oh! yes sir!"

Billy Bunter could, at least, read out the Latin, even if it conveyed no meaning to his fat mind.

"At pius Aeneas, per noctem plurima volvens—," mumbled Bunter.

"Construe!" snapped Mr Quelch.

Any fellow in the Remove could have told Bunter that that Latin line meant "But the good Aeneas, during the night revolving many matters—." To Billy Bunter it was an insoluble problem.

"I am waiting, Bunter!" Quelch's tone was ominous.

A faint whisper, which did not reach Mr Quelch at his high desk, reached Billy Bunter's fat ear. It was a whisper from Skinner, who sat beside him.

"Aeneas rolled over during the night," whispered Skinner.

"Oh!" gasped Bunter, in great relief.

Harold Skinner was not really the kind of fellow to help another fellow out of a jam. He was the kind of fellow to play malicious tricks. But Billy Bunter, in his present state of stress, forgot the kind of fellow Skinner was. He had no doubt that Skinner had given him the translation, and he burbled on quite happily—

"At pius Aeneas, per noctem plurima volvens—Aeneas rolled over during the night—."

"Oh, my hat!" gasped Bob Cherry, involuntarily.

"Ha, ha, ha!"

"Silence!" Quelch almost roared, "Bunter! How dare you?"

"Is—is—isn't that right, sir!" stammered Bunter.

"Upon my word! You have no knowledge whatever of this passage in Virgil. How dare you utter such absurdities?"

"Oh, crikey!" gasped Bunter. "You beast, Skinner." It dawned on his fat mind that Skinner had been pulling his fat leg. "I—I—I say, sir, I—I didn't mean that Aeneas rolled over during the night—."

"Then what did you mean, Bunter?"

"I—I—I." The unhappy Owl of the Remove stammered helplessly. He knew now that the translation supplied by Harold Skinner was not the genuine article. But that was all he knew. That Latin line was still a mystery to him.

"Well?" Quelch's voice was deep.

"I—I—I—."

"That will do, Bunter. Obviously you have neglected your preparation, and know nothing of the lesson. For that, Bunter, I should give you an imposition of fifty lines. But—," Quelch's voice deepened, "You must learn not to utter such absurdities in the form-room. You will take five hundred lines, Bunter."

"Oh, crikey!"

"You will go on, Todd."

Many commiserating glances were cast in Billy Bunter's direction, as Peter Todd took up the tale, and the lesson proceeded.

Bunter's "howlers" often caused merriment in the Remove form-room—to the juniors, if not to Mr Quelch. Quelch was often patient with the laziest and most obtuse member of his form. But this latest specimen was evidently too much for his patience. Aeneas rolling over in the night was the limit. Quelch had come down hard and heavy : and the hapless Owl sat in a state of collapse. Five hundred lines was an awful impot—really awful. It was likely to keep William George Bunter busy during all his leisure hours for days to come. Certainly it was also likely to impress upon his fat mind that it was worth while to give some attention to prep. But that was no consolation to Bunter.

"Oh, lor'!" mumbled Bunter, dismally.

The gimlet-eye glinted round at him.

"Did you speak, Bunter?"

"Oh! No, sir!" gasped Bunter, in alarm. "I never opened my lips, sir. I only said, 'Oh, lor',' sir. I—I mean I—I never said anything, sir."

"If you speak again, I shall cane you, Bunter."

"Oh, lor'! I—I—I mean, yes, sir." gasped Bunter.

The fat Owl was silent during the remainder of that lesson. But his looks were expressive—alternately at Skinner and at Quelch. Skinner had pulled his leg, and Quelch had given him five hundred lines—and Bunter could not help feeling that what they both deserved was something lingering, with boiling oil in it! It was a dismal Owl that rolled out of the form-room when the Remove were, at last, dismissed.

CHAPTER TWO

CALLED TO ACCOUNT

"I SAY, you fellows!"

"Hallo, hallo, hallo! Jolly old Aeneas still rolling over?" asked Bob Cherry. "Ha, ha, ha."

"Blessed if I see anything to cackle at!" hooted Billy Bunter, indignantly, "I've got five hundred lines—."

"Didn't you ask for them?" grunted Johnny Bull. "If you tell a beak that Aeneas rolled over—."

"I didn't!" howled Bunter, "It was Skinner."

"Eh! what?"

The Famous Five stared at the fat Owl. They had not heard Skinner's whisper in class, and knew nothing, so far, of Skinner's participation in that "howler" which had evoked Quelch's wrath.

They were talking of Soccer when Bunter rolled up in the quad. The St Jim's match on the morrow was the topic. Tom Merry and Co. of St Jim's were coming over the next day to play football, and it was a great occasion. Certainly they commiserated a fat Owl landed with five hundred lines: but they were much more interested in Soccer than in Bunter. However, they gave him their attention now.

"What the dickens had Skinner to do with it?" asked Frank Nugent.

"We all heard you hand out that howler," said Harry Wharton. "Where does Skinner come in?"

"He gave me the translation," explained Bunter, "He whispered it to me, and of course I thought it was fair and square, and passed it on to Quelch."

"Oh!" ejaculated all the five, together.

"Rotten trick!" said Bob.

"Rotten!" agreed Nugent.

"The rottenfulness is terrific!" said Hurree Jamset Ram Singh, with a shake of his dusky head.

Snort, from Johnny Bull.

"You might have known that Skinner was pulling your silly leg," he said, "Catch Skinner doing any fellow a good turn."

Harry Wharton glanced round at a group of three Remove fellows at a little distance—Skinner, Snoop, and Stott. All three were grinning and chuckling, evidently discussing something very amusing. The captain of the Remove could guess now what it was—Skinner's malicious trick on the obtuse fat Owl. He frowned. Skinner was as full of tricks as a monkey: and they were seldom good-natured. Evidently the fact that he had landed Bunter with a heavy imposition did not weigh on his conscience.

"I'd jolly well punch his head for it," said Bunter. "Only—only he would punch mine, you see—! But I say you fellows—I expect you to see fair play. Look here, Wharton, you're captain of the form, and it's up to you."

"I'll see fair play, if you're going to punch Skinner," said Harry. "But—you couldn't handle him, old fat man."

"I don't mean that. But look here, Skinner's landed me with five hundred with his rotten trick. Well, it's only fair for him to do the lines."

"Oh!"

Billy Bunter's fat brain had evidently been at work since the Remove had come out

"He wouldn't!" said Nugent.

"Not likely!" said Bob Cherry.

"Catch Skinner!" grunted Johnny Bull.

"You fellows make him!" said Bunter.

"Oh!"

"Fair play's a jewel!" said Bunter, "Skinner got me the lines, didn't he? Perhaps he'll think twice about pulling a fellow's leg in form, if he has to do them himself."

"By gum, it's only fair," said Bob, "Bunter can't help being a silly, fat-headed, blithering ass—."

"Oh, really, Cherry—."

"And it's a dirty trick to land him in a row with Quelch, when he hasn't sense enough to go in when it rains—."

"Beast!"

"Right!" said Harry Wharton, "Let's go over and talk to Skinner. We can't make him do Bunter's lines, if he won't, but we can jolly well bump him for landing the fat chump in a row. We'll give him his choice."

"Hear, hear!"

"I say, you fellows, come on!" chirruped Bunter.

20

The Famous Five came on! They walked across to the grinning group under the elms. The practical joker was to be called to account!

"Fancy even that fat ass falling for it!" Skinner was saying, as they came up, "Aeneas rolled over in the night! Ha, ha!"

"Ha, ha!" echoed Snoop and Stott.

"No wonder Quelch went off at the deep end," chuckled Skinner. "But fancy that fat chump taking it in!" He grinned round at Harry Wharton and Co. "You fellows haven't heard the joke—."

"Yes, we've just heard it—from Bunter," said Harry. "Very funny, if it hadn't landed Bunter in a row. But five hundred lines isn't a joke. What about that?"

Skinner shrugged his shoulders.

"Well, you've had your little joke," said Bob Cherry. "But the chap who calls the tune has to pay the piper. Are you going to help Bunter out with his lines?"

"What?"

"That's only fair!" said Nugent.

Skinner laughed.

"I say, you fellows—!" squeaked Bunter.

"Leave it to us, old fat man," said Harry. "Look here, Skinner, you can pull that fat chump's leg as much as you like: but you can't land him with a whacking impot for a joke. You got him that impot from Quelch, and it's only fair to do it for him."

"I'll watch it," said Skinner.

"You won't?"

"Not so's you'd notice it!" yawned Skinner.

"I say, you fellows—."

"Shut up, Bunter! Look here, Skinner, you're going to do those lines, or you're going to be bumped—hard! Yes or no," snapped the captain of the Remove.

Skinner made a move to back away. Five juniors surrounded him at once. There was no retreat for Skinner.

Snoop and Stott exchanged a glance, and strolled away. Skinner was left alone, scowling at five faces that encircled him.

"Can't you fellows mind your own business?" he snarled.

"We're minding Bunter's for a change," said Bob. "You wouldn't have played that trick on a fellow who could wallop you for it, Skinner. You're going to do those lines."

"Quelch would smell a rat, if I did," muttered Skinner. "My fist isn't like that fat scrawler's."

"You can make it near enough. Make it look as if a spider had swum in the ink-pot and then crawled over the paper. That would pass for Bunter's fist any day."

"Ha, ha, ha!"

"Oh, really, Cherry—."

"Well, I won't do a single line for the fat chump!" snapped Skinner, "And you can't make me."

"You'll get a bumping if you don't."

"The bumpfulness will be terrific."

Skinner made a sudden rush. But it booted not. Three or four pairs of hands grasped him at once.

Bump!

There was a frantic yell from Skinner, as he was swept off his feet, and landed on the hard, unsympathetic earth.

"Doing those lines?" asked Bob.

"No!" howled Skinner.

"Give him another!"

Bump!

"Ow! Oh! Leggo! Ow!" yelled Skinner. "I won't do a line! Wow!"

"One more for luck then," said Bob.

Bump!

"Yooo-hoooop!"

"Now boot him!"

A breathless, enraged, dusty Skinner fled from lunging feet—evidently no longer enjoying that joke on Billy Bunter.

The fat Owl blinked after him as he fled, and then blinked at the Famous Five.

"I say you fellows—!" he squeaked. "I say, if Skinner won't do those lines, what about you fellows doing them?"

"What?"

"I'll do some," said Bunter hastily. "Look here, I'll do twenty-five. Then you chaps can whack out the rest. It will be only seventy each, for the five of you, to make up the five hundred."

"Ha, ha, ha!"

"Blessed if I see anything to cackle at. I say, you fellows, don't walk away while a fellow's talking to you!" howled Bunter.

But the Famous Five did walk away, laughing. They had done all they could: and did not seem disposed to do Bunter's lines in addition. The topic of the St Jim's match was resumed, and Billy Bunter was left to waste his sweetness on the desert air.

CHAPTER THREE

BUNTER ON THE WAR-PATH!

HARRY WHARTON and Co. were looking merry and bright, when the Remove came out in the break the following morning. There was only one more lesson to come: after that, a half-holiday: and it was a fine, clear winter's day, and St Jim's were coming over to play football. So it was no wonder that the chums of the Remove looked as bright as the winter sunshine.

Their cheery looks contrasted with Billy Bunter's. The fattest face in the Remove was also the most lugubrious that morning. Five hundred lines impended over Billy Bunter's fat head. Like the sword of Damocles.

Some fellows, with so extensive an impot on hand, would have got going without delay. Not so Bunter. Bunter has not even started on his lengthy task. Not a single line, or a blot, had so far dropped from his pen. The lines had to be done: and if Skinner remained obstinate on the subject, in spite of bumpings, Bunter had to do them. There would be no lazy frowst in an armchair for Bunter, that afternoon, while Harry Wharton and Co. were playing St Jim's at Soccer. Only lines, and lines! It was an awful prospect for a lazy fat Owl.

Five cheery juniors, sauntering in the quad, came on a woeful Owl, who greeted them with a dismal blink through his big spectacles.

"Hallo, hallo, hallo! Enjoying life, old fat man?" asked Bob Cherry.

"Oh, lor'!" mumbled Bunter.

"Anything the matter?" asked Harry Wharton.

"Oh, really, Wharton—." Bunter gave the captain of the Remove a deeply reproachful blink. Actually, the Famous Five had forgotten about Bunter and his woes: just as if a football match was more important than Bunter! "My lines—!"

"Oh! Your lines! Haven't you done them yet?"

"There's five hundred—."

"Well, how many have you done, so far?"

"I—I haven't started on them yet—."

"Better get going," said Nugent. "Quelch will want those lines, fathead."

"Lazybones!" grunted Johnny Bull.

"Tain't fair!" hooted Bunter. "Skinner landed me with those lines, and it's up to him. Quelch will ask me for them to-morrow."

"Better get them done to-day," said Bob Cherry. "Quelch isn't exactly pleased with you already, old fat man. Might be whops!"

"That cad Skinner—."

"Skinner's a cad, but he won't do those lines for you," said Bob. "Make up your mind to it, you lazy old porpoise. After all, you did ask for them—you couldn't expect to please Quelch by telling him that jolly old Aeneas rolled over in the night—."

"Ha, ha, ha!"

"Oh, cackle!" said Bunter, bitterly. "Quelch is a beast—coming down on a fellow like that for nothing—well, next to nothing. But perhaps he'll be sorry for it," added Bunter, darkly.

"Eh! How come?" asked Bob, staring.

"Perhaps I know how to make him sit up for it," said Bunter. "Perhaps he will like sitting down in a lot of ink next time he sits down in his armchair. Perhaps he won't! He, he, he!"

Billy Bunter's lugubrious fat face cleared, and he chuckled. The idea of Henry Samuel Quelch sitting down in a lot of ink seemed to cheer him up.

The Famous Five gazed at him.

"You fat ass!" said Johnny Bull. "Are you thinking of playing tricks in Quelch's study?"

"Hasn't he given me five hundred lines?" hooted Bunter.

"He will give you something tougher than that, if he catches you playing tricks with ink in his study."

"He jolly well won't catch me," grinned Bunter. "You see, I heard him tell Prout that he's going out for a walk in break. He may come out any minute now. As soon as he's gone out, what's to stop a fellow nipping into his study, and pouring the inkpot into his armchair?"

"Fathead!"

"Ass!"

"Forget it!"

"Wash it out!"

23

"Yah!" was Bunter's reply to those remonstrances. Evidently, the fat Owl was on the trail of vengeance: and his fat mind was made up.

"Hallo, hallo, hallo, here comes Quelchy!" murmured Bob Cherry, as an angular figure, in coat and hat, emerged from the House. Mr Quelch walked briskly down to the gates, walked out, and disappeared.

"Now, look here, Bunter, you ass—." said Harry Wharton.

"Yah!"

"Keep clear of Quelch's study—."

"Yah!"

"Ten to one you'd be spotted," urged Bob Cherry.

"The ten-to-onefulness is terrific, my esteemed idiotic Bunter," said Hurree Jamset Ram Singh.

"Yah!"

Billy Bunter's replies were monosyllabic, but emphatic. The Owl of the Remove was on the war-path. Words of wisdom were wasted on him.

"Look here, Bunter," said Harry. "We'll go and look for Skinner, and bump him again if he won't help with the lines. But leave Quelch alone. Quelch isn't safe to rag."

"Yah!"

"Look here, you fat ass—"

"Yah!"

With that final monosyllable, Billy Bunter turned a fat back, and rolled away. Bunter was not losing this opportunity, while Quelch was out of gates! He rolled off to the House.

"Whops for Bunter, if Quelch catches him!" said Bob.

"The whopfulness will be terrific."

Harry Wharton knitted his brows.

"It's all that cad Skinner's fault," he said. "Let's go and look for him, and bump him again if he won't help Bunter out with the lines."

"Good egg!"

And the Famous Five went to look for Harold Skinner.

Meanwhile, Billy Bunter rolled into the House. Very cautiously he approached Masters' Studies. Bunter was not very bright: but he was bright enough to know that he had better not be seen going to his form-master's study, when the object was to tip his form-master's inkpot into his form-master's armchair, for his form-master to sit in.

To his extreme annoyance, the vicinity of Quelch's study was not uninhabited, as he had hoped to find it. Portly Mr Prout, the master of the Fifth, was standing at an open door, talking to Monsieur Charpentier, the French master, in the passage. Neither of them glanced at Bunter: but obviously the fat Owl could not roll undetected into Quelch's study while they were there.

"Beasts!" breathed Bunter.

He stopped at a window, and stood blinking out into the quad, hoping that they would go. Break did not last long, and Quelch would be back in time for third school. Minutes were precious. It seemed to the irritated fat Owl that Prout's drone, and Mossoo's squeak, would never end, as the precious minutes passed.

But they did end: Monsieur Charpentier, at last, came down the passage, and

Prout disappeared into his study and shut the door. Billy Bunter waited only till Mossoo was gone. Then he fairly shot along the passage to Quelch's door. That door was opened, and shut again, in a twinkling: and a breathless fat Owl panted for breath inside the study.

All was clear now.

Billy Bunter rolled across to the table, and reached to the inkstand. He jerked out the ink-well, grinning. Five hundred lines impended over Bunter: but it would be a consolation, while he was grinding through those endless lines, to think of Quelch sitting down in a swamp of ink!

Grinning, he rolled, inkpot in hand, towards Quelch's armchair, in the corner of the study—a dusky corner, where Quelch was not likely to discern ink on dark leather before he sat in it. He reached the armchair. In another moment, the inkpot would have been up-ended over the seat. But in that moment, he heard the door-handle turn!

Seldom was William George Bunter quick on the uptake. Seldom, very seldom, were his motions rapid. But the terror of being caught there by Quelch quickened his fat wits, and accelerated his movements. He had just time to whip round the armchair, and duck out of sight behind the high back, before the door opened. The next second it was open, and footsteps came into the study: and an invisible fat Owl, palpitating with dread, strove to suppress his breathing, as those footsteps approached the armchair behind which he huddled.

CHAPTER FOUR

SKINNER'S SCHEME

"RYLCOMBE one-O-one!"

Billy Bunter hardly refrained from jumping.

If Quelch had come in, no doubt he would sit down to rest after his walk, in the few minutes that remained before third School. Only the back of the armchair would be between him and Bunter. That was what the terrified Owl expected—and he could only hope to remain out of sight till the bell rang, and Quelch left the study to go to the form-room.

But, to his great relief, the newcomer did not sit down in the armchair. He stopped quite close to it, but apparently had no intention of sitting down.

A whirring sound reached Bunter's fat ears: and he understood. It came from the telephone, which stood on a little table close by the armchair. Quelch—if it was Quelch—had come in to telephone.

There was nothing surprising in that. But there was something very surprising in what followed. It was not Quelch's voice that Bunter heard: and that voice was asking for a trunk call! And the number given was one well-known to Remove fellows—St Jim's, the school in Sussex from which Tom Merry and Co. were coming to play Soccer that afternoon. Somebody was ringing up St Jim's on Quelch's phone.

It was not Quelch's voice,—even if the Remove master could have been supposed to have anything to say to anybody at St Jim's. Had it been Harry Wharton's, it might only have meant that the Remove captain wanted a word, for some reason, with the St Jim's skipper, before the team came over, and had borrowed Quelch's phone, for the purpose, in his absence. But it was not Wharton's voice—it was not a boy's voice at all, or at all events did not sound like one. It was a deep and rather husky voice that Bunter heard asking for the call to St Jim's.

Strangest of all, it was a voice unknown to Bunter. Bunter knew all the voices of the Staff at Greyfriars: from Prout's boom and Hacker's snap, to Wiggins' mumble and Mossoo's squeak. It was none of them.

"Is that St James's School?"

"Yes, the School House. Mr Railton speaking."

The telephone was so near the armchair behind which the fat Owl huddled, that the reply from St Jim's reached his fat ears. Railton, house-master of the School-House at St Jim's, had taken the call at the other end.

"Good-morning, Mr Railton. Mr Quelch speaking from Greyfriars School."

Again Billy Bunter barely refrained from jumping.

It was not Quelch's voice. Bunter knew that, though naturally a master at a distant school did not. Yet whoever was using Quelch's telephone was using his name also.

"Good-morning, Mr Quelch," came back from Mr Railton: in polite but slightly surprised tones. Obviously the house-master at St Jim's was not expecting a telephone call from the Remove master at Greyfriars, of whom he knew little more than his name.

"I am sorry to trouble you, Mr Railton—."

"Not at all, sir."

"But the matter is urgent—very urgent. I understand that a junior football team is to come here this afternoon from your school—."

"Yes, that is so."

"I am sorry to say that the fixture must be cancelled."

"Indeed! May I ask why?"

"Owing to a case of polio here—."

"Polio!"

"It was not known for certain till this morning, when the school doctor confirmed it. In the circumstances, every precaution, is of course, being taken and I felt it my duty to apprise you—."

"Bless my soul! I am sorry to hear such bad news, Mr Quelch: but very grateful to you for warning me in time. The football match must, of course, be cancelled: I will speak to Merry, the junior captain here, at once. Thank you very much, Mr Quelch."

"Not at all, Mr Railton. Good-bye."

"Good-bye, sir."

Billy Bunter, behind the armchair, listened like a fellow in a dream. In fact he could hardly believe his fat ears.

It was not Quelch speaking, though the speaker had used Quelch's name. There was not a word of truth in the statement made over the wires. Nobody at Greyfriars had even the most distant acquaintance with that dread disease, polio. Mr Railton, at St Jim's, had taken that statement at face value, naturally enough. Billy

Bunter knew that it was an invention. But the Soccer match, to which Harry Wharton and Co. were looking forward so keenly that afternoon, was going to be washed out. The expected visitors would not arrive: and the Remove footballers would be left wondering why. Somebody—evidently somebody with a bitter grudge against the Co.—had coolly and unscrupulously washed out the St Jim's match for them.

Who was it?

Bunter could not begin to guess. What man at Greyfriars could want to play a treacherous and unscrupulous trick on the footballers?

Then suddenly he was enlightened.

He heard the receiver jammed back on the hooks. That sound was followed by a low chuckle, and a muttering voice that Bunter knew.

"That's tit for tat, the rotters! They're going to keep on ragging me unless I help that fat idiot Bunter out with his lines, are they? Well, if they rag me, I'll give them something back as good, or better. If they make me stick in a study writing lines on a half-holiday, they can mooch about, wondering why St Jim's don't come over to play football, while I'm writing them. Ha, ha!"

It was Skinner's voice.

Then it dawned on Billy Bunter that the voice he had heard was not a man's voice at all, but an assumed one: the young rascal had assumed that deep husky voice to delude the St Jim's house-master at the other end.

"Beast!" breathed Bunter.

But he was careful to make no audible sound. He could guess what Skinner would feel like,—and what he would do—if he discovered that his cunning scheme had been overheard. At the mere thought of it, he could almost feel Skinner's fists hammering a fat face. Not a sound came from Bunter, and not a movement till he heard the door open. Then he ventured to raise a fat head above the level of the chair-back, as he knew that Skinner's back would be turned, and had a view of that unscrupulous youth as he left the study. The door closed on Skinner, and Bunter, at last, emerged from his hideout, the inkpot still in his fat hand.

"Oh, crikey!" breathed Bunter, at the sound of a voice from the passage. It was Prout's boom.

"What do you want here, Skinner?" Evidently, Prout had come out of his study, as Skinner emerged from Quelch's.

But Skinner's reply was prompt and plausible.

"I came to speak to my form-master, sir, but I found that he had gone out."

"Oh! Very well."

Skinner departed, and Bunter heard Prout's ponderous footsteps pass the door. Both of them were gone: and the fat Owl lost no more time. The inkpot was upended, and its contents flooded out into the seat of the armchair.

"He, he, he!" chuckled Bunter.

A cautious blink from the doorway revealed that the coast was clear. Billy Bunter rolled out of the study: and rolled into the quad, with startling news for Harry Wharton and Co. And a few minutes later Mr Quelch, coming in from his walk, sat in the armchair in his study to rest for a few minutes before going to his form-room—and his feelings, when he discovered what he had sat in, were deep—very deep indeed.

CHAPTER FIVE

"THIS way!" said Bob Cherry.

He linked an arm in Skinner's, when the Remove came out after third school. Johnny Bull linked on, on the other side of Skinner.

"Keep him till I come back!" said Harry Wharton.

"We'll keep him all right!" said Bob.

"The keepfulness will be terrific!" grinned Hurree Jamset Ram Singh.

Harry Wharton hurried away: leaving Skinner with the Co. Skinner wriggled in the grip on his arms, as the Co. walked him down the corridor.

"Will you let me go?" he breathed.

"Not so's you'd notice it."

"I tell you I won't do Bunter's lines for him, and if you start ragging again, I'll go to Quelch," hissed Skinner.

"We're not bothering about Bunter's lines at present," said Nugent. "Quite another matter."

"What do you mean?" snarled Skinner.

"You can go to Quelch as soon as you like," said Bob. "We'll walk you there if you like. Quelch would be interested to know what you had to say on his telephone while he was out in break this morning."

"Wha-a-t!" gasped Skinner.

"You rat!" grunted Johnny Bull. "I only half-believed—but there's no doubt about it now. Look at his face."

Skinner's face was quite sickly. Not for a moment had he dreamed that anything was known of that treacherous telephone call to St Jim's.

"I—I—I—," he stammered, 'I—I don't know what you mean. I—I haven't been to Quelch's study—I—I—."

"You didn't sneak there in break, and ring up St Jim's?"

"N-n-no!"

"You didn't spin a yarn that there was an outbreak of polio here, to keep Tom Merry's team away this afternoon?"

"I—I—I—No!" gasped Skinner. "Did—did—did anybody?"

"That's what Wharton's gone to make sure of. He's going to ask Quelch to let him use the phone for a call to St Jim's. Plenty of time to set the matter right, if you played that rotten trick."

"Oh!" gasped Skinner.

The Co. marched him out into the quad. They stopped at the fountain, to wait for Wharton to rejoin them. Skinner waited with them, having no choice in the matter, in a state of uneasy trepidation. The Co. had, perhaps, had some lingering doubt of the accuracy of Bunter's startling news: but Skinner's obvious uneasiness confirmed it. How they knew was a mystery to Skinner: but he knew that his cunning scheme had fallen to pieces like a house of cards, and that the consequences were likely to be extremely uncomfortable.

Harry Wharton came out of the House at last. His face was set and grim as he joined the group at the fountain.

"You cur, Skinner!" he breathed, as he came up. "I got on to Mr Railton at St Jim's. He was phoned this morning in Quelch's name, with a yarn about polio here. I've explained that it was a practical joke, and nothing in it: and Tom Merry's crowd will be coming over as arranged. It's all right now, Skinner, you rat."

"Good egg!" said Bob.

"The goodfulness of the egg is terrific."

"Okay now," said Johnny Bull. "Wasn't that St Jim's beak shirty about having his leg pulled like that?"

"He was!" said Harry. "He said that such a practical joke should be severely punished. I think you fellows will agree."

"Hear, hear!"

"Duck him!"

Splash!

There was a gurgling howl from Skinner, as his head went over the rim of the fountain into the water. It came out dripping.

"Ooooogh! Grooogh! Leggo! Gurrrggh!" gurgled Skinner.

"Give him another!"

Splash!

"Wurrrrgghh! Urrgggh!"

"Now, you rotter—!"

"Wurrrrrrgggh!"

"You're going to do Bunter's lines this afternoon—the whole five hundred of them!" said Harry Wharton. "If they're not done by the time we're through with the football, look out for squalls. Now boot him."

How many kicks he collected, before he escaped, Skinner could hardly have counted: it seemed to him like hundreds. It was a wet, draggled, aching and painful Skinner who got away at last, sadly and sorrowfully realizing that the way of the transgressor was hard.

"I say you fellows." Billy Bunter rolled up to the Famous Five in the quad. "I say, about my lines—I say, one good turn deserves another, you know. I put you wise about Skinner's dirty trick on Quelch's phone, didn't I?"

"You did!" agreed Harry Wharton.

"Fancy Bunter coming in useful for once!" said Bob.

"Well, he couldn't be ornamental!" remarked Johnny Bull.

"Oh, really Bull! But I say, about my lines—one good turn deserves another, doesn't it?"

"It does!" assented Harry.

"Well, then, suppose you fellows do my lines for me this afternoon—"

"While we're playing football?" asked Bob.

"You can cut out the football," suggested Bunter. "Lots of the fellows would be glad to take your places to play Soccer, but they wouldn't do any lines. What about it?"

"Ha, ha, ha!" roared the Famous Five.

"Blessed if I see anything to cackle at. I haven't said anything funny, have I?" yapped Bunter.

"Ha, ha, ha!"

"Look here, you fellows—"

"It's all right about the lines, old fat man," said Harry Wharton, laughing. "You can leave them to Skinner."

"But he said he won't—"

"If he doesn't, we're going to boil him in oil. It's all right."

"Well, if it's all right, all right!" said Bunter. "So long as I don't have to do them, I don't mind who does. I say, you fellows, I wonder what we're going to have for dinner!"

CHAPTER SIX

SIX FOR SKINNER

THERE were many cheery faces at Greyfriars that afternoon. Tom Merry and Co. duly arrived from St Jim's to play Soccer, and Harry Wharton and Co. went into the field with them, merry and bright. Billy Bunter, equally cheery though in a different way, settled down happily in an armchair before the fire in the Rag, with a bag of toffees he had found in Bob Cherry's study. Everyone in fact, seemed to be enjoying life, with the exception of Harold Skinner, whose cunning scheming had come home so painfully to roost. Skinner had Bunter's lines to write, lest worse should befall him: and even that was not all. He received a summons to his form-master's study: and he obeyed it in fear and trembling, in dread that Quelch had heard something about that telephone-call to St Jim's, so unexpectedly known to so many fellows.

He found Mr Quelch looking his grimmest.

"Skinner!" rapped Quelch.

"Yes, sir!"

"During my absence in break this morning, some Remove boy entered this study and poured ink into the seat of my armchair. I sat in it before I perceived it. I have made inquiries, Skinner, and I have learned that you were seen to leave my study during break. You were seen by Mr Prout." Quelch picked up a cane. "Bend over that chair, Skinner."

"But I—I—I didn't—I—I—I never—!" stammered Skinner.

"Did you enter this study, or not, without leave during my absence?"

"Oh! Yes! No! But—"

"That is sufficient. Bend over that chair. This is not the first time you have played disrespectful tricks in this study, Skinner. I trust it will be the last. Bend over that chair!"

Quelch had no doubts! He had sat in the ink, swamped in his armchair by a surreptitious hand. Skinner, whom he knew to be as full of mischievous tricks as a monkey, had been in the study at the material time. That was enough for Quelch. Six swipes from the cane were more than enough for Harold Skinner. From the bottom of his heart he wished that he had steered clear of Quelch's study that morning.

Skinner sat very uncomfortably while he scrawled five hundred lines that afternoon, what time Billy Bunter lolled at his fat ease in the Rag and consumed Bob Cherry's toffees, and Harry Wharton and Co. urged the flying ball on the football field.

THE END

THE DJAH OLD SCHOOL
by *Frank Richards*

SOLO: There are Eton and Harrow and Stowe,
      And Rugby and Winchester too,
    But I think you'll agree all you fellows, with me,
    That Barcroft's the bloom at the top of the tree.
    There's a something—a *je ne sais quoi*—don't you see?
      About us, don't you think so?

CHORUS: We do!

SOLO: I'm not slatin' Repton or Rugby, dear lads,
I'm not sayin' Eton men always are cads,
I'm not sayin' Winchester men can't be posh,
I'm not sayin' Uppingham men never wash,
Not that Harrow men are always seen at Bill
In bags as if they've just rolled down the Hill.
But Barcroft's the pick of the bunch, you'll admit,
Absolutely and finally, Barcroft is IT!

CHORUS: The djah old school,
The djah old school,
    Where the Head, *non compos mentis*,
    Stood *in loco*—ah!—*parentis*.
The djah old school,
The djah old school,
    Where we never swear in Rugger,
    When we're up for Confirmugger,
The djah old, djah old, djah old school!

SOLO: We were great men at games, don't you know,
      You remember the match with the 'Bricks',
When Viscount de Shine, son of Lord Palestine,
Our ripping three-quarter, went right through the swine,
And would have touched down, had he got to the line,
      But they fouled him, the rotters!

CHORUS: The Ticks!

SOLO: Slugger Parkinson, stout lad, got hold of the ball,
And would surely have scored, but he happened to fall,
Then Jackie de Boots—you remember old Jack?
Had a chance, but somehow he went down on his back,
The referee *stood* there, just blind, deaf, and dumb,
And never saw them put a spin on the ball in the scrum,
But right on the whistle, we had the swine licked,
If only Parkinson hadn't miskicked!

CHORUS: The djah old school,
The djah old school,
    You remember dear old Slugger,
    Quite the finest man at Rugger,
The djah old school,
The djah old school,
    Where a fellow who talked soccer,
    Was considered off his rocker,
The djah old, djah old, djah old school!

SOLO: Of course there were fellows, a few,
    Whom a chap couldn't possibly know,
One could not be seen, if you know what I mean,
In the quad with a rotten outsider like Greene,
Oh most frightfully poor, you know—hadn't a bean,
    A man couldn't know him!

CHORUS: Oh no!

SOLO: Of course bein' poor's not a crime, but good gad!
It's doocid bad form, oh, most doocidly bad,
Bein' hard up, I think, you'll acknowledge is one,
Of the things that most certainly never are done.
His hat, good gad, his trousers and his tie!
We barred the lout of course and passed him by.
Not a bad chap, you know in his way, but my Hat!
A man shouldn't be seen in bags such as that!

CHORUS: The djah old school,
The djah old school,
    Where the good old Head still totters,
    And we barred all cads and rotters,
The djah old school,
The djah old school,
    Where my name was on the panel,
    When I became House-Flannel,
The djah old, djah old, djah old school!

SOLO: There were others, a few, you recall,
    Who were barred by the House as too bad,
Perkins minor, the swot, was the worst of the lot,
He mugged up the classics and that sort of rot,
And cared not a bean if the House went to pot,
    He worked—really studied—.

35

CHORUS: The cad!

SOLO: A man doesn't come up to Barcroft to learn,
But because his dear pater has money to burn,
The rottenest thing you can say of a chap,
Is to call him a swot, or a greaser or sap.
At Barcroft we disdain to learn at all,
But think, you men, of Speecher in Big Hall,
And the pots on the sideboard in silver ranks,
Who cared if the brains are all perfect blanks?

CHORUS: The djah old school,
The djah old school,
  The old form-rooms that we sat in
    Picking up our scraps of Latin,
The djah old school,
The djah old school,
  We had little, but we had some,
    We could all, at Roll, say '*Adsum!*'
The djah old, djah old, djah old school!

SOLO: My fag, I remember, was Jones,
  A kid in the Shell don't you know,
It was really his joy, that seemed never to cloy,
To rush up the stairs when he heard me call 'Boy'!
Believe me, no man-servant that I employ
  Is as good as that fag was—

CHORUS: Bravo!

SOLO: You can't whop a valet who loses a stud,
Or leaves on your shoes a suspicion of mud,
You can't whop a butler who snaffles your port,
Or a cook if he doesn't do just as he ought,
At Barcroft School fag-masters kept a bat,
And if fags put on roll, just gave them that!
It's wonderful how little a kid ever lags
When he knows that it means for him six on the bags!

CHORUS: The djah old school,
             The djah old school,
               Where we gave our fags a whopping,
               For a plate or saucer dropping,
             The djah old school,
             The djah old school,
               Where they thought themselves in clover,
               If they weren't told to bend over,
             The djah old, djah old, djah old school!

SOLO: There's a game, at least so I've heard,
              Called soccer, a game we should bar,
            And the ticks have the gall to call soccer 'football',
            It's played by eleven or twelve men, that's all,
            And a man mustn't pick up or handle the ball,
              And it's footer they call it—

CHORUS: Ha, ha!

SOLO: There's something, I think, called a League, or whatnot,
            That encourages this sort of dashed, doocid rot,
            What the dooce do they know about games, or can know—
            Who have not been at Barcroft, or even at Stowe?
            Don't *they* know, as is quite well known to you,
            That Barcroft First Fifteen won Waterloo?
            Believe me, you men, this impertinent rot,
            Just shows that the country is going to pot.

CHORUS: The djah old school,
             The djah old school,
               Where we called our beak 'm'tooter',
               And we don't know soccer's footer,
             The djah old school,
             The djah old school,
               Where we barred off all outsiders,
               From our venerable walls—and spiders!—
             The djah old, djah old, djah old school!

The very first issue of *The Magnet* published on 15th February 1908.

Top right: The Magnet, 30th January 1915
Top left: The Magnet, 3rd June 1918
Bottom left: The Magnet, 13th June 1925

Two of C. H. Chapman's drawings of Bessie Bunter

CHAPTER ONE

"Never mind that," said Bessie, "I want—"

"Go away!" shrieked Clara.

"But I want—"

"Quiet!"

Clara Trevlyn was, in fact, working against time. She had a Latin translation to do for her form-mistress, Miss Bellew. That translation might have been, and really ought to have been, done long ago. But it had been left to the last minute—and a little

later! It was overdue in Miss Bellew's study. Now Clara was grinding at it.

Her friends were helping. Marjorie had an open dictionary, looking out words. Dolly had an open grammar, assisting with conjugations. But all three knew that Clara's belated effort was probably too late.

There was just a chance. Miss Bellew was in the Staff Room, where the tide of conversation always ran full and strong. She might remain talking in the Staff Room till Clara had had time to get that translation done, and conveyed down to her study, and placed upon the table there to meet her eyes. Otherwise, there was a spot of bother in store. Bellew might even come up to No. 7 to inquire after that wretched translation, if she did not find it in her study. In such circumstances, moments were precious: and Bessie Bunter, always a little superfluous, was more superfluous than ever.

But Bessie was a sticker. She had come to Marjorie's study because she wanted something, and she was not going away without what she wanted.

"I say, I want—!" Bessie began again.

Clara gave her a look that was almost ferocious.

"Do you want this inkpot at your silly head?" she demanded.

"Eh! No."

"You'll get it, if you interrupt again."

"Cat!"

"Another time, Bessie—!" urged Marjorie.

"Another time won't do," said Bessie

41

Bunter. "Bellew's in the Staff Room now, and I've got to get through before she goes back to her study. Have you got a bottle of gum?"

"Gum!" repeated Marjorie, blankly.

"Yes. I've asked Barbara and Mabel, and they won't let me have theirs. I know you've got some in this study. I want it for Bellew. Look here, Marjorie, I know you've got a bottle of gum, and I'm in a hurry. Suppose Bellew came back to her study and caught me there, putting gum in her Latin book—"

"What?" gasped Marjorie.

"Wha-a-t?" stuttered Dolly Jobling.

Both of them stared at the fat figure in the doorway. Even Clara, for a moment, looked up from that worrying translation, to stare at Bessie. Three horrified stares were fixed on Bessie Bunter.

"Gum—in Miss Bellew's Latin book!" said Marjorie. "For goodness sake, Bessie, don't think of anything of the kind."

"Forget it, you little duffer!" gasped Dolly Jobling.

Sniff, from Bessie.

"Bellew gave me a detention this morning," she said. "I'm going to put gum in her Latin book, and stick all the leaves together. Fancy her face when the book won't come open in class! What! He, he, he!"

Bessie Bunter chuckled, a fat chuckle.

"You little fathead!" exclaimed Clara.

"Oh, really, Clara—"

"Bellew would take you to the Head! You'd get into an awful row. Forget all about it, and now go away."

"I'll watch it!" said Bessie. "How's she to know? Think I'm going to tell all about it? I say, Marjorie, do give me your bottle of gum."

Marjorie shook her head.

"You can't play such a trick on Miss Bellew, Bessie—"

"I jolly well can!" declared Bessie. "All I want is a bottle of gum. Can I have yours?"

"Not to play tricks on Miss Bellew. Go away and forget all about it."

"Shan't!"

"Now, look here, Bessie—"

"Cat!"

Bessie Bunter frowned. Evidently, she was very much taken with her idea of gumming the pages of Miss Bellew's Latin book. Not only would it be a tremendous joke on the mistress of the Fourth, but it would be tit for tat, for the detention she had given the fat, fatuous Bessie. Bellew's face, in Bessie's opinion, would be worth watching, in the form-room, when she tried to open that book, and the leaves would not come apart. Certainly, Miss Bellew was likely to be quite furious about it: but what would that matter, so long as she did not know that Elizabeth Bunter was the culprit? She would have all the Cliff House Fourth to choose from, to discover who had gummed that book.

"I say, you girls, think what a joke it will be on Bellew," urged Bessie. "It will make the whole class laugh when she can't open that book—"

"It won't make you laugh, when she walks you off to Miss Primrose!" said Dolly.

"She won't know who did it! I keep on telling you that she won't know a thing. Where's your gum, Marjorie?"

Clara Trevlyn rose from the table and stepped to the door. She grasped two fat shoulders, and twirled Bessie Bunter into the passage. Then she slammed the door, and returned to the table.

But she had hardly restarted on the translation, when the door reopened, and a fat face looked in.

"Cat!" said Bessie.

"Go away!" hooted Clara.

"I'm going to find a bottle of gum, and I'm going to gum Bellew's Latin book, and you jolly well can't stop me!" snorted Bessie. "So yah!"

And with that, Elizabeth Bunter slammed the door, in her turn, and was gone. Her plump existence was forgotten a few moments later, as three heads bent over that troublesome translation.

Minutes were passing: and minutes were precious. Clara wished that she had devoted herself to that task a little earlier. If Bellew did not find it in her study only too probably she might come up to inquire: and if she found it unfinished—

It simply had to be done, and Clara slogged

on, and her friends gave all the aid they could: in dread every moment of hearing a well-known step in the passage outside.

But fortune favoured the industrious! Clara wrote her last line, and the thing was done—she threw down her pen, just as a firm—a very firm—tread was heard.

Clara gave a low whistle.

"That's Bellew!" she breathed.

And the next moment Miss Bellew's severe face was visible, as the door opened: and the form-mistress of the Fourth walked into No. 7 Study.

CHAPTER TWO

MARJORIE and Co. rose respectfully.

Miss Bellew's face was often kindly. Sometimes it was severe. It was severe at the moment. It was very unusually severe.

No doubt Miss Bellew was annoyed about that translation. Clara Trevlyn should, undoubtedly, have handed it in earlier. Even yet she had not handed it in, though fortunately—very fortunately—it was finished and ready for inspection. But the three junior girls could see that there was something more than that translation, belated as it was, the matter. It was not merely annoyance that was expressed in Miss Bellew's face. It was wrath. Her lips were set, and there was a glint in her eyes.

"I—I—I've done it, Miss Bellew!" stammered Clara. "I—I was just going to bring it down to your study, Miss Bellew."

"You should have brought your translation to me long ago, Clara!"

"Oh! Yes, Miss Bellew! But—"

"I have spoken to you more than once, Clara, about leaving tasks till the latest possible moment."

"Oh! Yes! I—I—"

"It is a fault you must correct, Clara."

"Oh, certainly, Miss Bellew! Yes."

The mistress of the Fourth picked up the translation from the table. But she did not look at it immediately. She looked at the three girls, in turn: and then looked at them in turn again. Obviously, it was not merely the belatedness of that translation that brought so grim an expression to her face. Marjorie and Co. wondered what it might be.

"Clara!" came in a rap.

"Yes, Miss Bellew!" murmured Clara.

"Have you been to my study since class?"

"Oh, no, Miss Bellew. I was going there as soon as I had finished that trans. but—"

"Have you been to my study since class, Marjorie?"

"No, Miss Bellew."

"Have you, Dorothy?"

"Oh! No!" gasped Dolly Jobling.

Something, the three girls could guess, must have happened in Miss Bellew's study. Whatever it was, she had discovered it when she returned there from the Staff Room. Involuntarily, Marjorie and Clara and Dolly exchanged startled glances, as they remembered Bessie Bunter. If the plumpest member of the Cliff House Fourth had carried on with that gummy scheme—

"Has—has—has anything happened Miss Bellew?" stammered Marjorie.

Miss Bellew's brows, already knitted became more closely knit.

"A foolish, reckless, and disrespectful prank has been played in my study!" she snapped. "The book I use in the Latin lesson has been drenched—soaked—with gum—"

"Oh!" gasped three girls together.

"A whole bottle of gum must have been poured into it! The pages are stuck together! I doubt whether I shall be able to use the book again. Someone must have gone into my study while I was in the Staff Room, and done this."

"Oh!" Three more gasps.

Evidently, Bessie had carried on! No gum had been available in her own study or in Marjorie's. But she had found gum somewhere: and carried on. Miss Bellew's Latin book had come to a sticky end!

Three girls could only hope that Bellew would never discover who had done it. Certainly they were not going to utter so much as a whisper to give a clue.

"Whoever has done this," resumed Miss Bellew, "will be taken to the Principal. The punishment will be severe. Such an outrageous act cannot be punished too severely.''

With that, Miss Bellew, at last, looked at the translation. She crossed to the window, for a better light, and stood scanning Clara's task. Apparently she was satisfied that Marjorie and Co. had had nothing to do with the gummy exploit in her study. But she looked like examining that translation even more meticulously than usual, in her present grim mood. Clara could only hope that she had not perpetrated too many howlers.

There was deep silence in No. 7 in the Fourth, while Miss Bellew stood by the window, and Marjorie and Clara and Dolly stood by the table, looking at one another eloquently, in a hushed group.

The silence was suddenly broken: as Bessie Bunter rolled into the study, chuckling, her fat face wreathed in grins.

CHAPTER THREE

"I SAY, you girls—"
    "Bessie!"
"He, he, he! I've done it!"
"Quiet!" gasped Marjorie.

"He, he, he!" cachinnated Bessie. Chuckling gleefully, she blinked at three horrified faces. She did not, for the moment, observe that another person was in the study standing by the window. Her eyes and spectacles were on Marjorie and Co. "I say, Bellew will be wild! What! Barbara wouldn't let me have her gum, and you wouldn't let me have yours, but I found some in Marcia's study and I've jolly well done it! Bellew will be hopping mad! He, he, he! I say, poured the whole bottle into her Latin book! Fancy her face when she finds it! What? He, he, he!"

Bessie chuckled explosively.

Evidently, she was tremendously pleased with her exploit.

Miss Bellew, by the window, stood as if petrified. Marjorie and Clara and Dolly could only gaze at Bessie Bunter in dumb horror.

Bessie chuckled on.

"I say, will Bellew be as mad as a hatter?

What? He, he, he! I say, nearly every leaf of her Latin book stuck together, in a chunk! She won't be able to use it in class again, I'll bet. He, he, he! I say, Clara, what are you making faces at me for? You needn't make faces at me. I say, what's the matter?" added Bessie, as it dawned on her fat mind that something was the matter.

"BESSIE!"

It was a deep voice from the window.

Bessie Bunter jumped.

In fact, she bounded.

She spun round like a plump humming-top, her eyes almost bulging through her spectacles at the unexpected figure by the window.

"Oooooooh!" gasped Bessie.

"Bessie!"

"Oh, dear! Oh! I—I didn't see you, Miss Bellew—oh." Bessie's fat brain almost swam, as she blinked at her form-mistress. She realized that Miss Bellew had heard every word.

"So it was you, Bessie—!"

"Oh! No! I—I—I haven't been to your study, Miss Bellew, and—and I never poured any gum into your book while I was there—I—I hadn't any gum, Miss Bellew—I never found any in Marcia's study—"

Miss Bellew laid Clara's translation on the table. The look she fixed on Elizabeth Bunter was like unto that of the fabled basilisk.

"You will come with me, Bessie!"

"I—I say, I—I never—"

"I shall take you to the Principal—"

"Oh, lor'!"

"Miss Primrose will deal with you. Come!"

"But—but I—I never didn't wasn't—"

"Come!"

Miss Bellew swept from No. 7. Bessie Bunter gave Marjorie and Co. one dismal, dolorous blink, and followed.

"Poor Bessie!" sighed Marjorie.

"Just like Bessie!" said Dolly.

"Just!" agreed Clara.

And they smiled. Really, they could not help it. They sympathized: but really and truly, it was just like Bessie Bunter!

THE END

ON THE BALL
A football song by
Charles Hamilton

1.
Here's a cheer for the grand old game,
  And a cheer for the men who play,
Here's a shout for the boys at home,
  And a yell for the lads away!
        Hurray!
CHORUS: On the ball, on the ball,
        Loud and clear it rings like a trumpet call!
        Hear the shouts excited roll,
        Buck up there! Look out in goal!
        On the ball, ball, ball
        On the ball, on the ball!

2.
Though the stormy winds do blow,
  And the sleet or rain may fall,
Hang the weather, lads, let it go,
  Buck up, and out with the ball,
        Hurray!
    CHORUS: On the ball, etc.

3.
If your goalie lets them through
  Or your crack man suddenly crocks,
Don't be downhearted boys,
  Play harder and give them socks!
        Hurray!
    CHORUS: On the ball, etc.

4.
If the finish is getting near,
  And you've had a knocking about,
Good old Soccer's all touch and go,
  There's a chance till they turn you out,
        Hurray!
    CHORUS: On the ball, etc.

46

5.

If a man doesn't come up to scratch,
   Don't say he's the worst you've seen,
It's all right to shout at a match
   But remember he's not a machine,
      Hurray!
      CHORUS: On the ball, etc.

6.

There's many a game been won,
   By a side that looked done in,
On the leather, lads! Bang it through,
   Just stick to your guns and win,
      Hurray!
      CHORUS: On the ball, etc.

EXTRA VERSES

1.

When a penalty's given against,
   And of course you don't agree,
Keep your temper—that's if you can—
   And don't kill the referee!
      Hurray!
      CHORUS: On the ball, etc.

2.

When the boys are off their form,
   And they don't know how to win,
Don't shout nasty things or swear,
   But stick to 'em, thick and thin,
      Hurray!
      CHORUS: On the ball, etc.

3.

When you've got a chance in a sweep,
   And the odd goal knocks you out,
It's better to cheer than to weep,
   Give the winning team a shout,
      Hurray!
      CHORUS: On the ball, etc.

4.

It's right to shout for your side,
   But never be carried away,
A sportsman's mind is wide,
   And he'll always cheer good play,
      Hurray!
      CHORUS: On the ball, etc.

5.

If you're drawn to play the Spurs,
   Or the Wolves in the final tie,
Or the Rovers or Blades—who cares?
   Line up, lads, and do or die,
      Hurray!
      CHORUS: On the ball, etc.

6.

When you get to the Palace ground,
   In the tie for the English Cup,
Put your beef in the game, my lads,
   Now or never, my lads! Buck up!
      Hurray!
      CHORUS: On the ball, etc.

Top left: The Gem, July 1908
Bottom right: The Gem, April 1919

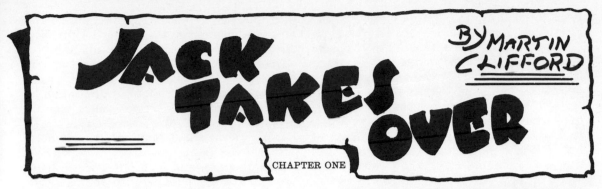

JACK TAKES OVER

BY MARTIN CLIFFORD

CHAPTER ONE

JACK of All Trades came to halt.

He was following a footpath across a sunny Sussex meadow. That footpath ended at a stile which gave access to Rylcombe Lane.

On the stile sat a burly youth, with a bullet head, a pimply complexion, and a cigarette sticking out of the corner of his mouth.

He had his back to the meadow, and seemed to be watching the lane, as if in expectation of seeing someone coming. But he glanced round at Jack's footsteps, stared at him, and then turned his head again, without otherwise moving. So Jack came to a halt. He had to cross the stile, to get out into the lane, and the bulky youth, sitting on the top bar with his feet on the step, barred the way. And apparently he had no intention of shifting.

"Mind letting me get over the stile?" asked Jack, mildly.

The commonest courtesy would have induced the big fellow to move and let him pass. But he seemed to have no use for courtesy, common or uncommon. He did not even answer the question, or turn his head again. He sat smoking and watching the lane.

Jack of All Trades breathed hard.

He was strongly tempted to grasp the uncivil fellow, and pitch him off the stile. And though the fellow was several inches taller, and twice his weight, he had no doubt that he could have done it. A rough life on the roads had taught the boy wanderer to use his hands, and landed him in more than one scrap with rough characters, in which he had not come out second-best.

But Jack was a peacable fellow, and he was not looking for trouble. He breathed hard, but he kept his temper. He gave the fellow on the stile a gentle tap on the elbow.

"Let a fellow get across!" he said, politely.

The pimply youth stared round again. He gave Jack a frown, and his jaw jutted threateningly.

"Keep your paws to yourself," he snapped. "I want to get across."

"You can want."

"Look here—."

"Jump it!" said the fellow on the stile, his frown changing to a grin, "Lots of room to jump! Chuck your bundle over, and jump after it, you young tramp."

A gleam like fire came into the blue eyes looking at him.

Who the fellow might be, Jack had no idea: but evidently he was the kind of fellow who prided himself upon being a "tough guy", and liked to "throw his weight about". Certainly it never occurred to him that the boy in the meadow, though nothing like his size and weight, could have knocked him right and left, had the spirit moved him so to do.

Jack was sorely tempted. His right hand clenched, almost itching to be planted in the grinning pimply face.

"Will you shift?" he asked.

"Shift me!" grinned the pimply one.

Jack almost took him at his word. But he restrained his temper. The fellow was not worth a scrap: neither did Jack want one: he wanted to get on his way. Quietly, though with deep feelings, he dropped his bundle over the stile, and clambered after it. The pimply youth watched him, grinning, as he negotiated the high bar, and jumped to the ground on the other side.

Taking no further notice of the offensive stranger, Jack picked up his bundle, slung it over his shoulder, and stepped out. In one direction, the lane led to the village of Rylcombe: in the other, it passed the gates of St Jim's, a school that Jack knew. It was in the latter direction that Jack stepped out, though his destination certainly was not the big school which he had visited once, and had never forgotten. But he liked the idea of catching a distant glimpse of it, before he turned off to get to the Wayland road.

A loud laugh from the fellow on the stile followed him, as he started.

Jack glanced round, with a flash in his eyes.

The fellow was laughing at him, evidently under the impression that he was scared, and amused by his lack of spirit. Jack came very near throwing down his bundle, and rushing back, to give that offensive "tough guy" what he was asking for. But once more he checked the impulse: and turned his back on the fellow and tramped on his way—that derisive laugh followed him as he went.

CHAPTER TWO

"BAI Jove!"

Jack of All Trades gave a little jump, as he heard that surprised exclamation. It was uttered in a familiar voice. It was not the first time that he had heard the aristocratic tones of Arthur Augustus D'Arcy, of the Fourth Form at St Jim's.

Half-a-mile or so from the stile, Jack had come to a stop again: this time standing by a gap in the hawthorn hedge, and gazing across the fields towards the big school to which he had once paid a happy visit. Even at the distance, he could make out the buildings, and innumerable chimneys and red roofs and the tops of tall elms. It was a pleasant sight, in the summer afternoon, and his sunburnt face was bright and cheerful as he gazed. He did not notice a schoolboy coming down the lane from the direction of the school, until that exclamation caused him to look round, when he beheld the elegant figure and gleaming eyeglass of Arthur Augustus D'Arcy.

D'Arcy stopped, at the sight of Jack of All Trades. He came towards him with a beaming smile, and held out a white hand that almost disappeared into Jack's larger brown one as he shook hands.

"Fancy wunnin' into you, deah boy!" said Arthur Augustus, evidently pleased by the unexpected meeting, "I wathah wondahed whethah I should evah wun into you again, and it is a weal pleasuah."

Jack smiled. He could hardly have expected that elegant St Jim's fellow, the son of a lord, to remember the wandering lad who had once done him a service. But D'Arcy, evidently, had not forgotten him: and was delighted to see him again: and apparently quite unconscious of any difference in social station between them. If there were fellows at St Jim's who might have turned up disdainful noses at the lad who tramped the road with a bundle on his shoulder, the Honourable Arthur Augustus D'Arcy certainly was not one of them.

"On the woad again, what?" asked D'Arcy.

"Yes. I'm heading for Wayland—."

"That is wathah a long step fwom heah," said Arthur Augustus, "But I wemembah that you are a wathah twemendous walkah. If you are staying in Wayland you must wun acwoss and see us at the school."

"I'd like to—but I've got to get on without stopping in Wayland," answered Jack. "But I'm very glad to see you again, and to know that you remember me."

"Yaas, wathah," said Arthur Augustus, "I wemembah you all wight, my deah boy. I'd be vewy glad to walk part of the way to Wayland with you, but I've got to keep an appointment a little furthah along the lane."

"I mustn't keep you, then!" said Jack: though he would have been glad of even a few minutes in the pleasant company of the swell of St Jim's.

"Oh, that's all wight," said Arthur Augustus, cheerily, "Punch Boggles can wait a few minutes anyhow, bothah him. It will not hurt him to wait a little longah before he gets a feahful thwashin'."

Jack started a little.

This well-dressed, elegant, easy-mannered schoolboy of St Jim's was hardly the kind of fellow he would have expected to find on the war-path. But from D'Arcy's words, it appeared that somebody was booked for battle further along Rylcombe Lane.

"Let's walk a little way what?" asked Arthur Augustus, "That wottah can wait at the stile and be bothahed."

Jack started again.

"At the stile!" he repeated.

"Yaas: Punch Boggles is goin' to wait for me there, and I have no doubt he is alweady waitin'."

"Oh!" exclaimed Jack, "A big fellow with a pimply face—?"

"That's the wottah!" agreed Arthur Augustus, "His name isn't weally Punch, you know—that's a nickname, because he's supposed to pack a twemendous punch. I twust that I shall punch a little hardah, though."

Jack of All Trades looked at him. He had had an idea that the bullying fellow at the stile was waiting for someone. Now he knew for whom he was waiting.

"Pwobably you passed him as you came that way," continued Arthur Augustus D'Arcy, "You seem to know what he looks like—."

"A big hulking fellow, more than twice your weight, D'Arcy," said Jack, and he could not keep a note of concern out of his voice. "Surely you're not thinking of tackling a ruffian like that."

"Yaas, wathah!" said Arthur Augustus, emphatically, "I twust that I shall be able to give him the thwashin' he deserves."

"But—!" Jack almost gasped. That the slim elegant swell of St Jim's could stand up, for a single round, against that big, strong, hulking fellow, was simply im-possible. Arthur Augustus D'Arcy had un-limited pluck, and no doubt he could box: but no amount of pluck, and no skill in boxing could avail him very much in combat with overwhelming size and weight and strength. Jack of All Trades knew, though D'Arcy evidently did not, that "Punch Boggles" would hammer him black and blue, and leave him lying a shattered wreck, if that combat came off at all. The swell of St Jim's had simply no chance, not the ghost of a chance, of thrashing that hulking rough. When the thrashing came off, Arthur Augustus D'Arcy could only be at the receiving end.

"Come on, deah boy," said Arthur Augustus, cheerily, "Punch Boggles can wait a little longah. Pewwaps you would like me to cawwy your bundle a bit."

"Oh! No! that's all right," said Jack, hastily. He walked with D'Arcy to the turning which led towards Wayland. He was glad of the elegant schoolboy's company: and gladder still to keep him, if only for a time, at a safe distance from Punch Boggles. Arthur Augustus, evidently wholly and happily unaware that he was rushing on destruction in keeping that appointment at the stile in Rylcombe Lane, chatted cheerily as they walked. But Jack of All Trades was feeling considerably worried.

"That chap at the stile is a lot above your weight, D'Arcy," he remarked.

"Oh, yaas," assented Arthur Augustus.

"Why not give him a miss?" hinted Jack.

"Imposs, deah boy. He would think I funked him."

"Oh! Yes! But—."

"I wathah think I shall handle him all wight," said Arthur Augustus, "Blake and Hewwies and Dig don't think so, and Tom Mewwy and Mannahs and Lowthah told me, one aftah anothah, to go to sleep and dweam again. They will be surpwised when they heah that I have thwashed him."

Jack had no doubt about that!

"I slipped away this aftahnoon without tellin' them," added Arthur Augustus, with a cheery grin, "They would vewy likely have twied to stop me."

Jack could not help thinking that it was a

pity they hadn't! Arthur Augustus's friends, evidently, did not share his happy confidence in his ability to handle the young ruffian at the stile.

"But—!" he said, uneasily. He could not help feeling deeply concerned, at a mental picture of that slim, elegant, kind-hearted fellow crumpling up, battered black and blue, under Punch Boggles's slogging fists. "But—the fellow isn't worth your trouble, D'Arcy—."

"Hardly," agreed Arthur Augustus, "But, you see, he kicked my young bwothah, Wally, and I am goin' to thwash him to teach him to behave. So I sent him a note wequestin' him to wait at the stile for me this aftahnoon, and I was on my way there when I wan into you. He is a vewy unpleasant and twoublesome person, always kickin' small boys or snatchin' their caps off, and it is time he had a lesson. I am goin' to give him one."

Jack walked on beside the elegant St Jim's fellow in silence,—thinking. That Arthur Augustus D'Arcy, with happy confidence, was going like a lamb to the slaughter, he knew quite well—just as well as Blake and Herries and Digby, Tom Merry and Manners and Lowther, would have known it, if they had known that D'Arcy had sallied out on the war-path that afternoon. While Arthur Augustus ran on with his cheery chat, Jack was trying to think of some way of saving him from himself, as it were. And Jack of All Trades, when he set his keen wits to work, seldom failed to find a solution to a problem.

CHAPTER THREE

"GOOD-bye, Jack!"

"Good-bye, D'Arcy."

"See you again some day, deah boy."

"I hope so."

"Cheewio!" said Arthur Augustus, and with a wave of the hand, he departed.

They had walked a mile on the way to Wayland, by a lane deeply wooded on either side. At that point Arthur Augustus had to tear himself away, in order not to be too late for his rendezvous with Punch Boggles. Jack watched him as he went—walking at an easy saunter, and smiled. It was not Arthur Augustus D'Arcy's way to hurry: and at that rate of progress, he was likely to take some considerable time in covering the mile back to Rylcombe Lane, and the further half-mile to the stile therein. Which was exactly what Jack of All Trades wanted, and upon what he had calculated.

Jack had thought that little problem out, and he fancied that he had found a solution. As D'Arcy disappeared at that easy and leisurely saunter, Jack stepped out of the lane into the wood adjoining. There he deposited his bundle out of sight in a bush. His next movements were to be rapid: very rapid: and he did not want to be encumbered.

Leaving his bundle hidden, to be picked up later, he set off through the wood, winding his way at a swift trot, back the way he had come, but keeping clear of the lane, in order to keep clear of the swell of St Jim's. Arthur Augustus, supposing that he had gone on to Wayland, was not to have the slightest intimation that he had turned back. Had Arthur Augustus guessed, and guessed his intention, his noble back might have been up. But Arthur Augustus was booked to remain in happy ignorance of his movements and his intentions.

Jack covered the ground fast, winding through the wood, till he was sure that he was well ahead of the sauntering schoolboy. Then he emerged into the lane, and ran on faster than before in the open. The boy wanderer was thoroughly sound of wind and limb, and running a mile cost him nothing. Indeed, his feet seemed hardly to touch the ground as he ran. He was well ahead of D'Arcy—and he had to get further ahead—as fast and far as he could.

He came speeding out into Rylcombe Lane, and turned in the direction of the stile. Without slacking speed for a moment, he ran on, and very soon came in sight of the stile, where he had left the pimply youth. "Punch Boggles"—Jack knew his name now,—was still sitting on the stile and smoking cigarettes. He stared at Jack as he came up, and stopped, panting a little after his long and rapid run.

"You again!" he said, aggressively.

"Little me!" assented Jack. He stood in front of the hulking fellow occupying the stile, looking at him. He was in no hurry to commence operations—he wanted to get his breath after his run. And he had no doubt that the leisurely swell of St Jim's was still a mile or so away. What Jack of All Trades had planned, would be over and done with, long before Arthur Augustus D'Arcy arrived on the spot. D'Arcy would never even guess that he had taken over!

"Well, what do you want?" growled Punch Boggles, puzzled by Jack's return, and by his look and manner. "If it's a thick ear, you'll get it fast enough, if you stand there staring at a chap."

"Get off that stile."

"Eh?"

"I said get off that stile."

Punch blinked at him.

"You said—what?" he stuttered.

"Deaf?" asked Jack, pleasantly, "I'll say again! Get off that stile, before you're knocked off it."

Punch Boggles fairly gaped at him. This was the fellow for whom he had refused to stir, and who had quietly allowed himself to be bullied, and gone on his way with Punch laughing at him. The change was quite startling. Having tamely tolerated Punch's offensive aggressiveness, he had gone off—now he had unexpectedly reappeared, with not the slightest sign of tameness about him: quite the reverse, in fact. Punch realized that he come back hunting for trouble, and a very ugly look came over the pimply face.

"You're asking for it!" he said, in a growl of menace. He threw away his cigarette.

"Exactly!" agreed Jack, "You wouldn't shift to let a fellow get over that stile. I've come back to shift you. You're getting off that stile, or I'm going to knock you off."

"By gum!" breathed Punch Boggles, "I'm waiting 'ere for a feller I'm going to make mincemeat of, but I'll make mincemeat of you while I'm waiting, you cheeky young tramp. Knock me off this 'ere stile, will you?

Look out that I don't knock your own block off. I'm coming for you."

"Come on then, and don't waste time gassing."

Punch Boggles came on, with a rush, with two big clenched fists sawing the air. His pimply face was red with rage. Under that savage rush, there was no doubt that the slim and elegant swell of St Jim's would have gone down like a ninepin. But the boy wanderer of the roads was built of tougher material than the elegant Gussy of St Jim's. He did not recede an inch, and he did not side-step the rush: he stood up to it like a granite rock, and met Punch with left and right, crashing in the pimply face.

"Oooooh" gasped Punch, again, as he staggered, Left and right came again, landing like hammers, and Punch's stagger became a totter, and he pitched over on his back, landing on Sussex with a resounding thud.

Jack stood, panting, and rubbing his knuckles. Contact with the pimply face had been hard and sharp.

"Oooooh" gasped Punch, again, as he sprawled. Jack of All Trades waited for him to get on his feet.

Punch was not long in doing that. He struggled up, and, almost hissing with fury, fairly hurled himself headlong at Jack of All Trades.

The next three or four minutes were wild and whirling.

Jack was hard as hickory, tough as steel. But the bullying Punch was big and strong, and had a longer reach and tremendous force in his hitting. Not a tithe of his wild and furious blows landed on his active opponent: but when they did land, they landed hard. But for every one that landed, Jack gave back two or three, with plenty of drive in them. Punch soon ceased his fierce rushes, and gave more attention to defence: but that did not save his pimply countenance, upon which fists that seemed to him like lumps of lead crashed again and again. It dawned on Punch Boggles that he was getting the worst of this: and he exerted every ounce. Not till his nose was swollen and streaming red, both his eyes blackening and blinking, and most of the rest of him feeling as if it had been under a lorry, did Punch Boggles admit defeat.

He had to admit it then: as a terrific right-hander, landing on his aggressive jaw, hurled him back against the stile, where he collapsed in a gasping, gurgling, groaning heap.

He did not even attempt to rise again. He could not. He sprawled helplessly, utterly spent, utterly knocked out and done for. There was not another punch left in Punch. He could scarcely have swatted a gnat. He lay on his back a complete wreck, blinking dizzily with blackened eyes, too far gone even to mop his streaming nose.

Jack made a step towards him: and Punch found energy enough for a gasping howl:

"You keep orf! I'm done! I give you best! Don't you touch me."

Jack laughed. He had had some hard knocks, and he was feeling the effects of them. But he could have gone on cheerfully, if Punch had wanted more. But Punch, evidently, didn't want more. Very much indeed he didn't. He was too utterly used-up even to be able to crawl away. He could only lie and gasp and gurgle and blink dizzily. And most undoubtedly he was in no state to "make mincemeat" of the St Jim's schoolboy when he arrived on the spot,—which was all Jack wanted.

"O.K!" said Jack, "Next time you pitch into a chap smaller than yourself, chum, better make sure that he isn't too tough! Cheerio!"

With that, Jack of All Trades swung himself over the stile, and cut away across the fields, to get back by a roundabout route to the spot where he had left his bundle, without risk of encountering Arthur Augustus D'Arcy on the way. He had saved that elegant and unsuspicious youth from a terrific hammering: but of that circumstance, the swell of St Jim's was to remain in happy ignorance.

"OH, cwumbs!" ejaculated Arthur Augustus D'Arcy.

He had arrived—about ten minutes after Jack of All Trades had disappeared into space.

He expected to find Punch Boggles at the stile. And he found him. But he did not find him as he expected to find him. He found him lying by the stile, feebly clasping an anguished nose with one hand, and feebly rubbing a darkened eye with the other. He gazed at him in astonishment.

"Oh, cwumbs!" he repeated, "Is that you, Boggles?"

Punch blinked at him.

"You!" he mumbled.

"Yaas, wathah! Weren't you expectin' me?" asked Arthur Augustus, "But you don't look much like scwappin'. Have you been havin' a wow with somebody else? You seem to be a vewy quawwelsome and aggwessive person, Boggles. I certainly shall not thwash you in your pwesent state."

"You keep orf!" moaned Punch, "Leave a bloke alone."

"Pway to not be alarmed," said Arthur Augustus, "I have no intention whatevah of hittin' a fellow when he is down. You seem to have been thwough it. You look an uttah w'eck. I have no doubt that you asked for it. It appeahs that somebody has saved me the twouble of thwashin' you. Pewwaps this will be a lesson to you, Boggles, not to be so vewy aggwessive and unpleasant. I weally twust so."

And, as there was evidently nothing doing now, Arthur Augustus D'Arcy turned, and walked back to St Jim's: leaving the once-aggressive Punch crumpled by the stile, caressing his eyes and his nose and other damaged spots almost too numerous to enumerate. It was quite a long time before Punch was able to limp away, a dismal, doleful, dizzy, dilapidated Punch.

By that time, Jack was miles on his way.

He had a cut lip, a swollen nose, and slightly darkened eye, and other traces of the fray. He was not feeling his best, after that strenuous combat. But his face was cheery, as he tramped on with his bundle on his shoulder: leaving Punch Boggles a sadder and perhaps wiser Punch: and Arthur Augustus D'Arcy, serene and undamaged at St Jim's, in complete and happy ignorance of what he owed to Jack of All Trades.

THE END

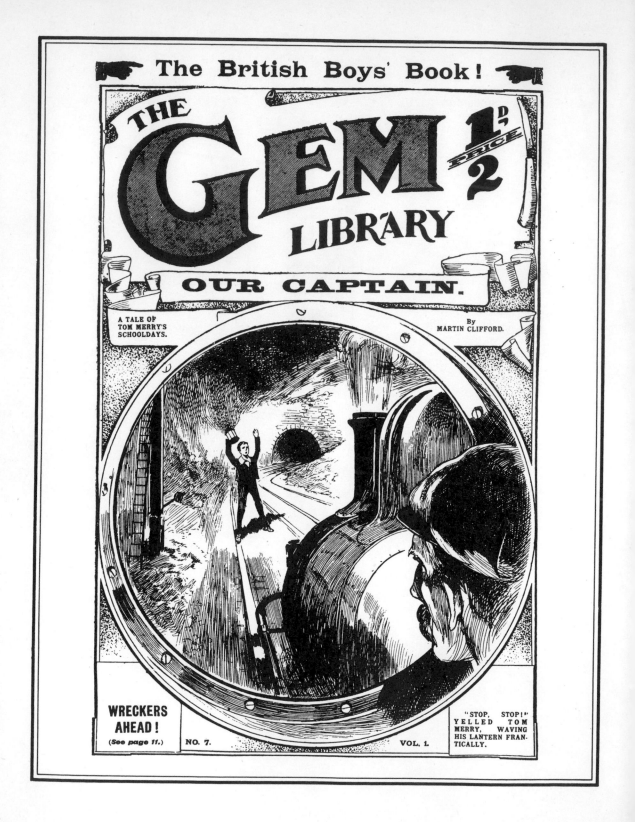

When *The Gem*, featuring Tom Merry &
Co., was launched in March 1907 it cost
½d an issue. When the paper folded,
thirty-three years later, it cost 2d.

"The CARCROFT" CHRONICLE

EDITED BY ~ HARRY COMPTON
SUB EDITOR ~ DICK LEE
SPORTS EDITOR ~ DUDLEY VANE-CARTER
BOXING EDITOR ~ BOB DRAKE
FOOD EXPERT ~ TURKEY TUCK

AN INTERVIEW WITH MARTIN CLIFFORD by Harry Compton

WE thought it a top-hole idea, in the editorial office, otherwise the corner study, to interview Mr Martin Clifford, the celebrated author of "Tom Merry". If it came off, the *Carcroft Chronicle* would be the only school magazine ever to pull off such a scoop. So, provided with a large new note-book and having borrowed Vane-Carter's fountain-pen, I took the train from Sussex to Kent, and arrived ultimately at Mr Clifford's door.

It was opened by a lady whom I concluded to be the great man's housekeeper.

"Does Mr Martin Clifford live here?" I asked.

"Yes."

"Can I see him?"

"Mr Clifford is busy."

"I represent the Press," I explained.

"Mr Clifford sees reporters only by appointment," she explained in her turn: and the door closed.

I was a little dashed. I realized that I was probably not the only representative of the Press seeking interviews with the author of Tom Merry, and that no doubt a busy man had to ration them, as it were. On the other hand, I did not want to return to Carcroft and explain to Lee, and Drake, and V.C., and the rest of the Staff, that all I had learned of Martin Clifford was that he saw Press-men only by appointment. So I stood considering my next move.

I was still standing and considering, when a French window opened, and a rather kindly face, surmounted by a velvet skull-cap, looked out. I had seen photographs in the papers—I knew him at once! This was the man!

"Haven't you brought it?" he asked.

"Eh! Brought what?" I stammered, taken aback.

"The evening paper."

"The evening paper!" I repeated, blankly.

"Aren't you the boy from the newsagent's?" asked Mr Clifford.

I think I breathed rather hard.

"I am NOT the boy from the newsagent's, Mr

Clifford," I said, very distinctly, "My name is Harry Compton. I am captain of the Fourth Form at Carcroft. I am also Chief Editor and Roving Reporter of the *Carcroft Chronicle*. I represent that journal. I am here to interview you, Mr Clifford."

"Oh!" said Mr Clifford, taken aback too, "The fact is, I never see reporters except by—"

I ventured to interrupt him.

"I've heard that one!" I said. "I've just heard it from your housekeeper. Please give me a few minutes."

'I am rather busy to-day," said Martin Clifford. He hesitated. But as he has remarked in his own stories, the man who hesitates is lost. His kindly nature prevailed. He nodded. "Step in," he said.

I did not wait to be asked twice!

A moment later, I was seated in the Presence: and could scarcely believe in my good luck. Here was I, in a comfortable armchair, face to face with the man whose name was a household word. I whipped out my note-book.

"Now, a few questions, Mr Clifford," I began, in a business-like manner.

"Fire away!" said Mr Clifford, good-humouredly.

"Many of my readers," I said, "would like to know just how old you are, Mr Clifford."

"I am not old at all," explained Mr Clifford, "But I have been young for more years than I ever confide to reporters."

"Will you tell me when you were born?" I inquired.

"Certainly," said Mr Clifford, "on my first birthday."

"Hem! Another interesting question is your various pen-names," I said. "You wrote the old *Gem* as Martin Clifford! What were your other pen-names at various points of your life?"

"Too numerous to mention," answered Mr Clifford.

"Hem!" I tried again. "I have heard that you were a great traveller in your younger days, Mr Clifford—France, Germany, Austria, Switzerland, Italy, Holland, Belgium—is it true that you once descended into the crater of Mount Vesuvius?"

"Quite true."

"What was it like?"

Martin Clifford seemed to consider for a moment or two.

"It was quite like the crater of Mount Vesuvius!" he answered, at length. "Very like indeed!"

"Hem! Do you ever broadcast, Mr Clifford?"

"Sometimes."

"How often?"

"As often as the B.B.C. asks me," said Mr Clifford, with a smile. "Speaking of the B.B.C., it may interest you to hear of one of my own little personal customs."

I was all eagerness at once. Note-book and fountain-pen were ready. In fact I was almost breathless.

"Please go on, Mr Clifford," I exclaimed. "Anything of that kind—the personal touch, you know—will delight my readers. Please tell me."

"You see," said Martin Clifford, "It sometimes happens that some boring person may drop in, and stay too long and talk too much. Hospitality forbids me to tell him to cut it short and travel. So I have instituted this little custom I am going to tell you about to solve the difficulty. I have a press button under this rug—!" He indicated the spot with his foot.

"A press-button under the rug," I repeated, scribbling away busily in my note-book.

"Unseen by my boresome caller, quite unnoticed, I press it with my foot," continued Mr Clifford. 'It rings a bell in my house-keeper's room."

"—in the house-keeper's room," I repeated, scribbling down Mr Clifford's words as fast as he uttered them.

"Edith then taps at the door," went on Mr Clifford, "and announces 'A telephone call from the B.B.C., Mr Clifford! They are holding the line'."

I made more hurried notes.

"My boring visitor then takes his hat, and his departure," said Mr Clifford. "We part on the pleasantest of terms, with feelings unruffled. Rather neat idea, what?"

"Excellent!" I exclaimed, heartily, "An excellent idea, Mr Clifford. Bores never know they are boring, do they?"

"Seldom," agreed Mr Clifford.

"And they wouldn't like to be told," I remarked, with a smile.

"They wouldn't indeed."

"By that simple dodge, you get rid of a bore who is wasting your time, and without ruffling his feathers," I said.

"That is the big idea," said Mr Clifford.

"Very, very tactful!" I said.

"Very!" assented Martin Clifford.

"I am sure that will interest the readers of the *Carcroft Chronicle*," I said, "Now, I have a few more questions to put, Mr Clifford—" I was going on, when I was interrupted by a tap at the door.

It opened, and the trim house-keeper appeared.

"What is it, Edith?" asked Martin Clifford.

"A telephone call from the B.B.C. Mr Clifford," said Edith, "They are holding the line!"

I looked at Edith. I looked at Martin Clifford. A few moments more, and I was heading for the railway station!

Martin Clifford, the creator of Tom Merry, admires one of *Tom Merry's Annuals*

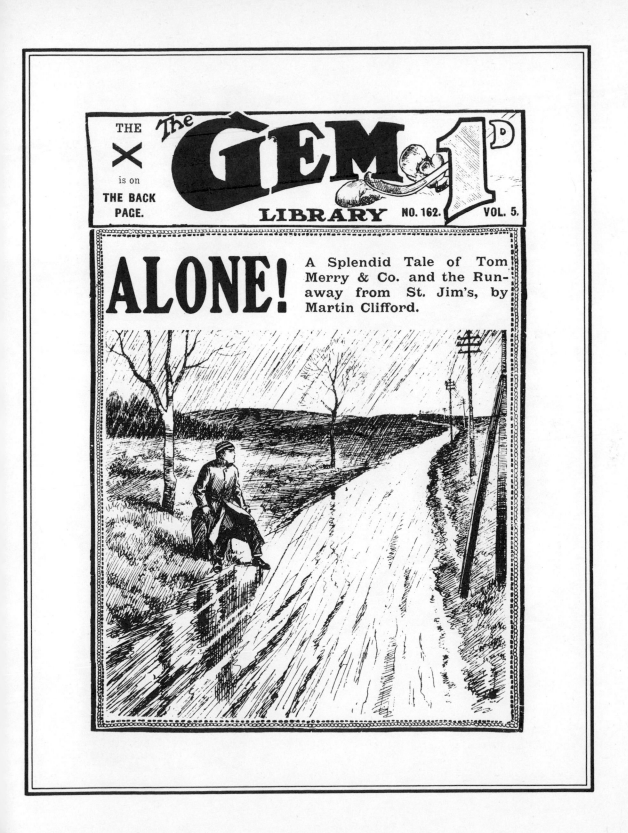

'The Beaks at Greyfriars' as seen by
C. H. Chapman

PRICELESS EDUCATION

A poem by Frank Richards sent to his sister, Una Harrison,
on the occasion of the Teachers' threatened strike during the Autumn of 1961

The Teachers struck. The schools were closed: each little fellow grew
From youth to age in ignorance, and never, never knew,
How many wives King Henry had, and which of them he slew.

He had to face the facts of life, its problems and its pain,
Not knowing when or wherefore the Armada sailed from Spain,
Or whether Alfred burned the cakes while hiding from the Dane.

Geography, too, passed him by: no more than any mouse,
Could he have told the difference between Siam and Laos,
How then could he wield pick or spade, or help to build a house?

How could he handle bricks or lime, or mortar in a pail,
Who knew not that a man named Shakespeare wrote The Winter's Tale.
Or that old Johnson used to take his tea with Mrs Thrale?

Who, who would care to risk his life, in train or motorbus,
Driven by some benighted chap, some ignorant young cuss,
Who'd never heard of Picts and Scots, and how they raided us?

O give us back our teachers: let us pay them what they will,
Give their scholastic fingers freest access to the till,
Let aching heads be crammed again, and never mind the bill!

Aspects of Bunter. Five faces of the Fat Owl drawn by C. H. Chapman

BILLY BUNTER'S BOUNDARY

By FRANK RICHARDS

CHAPTER ONE

"WHY not?" asked Bob Cherry.

Harry Wharton shook his head.

"Rot!" he said, tersely.

"Bunter's keen—"

"Is he? First time he's ever been keen on anything but tuck."

"Well, yes," admitted Bob. "But he really is keen now, and when a chap's keen, why not give him a chance? After all, it's only the Fourth we're playing—and we can beat the Fourth hands down, with a passenger on board. Bunter won't do any harm if he doesn't do any good."

Harry Wharton laughed.

"That's one way of looking at it!" he said. "But cricket's cricket, and we can't take chances."

"Safe as houses!" said Bob. "And dash it all, old man, we've ragged the fat ass often enough, for slacking: and now he's keen for once, why not give him a look in, when there's no real risk?"

"What's made him so jolly keen, all of a sudden?" asked the captain of the Remove. "He's usually keen on dodging games."

"Blessed if I know but—he is! Keen as mustard!" said Bob. "Look here, what do you fellows think?" He glanced round at Johnny Bull, Frank Nugent, and Hurree Jamset Ram Singh.

"Oh, give him a chance," said Nugent. "We can beat the Fourth playing a man short—and that's what it comes to."

"The beatfulness is a deadly cert," agreed Hurree Jamset Ram Singh.

Grunt, from Johnny Bull.

"Cricket's an uncertain game," he said. "Temple's crowd aren't much good, but you never know."

There was a pause.

That afternoon, the Greyfriars Remove were playing the Fourth, in a Form match. They had no doubt of the result, which every Remove man regarded as a foregone conclusion. Temple, Dabney and Co. of the Fourth, were simply not in the same street, when it came to games, with the Remove. Not a member of the Famous Five doubted that they would beat the Fourth by a bagful of runs.

In such circumstances, it was possible to stretch a point.

Billy Bunter, the fattest and most fatuous member of the Remove, was keen to

65

play. It was, as the captain of the Remove remarked, the first time he had displayed keenness. But for once, wonderful to relate, Bunter was keen as mustard: and he had pestered the captain of the Remove for days on end to give him a chance. Now Bob Cherry, always good-natured, and more than willing to welcome a stray sheep into the fold, as it were, had taken up the cudgels for the fat Owl. Certainly, in a match with Rookwood, or St Jim's, or Felgate, Bob would not have dreamed of it. But it was only the Fourth, whom the Remove were accustomed to walk over. Even if Bunter scored ducks at the wicket, and fielded like a sack of coke, it wouldn't affect the result, unless by reducing the margin by which Temple, Dabney and Co. were licked. There would be a good margin anyway.

Harry Wharton nodded, at last.

There was only one dissentient voice among the five: Johnny's. Cricket, as Johnny remarked, was an uncertain game. But even Johnny was not emphatic about it.

"Oh, all right!" said Harry. "I'll tell the fat ass he's to play. And if the Fourth beat us, Bob—"

"They couldn't."

"Well if they do—"

"They won't."

"If they do, we'll boot you all round the field after the game," declared Harry Wharton.

Bob Cherry chuckled.

"Do!" he said.

And the point having been settled, the captain of the Remove went to look for Billy Bunter, with good news for that fat and fatuous youth. He found the Owl of the Remove leaning on a buttress, breathing rather hard. Billy Bunter had done well at dinner, and he was slowly recovering from his exertions. Certainly he did not look a promising recruit for a cricket team.

He blinked at Harry Wharton, through his big spectacles, with a reproachful blink, as the captain of the Remove came up. How often his form-captain had answered "No!" to his requests to play for the form. Bunter could hardly have computed: but the negatives had been frequent enough to convince him that there was nothing doing.

"Oh, here you are," said Harry. "You're playing this afternoon, Bunter."

"Eh?"

"I'm shoving you into the team."

"Oh!"

"Get changed in time, if your flannels will go round that dinner you parked in hall."

Billy Bunter's fat lip curled.

"So you want me, after all?" he said. "I've a jolly good mind not to play, now."

"What?"

"You've found out that you were throwing away a good man," jeered Bunter. "Well, now you've changed your mind, and come and ask me to play, I'm not at all sure that I will, so yah! Still, if you want me—"

"You fat, foozling, frabjous, footling fathead!" said Harry Wharton, in measured tones. "You're not wanted, and you can go and eat coke." And he turned away.

A fat clutch on his arm stopped him.

"Hold on, old chap—!" bleated Bunter.

"Rats!"

"I was only jig—jog—joking, old chap! I'll play all right," gasped Bunter, "I'm awfully keen. Rely on me, old fellow! I'm your man!"

"Oh, all right, then. Stumps pitched at two!" said Harry. "And for goodness sake, Bunter, don't let us down if you can help it."

"Trust me!" said Bunter, cheerfully, "I suppose you'd like me to open the innings—"

"Oh, my hat! Hardly."

"Well, it would encourage the other fellows, you know, to see some really good batting at the start—"

"Ha, ha, ha!"

"Blessed if I see anything to cackle at! What are you cackling at, I'd like to know?" hooted Bunter.

Harry Wharton did not stay to explain what he was cackling at. He walked away, still laughing. Billy Bunter frowned after him as he went. Bunter, at any rate, fancied that he could play cricket, and did not see where any element of the comic came in.

Bob Cherry met the fat Owl when he rolled in to change, and clapped him on a plump shoulder.

"Gratters, old fat man," he said. "Glad you're playing. Look here, Bunter, do your best—I talked Wharton into playing you, and he's promised to boot me round the field if we lose the game. So pull up your socks."

"Oh!" said Bunter. "Thanks, old chap! Jolly decent of you to put in a word for me."

"Well, as you're so jolly keen for once—!" said Bob.

"Yes, rather! Keen as billy-o!" said Bunter. "And look here, old fellow, you come to the feed in my study to-morrow."

"Eh? is there going to be a feed in your study to-morrow?"

"What-ho! I'm going to blow the whole quid on one!" said Bunter, impressively.

"What quid?"

Billy Bunter grinned.

"It's coming from the pater," he explained. "He's heard from Quelch that I'm slack at games. You know Quelch—he never does a fellow justice in his reports. I've told the pater a lot of times that I'm the best cricketer in the form, and chance it—"

"Oh crumbs!"

"Well, the pater's standing me a quid, if I play for the Form!" said Bunter. "And now I'm jolly well playing—he, he, he! Jolly good of you to help a fellow out, Cherry—"

"You fat villain!" roared Bob Cherry.

"Eh?"

"So that's why you're so keen all of a sudden!" howled Bob. "By gum, I've a jolly good mind to boot you all over the school—"

"Beast!"

Billy Bunter threw that monosyllable over his shoulder as he hurriedly

departed. Bob glared after him. Bunter's unusual and unexpected keenness on cricket was explained now. It was not a sudden and very commendable yearning for the summer game that moved him. It was the prospect of a tip from his pater if he played for his Form! Certainly Bob would never have put in that word for him, had he known that little circumstance earlier. But it was done now: for one occasion, if one only, the fat Owl was booked to display to all Greyfriars what a cricketer he was!

CHAPTER TWO

"LOOK out, Bunter!"
     "Oh, fathead!"
"Butterfingers!"
Bunter was fielding.

To do the fat Owl justice, he was, if not exactly a keen games-man, at least keen to show the Remove, and all the rest of Greyfriars that he could play cricket. Billy Bunter often fancied that he could do things, until he came actually to do them. Then he generally woke up.

On the present occasion, it was an undoubted fact that Bunter was thinking most of all of the promised tip from his pater. That was the most important consideration in the game: indeed, in the whole universe. That "quid" was to be expended on a royal feast in Bunter's study: and compared to a study spread, a cricket match was merely an also ran. Nevertheless, Billy Bunter fancied himself as a cricketer, and was willing, in fact eager, to let the Remove see what a mistake it had been to leave him out of matches.

Temple of the Fourth had won the toss, and elected to take first knock. The Fourth-form batsmen grinned at the fat figure that looked twice as wide as any other in the field, and gave him many chances. They seemed rather to rely on Bunter missing the ball, even if it dropped fairly on his fat little nose. If that was the idea, it paid dividends: for never by any chance did Billy Bunter's fat fingers contact the leather.

Now Hurree Jamset Ram Singh was bowling to Cecil Reginald Temple at the wicket. The Fourth had made forty, so far, and last man was in. So a catch in the field would have dismissed the Fourth: and as it happened, Temple landed a perfect "sitter" right into Bunter's hands—if those hands had not been so extensively what the juniors called "cack-handed".

Billy Bunter blinked at the ball. Perhaps he saw it. If he did that was all he did. It dropped lightly at his feet, and Temple and his partner were running.

"Butterfingers!"
"Fathead!"
"Send in that ball."

Bunter sent it in, in the wrong direction. By the time it came home, four had been scored, and Temple was back at his wicket, grinning. And six more were taken before a catch in the field by Vernon-Smith put paid to the Fourth. Temple and Co. retired for fifty. It was more than they were accustomed to take, against

68

doughty men like the Remove. Bunter in the field had been a present help in time of need!

"We shall have to pull up our socks, after all," Bob Cherry remarked at the pavilion.

"I say, you fellows—"

"Oh, dry up, Bunter!"

"But I say, what about me to open our innings?" asked Bunter. "It's a good rule in cricket to put the best men in first."

"Just what we're going to do," said Harry Wharton. "You come in last you fat Owl—"

"Me last man!" exclaimed Bunter, indignantly.

"Yes: and if you don't like it—"

"I jolly well don't!" said Bunter, emphatically.

"Then you needn't come in at all. You can sit it out in the pav.—it won't make any difference."

"Beast!"

Billy Bunter watched the Remove innings with a frowning brow. He admitted that he hadn't had luck in the field: but he had a happy delusion that he was good for a century at the wicket, given a chance: indeed, in his mind's eye, he could see himself first in and not out! What he actually did see, when at long last he rolled out to bat, was a wrecked wicket, wrecked by the first ball he received. He blinked at that spread-eagled wicket, in surprise. He was the only person who was surprised.

"Oh, crikey!" said Bunter.

And he rolled on his homeward way.

"All down for forty-six!" Bob Cherry whistled.

"Did I say that cricket was an uncertain game?" queried Johnny Bull. "Temple's crowd are in better form than usual—and Bunter's helping them all he can—"

"Oh, really, Bull—!" squeaked an indignant fat Owl.

"You're an ass, Bob!" said Harry Wharton.

"And a chump!" said Nugent.

"The chumpfulness is terrific!" concurred Hurree Jamset Ram Singh.

Bob Cherry made a grimace.

"We'll lick them yet," he said.

"Better hope so!" said the captain of the Remove. "There's somebody who's going to be booted all round the field, if we don't."

"I suppose it was a bit risky, playing Bunter—", admitted Bob.

"More than a bit."

"I told you so!" remarked Johnny Bull.

"I say you fellows, chuck it!" hooted Billy Bunter. "Any fellow might have a spot of bad luck. If you'll let me open our next innings, Wharton—"

"Kill him, somebody!"

"Beast!" hooted Bunter. "Well, I'll jolly well show you something in the field, anyhow."

And he did, when the Fourth batted again. As Bunter, in the field, was precisely as useful as a sack of coke, or a stone image, the Fourth-form batsmen seemed to

delight in giving him chances. But Billy Bunter was on his mettle now—he was going to show them! And for once, marvellous to relate, his fat fingers did contact the ball. Temple, in fact, delivered it into his hands like a postman delivering a parcel.

Smack!

"Wow!"

Actually the ball smacked the fat palm. Then it dropped, and Bunter sucked that fat palm, which apparently had a pain in it.

"Oh, my hat!" gasped Bob Cherry.

"Oh, the fat chump!"

"Butterfingers!"

"Ow! ow!" gasped Bunter. "Wow!"

That was Billy Bunter's last chance to distinguish himself in the field. The innings ended with the Fourth Form another fifty up: and the Remove were left with fifty-five to get if they were going to pull off that match. So far from beating the Fourth by a wide margin, there seemed to be an element of doubt whether they would beat them at all: undoubtedly, cricket was an uncertain game, as Johnny Bull had sapiently remarked.

CHAPTER THREE

"**B**OB you ass—!"

"Bob, you fathead—!"

"Bob, you ditherer!"

"Bob you terrific ass!"

Bob had nothing to say. He could have kicked himself. Still more willingly, he could have kicked Bunter. Good-naturedly, he had urged Bunter's claims: only to discover that the fat Owl's main object was to bag a tip from his pater. But at least he had banked on Bunter doing no harm if he did no good. Even if the fat Owl scored a pair of spectacles, he did not think the result less assured. Ten Removites were as good as any eleven of the Fourth: he was sure of that. But the proverbial uncertainty of the summer was his undoing. Temple and Co. were playing a better game than usual, and there was no doubt that a man in the field like Bunter was a considerable help to batsmen. The expected margin of victory was not only narrowed down. It looked like disappearing.

Bob, generally a mighty man with the willow, couldn't forsee that he was going to have awful luck, and be dismissed for two! Neither could he have guessed, or dreamed, that Smithy would be out for three. Such sad and unlooked-for things do happen on the cricket field.

Now the Remove were taking their second knock. The best men had not been quite up to their best: and the "tail" went down rapidly. When last man in was called, the Remove score stood at fifty-one for the innings. They wanted three to tie, four to win. And the over was unfinished: the last man was to take the bowling! And last man was William George Bunter!

So the other men told Bob what they thought of him, and Bob felt like kicking himself. Any man in the Remove—excepting Billy Bunter—might yet have pulled that game out of the fire. Wide margins were forgotten: but a win by a single run was a win. Instead of which, they were going to be beaten by three: for who could doubt that Bunter was going to repeat his earlier performance and remain at the wicket just long enough to turn his duck into a pair of spectacles!

"It's rotten!" mumbled Bob.

"Fathead!"

"You priceless ass!" said Harry Wharton. "You know what's coming to you if you've got us licked! Get ready to boot him all round the field, you men, after Bunter's scored his duck."

"Oh, really, Wharton—"

"Get a move on, fathead! Get it over!"

"Yah!" retorted Bunter. "You just watch out, and you'll see what you will see! I fancy I can handle that bowling, if you fellows can't."

"Kick him!"

"Beast!"

Bunter rolled out to the vacant wicket. The Fourth-form field grinned, as he took his stand there, with the ease and grace of a coal-sack. Fry of the Fourth, who had the ball, winked at Temple, who chuckled. They all knew what was going to happen. For once in a way, they were going to beat the Remove at cricket: and undoubtedly the Remove had asked for it. One ball would be enough for that fat batsman: and all would be over. They could see it just as clearly as if it had already happened: and so could the Remove men at the pavilion: only one fellow couldn't, and that one was William George Bunter.

Bunter blinked along the pitch through his big spectacles. He took a business-like grip on the handle of his bat. Bunter was going to swipe—he was going to put his beef into it: and whatever else Bunter lacked, it was certain that he did not lack beef. If the bat met the ball, quite probably that ball might go on distant travels. It was more likely to miss it by a foot, if not by a yard.

"All up!" sighed Bob, as Fry sent down the ball.

Johnny Bull barely refrained from saying "I told you so!"

And then—!

Clack!

All ears heard the clack of bat and ball. Bunter had swiped—and by one of those miracles which happen in cricket, Bunter had got the ball fair and square! It was a tremendous swipe! The impetus of it tipped Bunter over when it was delivered, and he landed on fat knees.

But where was the ball?

It soared far away, far over heads and uplifted hands. Amazed eyes followed it in its flight. Bob Cherry gave Harry Wharton a thump on the back that made him stagger.

"It's a boundary!" he yelled.

"Ow! Don't break my backbone! wow! By gum, so it is!"

If runs had been needed, certainly they could not have been provided from Bunter's end of the pitch. That tremendous swipe seemed to have expended all his limited supply of wind. He sagged on fat knees and gasped for breath.

But no runs were needed!

That swipe had done it!

Bunter had hit a boundary!

It was incredible, unthinkable, a chance in a thousand, if not in a million: but Bunter had done it! There was a roar from the Remove.

"Four!"

"Good old Bunter!"

"Good old porpoise!"

"Ha, ha, ha!"

"Who'd have thought it?" gasped Harry Wharton. "Bunter—a boundary! A boundary—Bunter! I suppose we've not gone to sleep and dreamed it!"

"Ha, ha, ha!"

"Anybody going to boot a chap round the field for pushing Bunter into the team?" grinned Bob Cherry. "By gum—cricket is an uncertain game, and never so jolly uncertain as when Bunter's playing it."

"Ha, ha, ha!"

It was over. After so many doubts and uncertainties, the Remove had won by a run with a wicket in hand. Later, Billy Bunter pointed out to Harry Wharton that he simply couldn't afford to leave out such a batsman when Rookwood came over. To which the captain of the Remove replied only with the classic monosyllable "Rats!" Nevertheless, Remove fellows did not forget—Billy Bunter took care that they shouldn't—that Form match had been won by Bunter's boundary!

THE END

BOYS! THIS IS YOUR PAPER!

No. 899. Vol. XXVII.   Week Ending May 2nd, 1925.

The **Magnet 2ᵈ** Library *of* **EVERY MONDAY** Complete School Stories.

"HOW'S THAT?"

THE BOUNDER'S BOWLING BEATS TEMPLE OF THE FOURTH!

(A diverting incident from the long complete story of Harry Wharton & Co. inside.)

THE CRICKET CAPTAIN
A song by Frank Richards

When I was a kid in the Lower Fourth,
I slacked and ragged for all I was worth,
   I scamped my prep, and I skewed my con,
Whenever my Form beak put me on.
   But I held my bat so straight and true,
That nothing mattered that I could do,
   The balls I slogged, and the runs I ran,
They marked me out as a coming man.

CHORUS: The balls he slogged, and the runs he ran,
            They marked him out as a coming man.

My tutor's tears ran down his nose,
Only just to look at my Latin prose,
   If anything was a trifle worse,
It must have been my Latin verse.
   But I held my bat so straight and right,
Though the beaks might bark, they'd never bite,
   For, hic, haec, hoc, amo, 'mas, 'mat,
What the dooce were they to a good straight bat?

CHORUS: For hic, haec, hoc, amo, 'mas, 'mat,
            What the dooce were they to a good straight bat?

I really don't know how the . . . well,
I pushed up through Remove and Shell,
　But I'd worn my charity tails so long,
They had to give me a shove along.
　But I held my bat so straight and clean,
That everything was all serene,
　Compared, you see, with such a man,
The Head himself was an also-ran!

CHORUS:　Compared, you see, with such a man,
　　　　　The Head himself was an also-ran!

Somehow I did contrive to get,
To the Lower Fifth, where I'm sticking yet.
　I can't mug up that classic rot,
I shall never be a Sixth Form swot,
　But I hold my bat so straight and stiff,
I've never had the slightest tiff,
　I hold my bat so stiff and straight,
They dare not superannuate.

CHORUS:　He held his bat so stiff and straight,
　　　　　They dare not superannuate.

My tip to every Greyfriars chap,
Is this 'Don't swot, and never sap!
　Keep a straight, straight bat, and a steady eye,
Be worthy to wear your old school tie.
　In the big wide world it's just the same,
Keep your willow straight, and play the game!
　Wherever you are, remember that,
Keep your wickets up, with a good straight bat!'

CHORUS:　Wherever you are, remember that,
　　　　　Keep your wickets up, with a good straight bat!'

Five issues of *The Magnet* out of the 1,683 that appeared between February 1908 and May 1940

RAG'S CATCH!

BY FRANK RICHARDS

CHAPTER ONE

RAG KNOWS WHAT!

"I KNOW what!" said Rag Pickles.

Nobody heeded that remark.

There were three other fellows in the junior day-room at Dilcombe: Jimmy Denver, Carr, and Paget.

They stood at the big window, looking out into the wintry sunshine in the quadrangle. That bright sunshine was not reflected in their faces.

Generally, Jimmy Denver and Co. looked as merry and bright as any fellows at Dilcombe. And on this particular afternoon, had circumstances been normal, they would probably have looked merrier and brighter than usual. For it was Wednesday, a half-holiday, and the Soccer match at Walcot was due.

But circumstances were not normal. And they were looking grim and glum and gloomy, as if they found life hardly worth living, even at Dilcombe!

"Gated!" said Jimmy Denver, dismally: heedless of Rag.

"On Walcot day!" mumbled Carr.

"Rotten!" groaned Paget.

"I say, do listen to a chap," urged Rag, "I tell you I know what—."

"Oh, dry up, you!" snapped Jimmy Denver. "You've got us into this jam, with your fathead rags. You can't get us out of it. Pack it up."

"But I say—!"

"Pack it up!" hooted Carr and Paget together.

Rag looked indignant.

Rag—his full name was Albert Edward Pickles—was feeling the blow, just like his chums. Rag was as keen to play Soccer at Walcot that afternoon, as any other fellow in Randall's House at Dilcombe. The housemaster's sentence of "gates" had fallen as heavily on Rag as on his comrades. And Rag couldn't see that he was to blame, as his friends quite clearly could!

"Was it my fault?" demanded Rag, hotly.

"Wasn't it?" hooted Jimmy, "You had to get that ass Crawley of the Fifth with your silly pea-shooter—and start a row—."

"I didn't think he would spot me—."

"Catch you thinking!" said Jimmy, witheringly. "You've got nothing to do it with, if you come to that. He did spot you, and pitched into you, and then what could we do but drag him off and sit on his head?"

"And Randall had to barge in at that very moment!" said Carr. "Randall all over—poking his nose in where it wasn't wanted."

"And a gating all round for the four of us, for ragging in the Quad!" said Paget, "And what's going to happen at Walcot, with the four of us left out of the eleven? We've got to stay in gates, kicking our heels, while the Walcot men wipe their boots on Dilcombe."

"I know it's rotten," said Rag, "But—."

"Oh, give us a rest."

"But I say—!" persisted Rag.

"The question is," said Jimmy Denver, ruthlessly regardless of Rag, "Can we do anything about it? Might Randall let us off, if we explained about Walcot? Might catch him in a good temper after dinner. He's often in a good temper after tiffin."

"Um!" said Carr and Paget, very dubi-

77

ously. It did not seem very hopeful to them. Mr Randall, house-master of Randall's House, was a stern and severe gentleman. An edict from Randall was like the laws of the Medes and the Persians: fixed and immutable.

"Looks like the only chance," said Carr, slowly, "But—!"

"But—!" sighed Paget.

"If you let a fellow speak—!" hooted Rag. "I've told you I know what."

Three impatient juniors stared at Rag. They were in a jam: but they did not expect any help out of it from Albert Edward Pickles. True that Albert Edward was the best junior winger at Dilcombe, worth his weight in gold, if not in banknotes, on the Soccer field. But off the football field, he was, as his best chums agreed, the biggest ass at Dilcombe or anywhere else.

They did not expect any sense from old Rag. Still, in the dire circumstances, they were prepared to give him a hearing, if he had anything in the least useful to suggest.

"Well, if you know what, what's what?" yapped Jimmy, "Get it off your chest, and don't talk out of the back of your neck if you can help it."

"We're gated," said Rag. "That washes out the Walcot match for us. No good asking old Randy anything—you'd only get a snort from him! But it's all Crawley's fault—kicking up a shindy just because a chap got him in the ear with a pea-shooter. Crawley's a swanking ass—."

"Never mind Crawley now—."

"But that's it!" explained Rag, "Crawley's got lines to do for Randall this afternoon. I heard him telling Hart that he'd a good mind to give them a miss, because he wants to go to the pictures at Dilford—."

"Bother Crawley and his lines."

"He will be in his study, writing lines—." continued Rag.

"What about it?" hooted Jimmy.

"I'm going to lock him in."

"Wha-a-a-t?"

Rag grinned. His three chums stared at him blankly. Rag tapped the pocket of his jacket.

"I've got his study key here," he said,

"Nobody was about when I snooped it. I'm going to wait till Crawley gets busy on his lines in his study. Then I'm going to tiptoe along and turn the key on him. Tit for tat, you know—he's dished us over the Walcot game, and I'm going to dish him over his trip to Dilford this afternoon—see?" Rag chuckled. "When he's through his lines, and ready to start, he won't be able to get out of his study! Rather a rag on Crawley, what! Ha, ha, ha!"

Albert Edward Pickles laughed loud and long: evidently greatly taken with the idea of a rag on Crawley of the Fifth. He seemed to expect his chums to join in his merriment.

But they did not! Rag had the laugh all to himself! So far from laughing, Denver and Carr and Paget glared at him, almost as if they could have eaten him!

"You silly ass!" gasped Jimmy Denver.

"Look here—!" protested Rag.

"You dithering chump!" roared Carr.

"I say—."

"You frabjous, frumptious fathead!" hooted Paget.

"I tell you it will be no end of a rag on Crawley—bottling him up in his study for the afternoon—."

"You and your rags!" said Jimmy Denver, "You've got us gated on Walcot day with your silly ragging: and now all you can think of is another rag! We've got to let the team go over to Walcot without us, and get licked to the wide, and you—you—you—." Words seemed to fail the captain of the Dilcombe Fourth. He spluttered with wrath. "Bump him!" he added.

"Good egg!" said Carr and Paget together.

Rag jumped back, in alarm.

"Here, I say, hands off—I say—leggo—Yooooop!" roared Rag, as three exasperated juniors grasped him, and swept him off his feet.

Bump!

"Ooooooooh!" spluttered Rag, as he sat down—hard—on the old oaken floor of the day-room, "I say—oooooh!"

"Give him another!"

Bump!

"Oh, crikey! Ow! Ooooooh!"

"One more for luck," said Jimmy Denver. Bump!

"Urrrrrrggh!" gurgled Rag.

He sat and spluttered for breath. Jimmy Denver and Co. walked out of the day-room, and left him to splutter. Their problem was unsolved: but there was some solace in having given Rag that for which he had asked, and they were feeling a little better. Rag, sitting and spluttering, was feeling considerably worse!

CHAPTER TWO

CAUGHT!

MR RANDALL, house-master of Randall's House, frowned.

Randall was walking in the Quad, after dinner.

As Jimmy Denver had told his friends, Randall was often in a good temper after tiffin. But he did not look in the best of tempers now.

Pacing sedately under the old Dilcombe oaks, Mr Randall passed, at a little distance, a group of three juniors of his House. With gloomy looks, they seemed to be discussing some absorbing topic: so absorbing that they did not notice their house-master in the offing.

Had they noticed him, no doubt, they would have subdued their voices. Not noticing him, they didn't. As a result, three successive remarks floated to Mr Randall's ears as he passed.

"No good asking old Randy anything!" said Paget.

"Bother old Randy!" said Carr.

"Bother and blow him!" said Jimmy Denver.

Mr Randall walked on, with hard-compressed lips. Randall was not the man to take official note of words not intended for his ears, heard by chance. He walked on as if he had heard nothing. But a deep frown knitted his brow.

Those three juniors, and their chum Pickles, who was not with them at the moment, were "gated" for the afternoon: quite a light punishment, in Mr Randall's opinion, for a reckless rag in the Quad. Possibly Mr Randall might have given consideration to a plea for leave out of gates in view of the fixture at Walcot. If so, that chance was gone now—after what he had inadvertently heard. "Old Randy" was not a phrase pleasing to his ears: neither did he like being "bothered" and "blowed" by juniors of his House. Jimmy Denver and Co. continued their anxious discussion, happily unconscious that their goose was already cooked.

Randall was frowning—and a few minutes later, his frown intensified. This time his glinting eyes fixed upon a senior of his House—Crawley of the Fifth Form.

Crawley had been mixed up in that rag, for which the juniors were gated. Crawley had been given two hundred lines, with orders to deliver them in his house-master's study before the tea-bell rang.

Crawley, therefore, should have been sitting in his study, in the Fifth, at that moment, grinding at Virgil. Two hundred lines of Latin was a task to take time. Crawley had to write two hundred lines from the Second Book of the *Aeneid*, from "*conticuere omnes*" to "*improvida pectora turbat*".

He couldn't have written them already, unless at supersonic speed. Yet there he was, sauntering down to the gates, with his hands in his pockets, as casually and carelessly as if house-masters and lines did not exist at all. As Mr Randall, from a distance, stared at him grimly, Crawley called out to another Fifth-form man.

"Come on, Hart."

Hart of the Fifth joined him.

"Going?" he asked. "Dilford Regal?"

"Yes—lots of time if we step out."

"But—."

"Oh, come on: we don't want to be late."

"Oh, all right."

They walked down to the gates together.

Mr Randall made a step to follow—to call Crawley back. But he paused. It was possible, after all, that Crawley had done his lines, and that they lay on his study table in

79

the Fifth, ready for delivery by tea-time as commanded. In which case, Crawley had every right to walk down to Dilford to the picture-palace, if the spirit moved him so to do. But if he had walked out, regardless of lines, and of his house-master, to turn up at tea-time with an excuse instead of lines—Mr Randall's lips set in a tight line at that idea.

Mr Randall turned and walked to his House. It was a simple matter to step into Crawley's study, and see for himself. If the lines were there, done according to orders, well and good. If not, a House Prefect would be despatched immediately to call Crawley in: with a double imposition to reward him for his disregard of authority.

Mr Randall whisked into his House, and up the staircase to the Fifth-Form studies. Randall's House at Dilcombe was a very ancient building, with dim old passages that seemed to lead nowhere in particular. Crawley's study was at the end of one of those passages. Not a soul was about, as Mr Randall billowed up the passage: everyone was out of doors that bright afternoon: most of the fellows interested in football.

Certainly it was not likely to occur to the house-master that a Fourth-Form fellow had parked himself in one of the deserted studies, where he was listening with intent ears for the sound of footsteps going into Crawley's study! Mr Randall, naturally, had no idea of Rag Pickles' astute plans for that afternoon: and had, indeed, quite forgotten Rag's unimportant existence.

He arrived at Crawley's study, at the end of the passage. He walked in, leaving the door ajar behind him.

He stepped to the study table.

There were books and papers, an inkpot and some split ink, and an odd football boot on the table: Crawley was not a tidy fellow. Mr Randall scanned that untidy table with grim eyes. If the lines were not there—!

They were not! There was not a sign of lines. Crawley had not even started on his imposition. Probably he had not come up to his study at all since dinner. Grimmer and grimmer grew Randall's brow. Crawley had gone off to the pictures that afternoon, passing by his house-master and his house-master's commands like the idle wind which he regarded not!

Randall, with glinting eyes, turned to the door again.

Then he jumped.

The door, which he had left ajar, suddenly closed, with a snap, under his eyes. Randall jumped, and stared at it, blankly.

Obviously, that door could not have snapped shut of its own volition. Someone in the passage outside, unseen, had dragged it shut.

The next moment, there was a scraping sound of a key jammed into a lock—and click.

Click! Then a scrape of a key withdrawn. Randall stood petrified.

There was a low chuckle outside. Then a sound of hurriedly retreating footsteps. That sound died away almost in a moment.

"Bless my soul!" ejaculated Mr Randall.

He made a stride to the door.

He grasped the door-handle, and dragged.

The door did not open.

Then he knew beyond doubt, what his ears had already told him, that the door was locked on the outside.

He was locked in Crawley's study!

"Bless my soul!" repeated the house-master.

For a long minute, he stood staring at the door. He could hardly believe that this thing had happened! But it had!

Someone—he could not begin to guess who—had seen him, or heard him, come to Crawley's study, and tiptoed to the door and locked him in. He was a prisoner in Crawley's study.

He rapped on the door with his knuckles.

"Come back! Come back and unlock this door instantly! Do you hear me?"

But he knew that the unknown locker-in was gone, taking the key with him! He ceased to rap on the oak. There were no ears to hear: but even if he could have drawn a crowd to the spot, the door could not be unlocked without the key. And he did not want a crowd of fellows outside grinning over his predicament.

He crossed to the window and looked out. It gave a view of kitchen gardens at the back of the House, with nobody in sight. Clambering down from a high window was not a feat to be performed by a middle-aged house-master. He turned back from the window: his feelings deep, the frown on his brow rivalling the frightful, fearful, frantic frown of the Lord High Executioner. He was a prisoner in Crawley's study—until the unknown ragger chose to let him out! He had to wait—and his feelings grew deeper and deeper and deeper as he waited!

CHAPTER THREE

ALL CLEAR?

"GOT him!" trilled Rag.

Rag was jubilant, as he joined his friends in the Quad.

He had rather avoided them, since the bumping in the day-room. But he had to seek them now, to tell them of the complete success of his astute scheme to dish Crawley of the Fifth that afternoon.

They did not heed him. The Walcot match, and the faint hope of something coming from an appeal to Randall for leave out of gates, occupied their minds. But Rag ran on happily:

"Got him! Got that swanking ass Crawley! I say, do listen you fellows. I got him all right! I say, I waited in Hart's study till he came up. I heard him pass the door, and go into his own study. And then—."

"Shut up!" hooted Jimmy Denver.

"Then I tiptoed out, pulled his door shut, and locked it on the outside!" trilled Rag. "I've got the key! Even if he yells, nobody will be able to let him out! Ha, ha, ha!"

Again Rag had his laugh all to himself. Jimmy Denver and Co. were not amused. They did not care two hoots about Crawley of the Fifth, or whether he was locked in his study, or sitting watching the pictures at Dilford.

"You dithering dunderhead," said Jimmy, "Dry up! Bother you and bother Crawley! Look here, you men, it's time to start for Walcot: and if the team go without us, they're going to be wiped off the earth."

"Might cut!" suggested Paget.

Jimmy Denver shook his head.

"Too jolly risky—Randall's as sharp as a needle. But—there's just a chance that he might let us off, if we explained about Walcot—."

"Try it on!" said Carr.

"Well, it won't do any harm, if it doesn't do any good," said Jimmy, "Let's go and ask him, anyhow. He's not a bad old bean, really, and he might go easy, with a Soccer match on."

"I say—!" recommenced Rag Pickles.

"Oh, pack it up, you!" snapped Jimmy. And, having finally made up his mind that an appeal to Randall was the only hope, he walked off to the House with Carr and Paget.

Jimmy Denver tapped at the door of his house-master's study. There was no reply from within: and he opened the door.

"If you please, sir—!" he began, in his meekest tones.

He broke off at that. Randall's study was vacant: his house-master was not there!

"Oh, blow!" grunted Jimmy. "Randall's not here."

"Common-Room, most likely," said Carr.

"Come on, then."

The three walked on to Masters' Common-Room. Jimmy tapped at the door of that august apartment, and opened it, and looked in. Three or four "beaks" were there, taking their ease in armchairs after "tiffin". But Mr Randall was not to be seen.

Jimmy Denver breathed hard, as he closed the door again.

"Bless him!" he breathed, "We shall be late at Walcot, even if he does give us leave, at this rate. Where the dickens is Randall?"

It was an unexpected set-back.

"Trotting in the Quad," suggested Carr. "He often does after tiffin. Let's go and look for him there."

They went to look for him there! But Mr Randall was not to be found in the Quad. They asked fellows right and left: but nobody seemed to know where Randall was. As a last hope they repaired to his study again, thinking that he might have returned there during the search. But the housemaster's study was still vacant.

"Not here!" said Jimmy Denver.

"Not anywhere!" said Carr, "Look here, it's pretty plain that he's gone out. And if he's gone out—!"

The three looked at one another. The same thought was in all three minds. For gated fellows to "cut" with Randall on the spot, was impracticable. But if Randall had gone out—!

"While the cat's away—!" said Paget.

Jimmy drew a deep breath.

"Must have gone out," he said, "Mightn't be back till we get home from Walcot—and he couldn't know a thing. But—even if he came in, and missed us, we'd get the game—we could stand a row afterwards. You fellows feel like chancing it?"

"What-ho!" said Paget and Carr together.

"That's that!" said Jimmy.

And "that" being "that", the chums of the Dilcombe Fourth lost no more time. In the unexpected circumstances, there was no need to make hurried last-minute changes—the Dilcombe junior team was not, after all, losing them. All that was necessary was for the motor-coach to roll off with its crowd: and four gated juniors to leave quietly and unostentatiously over a secluded wall, and pick up the coach later on the road.

Which they duly did.

Jimmy Denver and his chums were feeling cheerful as they rolled over to Walcot with the football crowd. From all appearance, Mr Randall was absent from Dilcombe: and while the cat was away, the mice, proverbially, could play. Quite possibly he might not return till after the footballers were home again: in which case he would never know that four juniors, supposed to remain within gates, hadn't done so. Anyhow they were going to play Walcot, and that was that.

Rag Pickles was the most jubilant of the four.

Rag, of course, was as glad as the others that Randall had gone out, and left the coast clear. But he had additional cause for jubilation, in the success of his rag on Crawley of the Fifth. Albert Edward Pickles was a born ragger: he lived and moved and had his being in ragging: hence his nickname in the Dilcombe Fourth. Often, only too often, his "rags" ended in disaster: for if there was a blunder or a bungle to be made, Rag was the man to make it. But this time everything had gone like clockwork—at least Rag was sure that it had.

"Just think of that swanking ass Crawley!" chuckled Rag, "Raging, I expect—simply raging, in his study—locked in—and he won't get out till we come back from Walcot! Fancy Crawley's face, you men—locked in, and raging! Ha, ha, ha!"

"Ha, ha, ha!" echoed Jimmy Denver and Paget and Carr. They could join in Rag's laugh now: now that it was all clear for Walcot. They laughed: and all the football crowd laughed, at the idea of the swanking ass, Crawley of the Fifth, raging in his study till the Soccer team came home. Fortunately for their peace of mind, nobody had the faintest suspicion who it really was that the ineffable Rag had locked in Crawley's study!

OKAY!

IT was a great game at Walcot.

Walcot men were good at Soccer. When the Dilcombe junior eleven met the Walcot junior eleven on the football field, they had to put their best foot forward, and go all out: and even then the result was generally on the knees of the gods. What would have happened, had the Dilcombe team gone over minus its four star players, their places filled by second-rate men, was a question that had only one possible answer: Dilcombe would have been wiped off the face of the earth.

Now, however, it was O.K. With Jimmy Denver at centre-forward, Dick Paget at centre-half, Chris Carr in goal, and Rag Pickles as fleet as a deer, and nimble as a monkey, on the right wing, the Dilcombe junior eleven was at the top of its form. Rag, in exuberant spirits, excelled himself. Rag, who bungled everything else, was always worth watching on the Soccer field. Off it, he might be an unmitigated fathead and a priceless ass, as his chums often told him: on it, he was a pearl of price! And in fact, the first goal came to Dilcombe from Rag, with a long shot from the wing which hardly any other fellow could have brought off. And the second came to Jimmy Denver, from a pass that Rag gave him at exactly and precisely the right moment. The first half ended with Dilcombe two up.

In the second half, Walcot equalized. But they did not keep equal. The game went on ding-dong, till in the last few minutes, the ball whizzed into the home goal and stayed there. Dilcombe came off the field winners by three goals to two.

Which was a very satisfactory result for the visitors. They were all looking merry and bright as they piled into the motor-coach for home.

"Okay!" said Jimmy Denver, as they rolled away from Walcott. "But if Randall hadn't gone out—!"

"Let's hope that he hasn't come in yet!" said Carr.

"If he has—and if he's missed us—!" murmured Paget.

Jimmy Denver whistled. He was happy and satisfied, so far as Soccer was concerned. But now that the Walcot game had been fought and won, he had more leisure to think of possible consequences. Randall was as keen as a razor: and he had a watchful eye. If he had come in, and noticed that four juniors of his House, supposed to be within gates, were absent, there was going to be a row—a royal row. The Walcot game, no doubt, was worth it: but it was not going to be pleasant, all the same.

Three juniors were rather thoughtful, as they rolled homeward. Rag, who was never known to think, was as cheery as ever. The mental picture of that swanking ass, Crawley of the Fifth, raging in his study, was enough to keep Rag merry and bright.

Some distance short of Dilcombe, four juniors dropped from the motor-coach. It rolled on without them: and they walked the rest of the way: and re-entered the school in the same quiet and unostentatious way that they had left it. As they were supposed to be gated, it would never have done, of course, to roll in with the crowd. Caution was their cue.

Having clambered in by an ivied wall, in a spot where it was nicely shaded by one of the old Dilcombe oaks, they breathed more freely.

"All serene—if Randall isn't back!" said Paget.

"We'll soon see!" said Jimmy Denver.

They strolled, with a casual air, into the Quad. If Randall wasn't back yet, it was all right—right as rain! If he wasn't in yet, they were prepared to be quite prominently on view when he did come in: and how was even old Randy, with his pin-point eyes, to know that they hadn't been in gates all the time! If only Randall hadn't come in yet—!

Apparently he hadn't! Jimmy Denver called to the first fellow they met:

"Is Randall in, Bates?"

"Haven't seen him," answered Bates.

Three or four other fellows answered the same question to the same effect. Jimmy Denver and Co. exchanged blissful glances. Somebody would have seen Randall, if he was about. Nobody seemed to have seen him. So—as far as the Co. would see—he was still out.

"Thank goodness," said Jimmy, "We just had to play Walcot—but we didn't want a row with Randy."

"We jolly well didn't!" agreed Carr.

"Not a lot!" grinned Paget.

"Might have been six of the best, all round," said Jimmy, "We can do without them!"

"Sort of!" chuckled Carr.

They strolled in the Quad, quite at their ease now. They had played Walcot, and beaten Walcot: and there was nothing to come! Wherever Randall was, and whatever might be the cause of his happy and fortunate absence, he was never going to know that four "gated" juniors had "cut". Everything was all serene.

"But I say," said Rag, "What about Crawley—?"

Jimmy laughed.

"You'd better cut in, and let him out," he said, "And if he skins you alive for playing potty tricks on him, serve you jolly well right!"

"Well, I'm going to let him out," said Rag, "I daresay he's had enough, by this time. But if he cuts up rusty—."

"Not much 'if' about that," said Jimmy.

"Well, look here, you fellows come with me," said Rag, "I can't handle a Fifth-Form man—too jolly hefty for me. If he cuts up rusty, the four of us can give him all he wants, and some over."

"Oh, all right!"

They went into Randall's House, and up to the Fifth-form studies. There was little doubt that if Crawley of the Fifth had been raging in his study for hours on end, he would be in a rather dangerous state when he was let out: and Rag was very likely indeed to be in need of help from his friends. The Co. were prepared to stand by him strenuously if Crawley cut up rusty!

Rag grinned, as he drew a study key from his pocket. They could see, as they came up the passage, that the door of Crawley's study was shut: plainly it had not been opened since Rag had turned the key. But there was no sound from the study: the occupant did not seem to be "raging". perhaps he had got tired of "raging", and was patiently sitting it out!

Rag, key in hand, bent to the keyhole. His face was wreathed in grins.

"Hallo, in there!" chirruped Rag, through the keyhole, "I'm going to let you out now, fathead!"

There was a gasping sound in the study.

"Hear me?" went on Rag, cheerily, "I'm going to let you out now, you swanking ass! I hope you've had a pleasant afternoon. Ha, ha, ha!"

There was another gasp within: it sounded as if that address through the keyhole had taken somebody's breath away.

Rag jammed the key in the lock, and turned it back. He pitched the door wide open.

"Now, you silly ass, you can come out!" he said, "and—!" Rag broke off, suddenly, as a figure appeared in the study doorway.

Rag's eyes bulged from his face. Jimmy Denver and Carr and Paget gazed in horror. It was not Crawley of the Fifth who emerged from Crawley's study. It was quite a different person. It was Mr Randall, house-master of Randall's House, his face crimson with wrath.

CHAPTER FIVE

RAG, ALL OVER!

"OH!" gasped Rag Pickles.

He stared at Mr Randall.

He goggled at him.

He could not believe his eyes. The ghost of Banquo did not startle Macbeth more, the shadowy form that drew his curtains at dead of night did not startle King Priam more, than the sight of his house-master in Crawley's doorway startled Rag Pickles.

It seemed like magic—black magic—to Rag. He had locked Crawley in that study—at least he was sure that he had! And it was his house-master who emerged in towering wrath.

"Oh!" babbled Rag. "Oh! Oh, crumbs! Ooooooh!"

His friends looked on, in utter dismay. Evidently, Rag had made one more of his many bungles. Randall's happy and fortunate absence that afternoon was accounted for now. He had not gone out—he had been locked in Crawley's study, in mistake for Crawley, by that ass, that ineffable fathead, that priceless goat, Rag Pickles. It was not Crawley, it was Randall, whom that unmitigated ass, Rag, had locked in: and whom he had just addressed through the keyhole! Three juniors stood dumb with horror while Rag babbled incoherently.

"So it was you, Pickles, who locked me in that study!" Randall's voice was deep, with an edge on it. "You!"

"I—I—I—!" stammered Rag.

"Come with me!"

"I—I—I—!"

"Come!"

Randall's grip closed on Rag's collar. By the collar he led him away. Jimmy Denver and Carr and Paget watched them go. They were there to back up Rag if Crawley cut up rusty: but it was not Crawley, it was his house-master: there was no help for Rag. Rag was led away to his house-master's study. Only too well he knew, and his chums knew, what awaited him there.

"Well, my hat!" said Carr, with a deep breath, "Rag, all over."

"Poor old Rag!" said Jimmy.

And they sadly went their way: deeply sympathetic for poor old Rag. He needed sympathy!

———————

ALL the Dilcombe Fourth, with a single exception, chuckled over the story of Rag's catch. The exception was Albert Edward Pickles. Other fellows might smile over that extraordinary bungle: but Rag, after his house-master had dealt with him faithfully—very faithfully!—did not feel like smiling. Indeed, for a long, long time, Rag seemed to be understudying that ancient monarch who never smiled again!

THE END

EDUCATING UNCLE

A number from a 1920s musical comedy by Frank Richards

UNCLE: In my young days, the girls wore stays,
         And skirts below their knees,
No jazz was there, no backs were bare,
         There were no tango teas,
They never sat on the floor like that,
         With such display of stocking,
         In those days long ago, they were all *comme il faut*,
But now . . . oh, isn't it shocking?

CHORUS
OF GIRLS: What, shocking?

UNCLE: Yes, shocking.

CHORUS: He thinks we're awfully shocking.

UNCLE: In my young days girls had no craze
         For sports or backing horses,
No cigarettes, or gambling debts,
         Nor mixed up in divorces.
They used to sit, and sew or knit,
         Or else read Silas Hocking,
They did not vote, or play the goat,
         But now . . . oh, isn't it shocking?

CHORUS: What, shocking!

UNCLE: Yes, shocking.

CHORUS: He thinks we're awfully shocking!

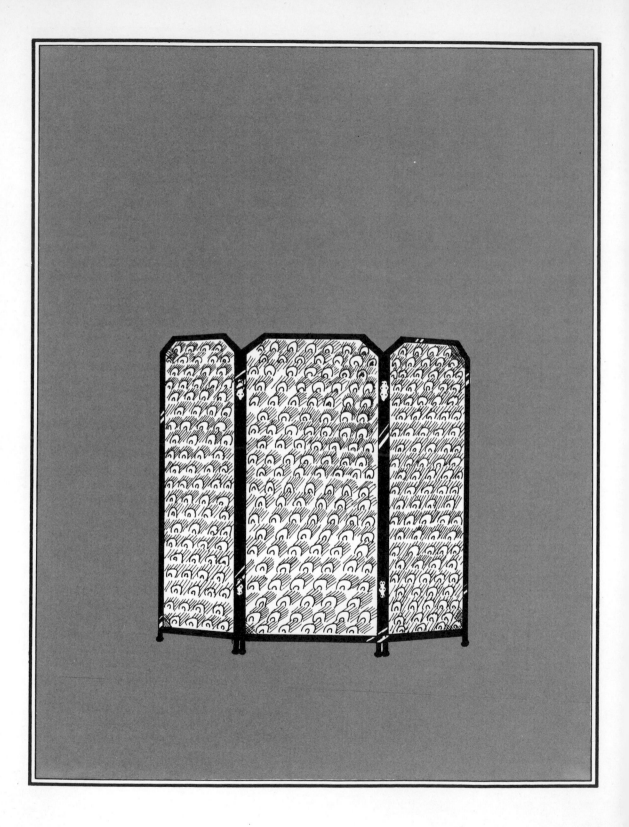

THE PEACOCK-FEATHER SCREEN

BY CHARLES HAMILTON

HER eyes turned upon the peacock-feather screen as she came into the room, and a slightly ironical smile curved her lips.

It was one more curio—and the room was stacked with curios already. Sir Paul was an indefatigable collector, and he was continually adding to his collection. Sometimes she thought that he lived for nothing else: and she was glad, in a cool scornful way, that he had an occupation. Certainly, he gave her little of his society, even if she had wanted it, which she did not. They dined together, with cool politeness on her side, grave courtesy on his: for the rest, they might almost have been the veriest strangers. She always knew when he was in the house: but he, she was quite sure, did not always know when she was at home, even for days or weeks at a time. Probably he did not care—charitably, she hoped that he did not. For if he had cared it would have made no difference.

She came in by the French windows from the balcony, her cloak draped about her tall graceful figure, her face, wonderfully beautiful, looking more beautiful than ever. Sir Paul Trench did not seem to hear her enter—he was seated before the peacock screen—the latest addition to the famous Trench collection—gazing at it, absorbed, as it seemed, in the contemplation of its gorgeous colouring. The screen stood before an alcove, in the wall opposite the windows: her husband's face was partly turned from her as he gazed at it, but she could see how fixed and rigid was his gaze.

The mocking curve of her red lip grew more pronounced.

The screen was a beautiful thing, doubtless—the work of patient dusky hands in Hindustan: the gorgeous colours of the peacock-feathers glowed and gleamed in the shaded electric light. It was doubtless costly—Sir Paul Trench was rich, and could afford not to count the cost when his fancy was taken by anything. He was rich—if he had not been rich, Myra Mainwaring would never have become Lady Trench. She wondered sometimes whether he knew that. He could not have known it, could not have dreamed it, at the time of his earnest, impassioned courtship. Much water had passed under the bridges since that time—much had happened to open his eyes. Indeed, their drifting apart indicated that he understood the situation and accepted it. No word of reproach had ever passed his lips: not by word or look had he reproached her, or hinted that she had done him wrong. As she had drawn away from him, he had let her go—somewhat to her surprise, immensely to her relief. She was Lady Trench, and all that money could buy was hers for the asking, or without the asking: and on her side she gave—nothing. And he did not complain—he did not seem to think that he had any cause or right to complain.

But he had his collection, she told herself with ironic contempt. His manuscripts, his bronzes, his statues, his first editions, and now—his peacock screen! And her lip curved still more mockingly and contemptuously, as she gazed at his half-turned face. It was as if she looked at a child with a new toy, a child oblivious of all other things so long as the toy was novel. That was how she thought of him.

And he was her husband, and had loved her, and fancied once that she loved him! Now as she stood in his room, tall, graceful, beautiful, her lovely face circled by costly furs, he did not heed her presence—his gaze was fixed on the gorgeous, glowing screen of peacock-feathers. Well, it was better so—if he had thought less of his curios, he might have thought more of other things—he might have suspected—he might have known—It came into her mind, with a dim wonder, to imagine what he would have thought, had he known of Eustace. Had he known that that very night she was to meet Eustace Tracey, as she had met him many times—that her husband's message had called her there, only a few minutes before she had intended to leave—that if his message had not interrupted her, by this time she would have been in Eustace Tracey's arms, feeling his kisses upon her lips . . .

She tried to imagine it, but she could not. Would such a discovery have disturbed his grave calmness? Would it have brought upon her a storm of angry reproaches? Or would he have dismissed the matter and turned again to his collection—to his illuminated missals—to his peacock-feather screen? She did not know—she could not even guess, so much was the man she had married a secret to her.

At all events, he suspected nothing: his manner to Eustace Tracey, when her lover came to the house, was irreproachable. Indeed, when she had seen the two men together, she had felt something like pang of shame—not for her husband. Whether it was blind faith or indifference, he trusted her—it did not seem to enter his thoughts that she could be false, that his friend could be false. She hated to see them together—it made Eustace seem false in her eyes. It perplexed her that Eustace was willing to meet him, to come under his roof, to speak to him in cordial tones . . . the man whose confidence he betrayed. Eustace did not seem to think that it mattered, and she tried to think that it did not, for she loved him, and she would believe nothing less than the best of the man she loved.

That evening, she knew, Eustace had accepted an invitation to look at Trench's collection: to be shown the latest addition to it—the peacock-feather screen. She had been dining out, and had not seen him—but she knew that he had been there. Only an hour ago he had stood in that room, where she now stood, and the thought troubled her.

But Eustace, after all, was not rich like her husband: he had his way to make in the world, and he could not afford to abandon the friendship of a man in the position of Sir Paul Trench. But it troubled her.

The silence in the room was oppressive.

Sir Paul did not move: his strange, intent gaze was fixed on the peacock-feather screen as if it fascinated him. Myra tapped with her foot on the parquet: and still he did not turn his head. It seemed almost as if he were in a trance.

She spoke at last; her impatience growing. Eustace would be waiting—the minutes—the precious stolen minutes—were fleeting away. Why had her husband sent for her to come—did he imagine that she was interested in an addition to his collection?

"Paul!"

He started, and turned his head.

She saw that his face was pale, as he rose to his feet. He seemed to draw himself with a palpable effort from deep reverie.

"My dear! I did not hear you," he said, "You came in very quietly."

She looked at him.

It was months—or was it years?— since he had used any endearing word in speaking to her. Sir Paul Trench was not himself tonight.

"I have disturbed you," she said.

"No! no."

"You sent a message that you wished to see me, Paul. What is it?"

He drew out a chair for her.

"Will you sit down, Myra?"

She shook her head.

"I have something to tell you," he said, gravely.

"Will it take long?"

"I am afraid so."

She made a movement of impatience. By this time, Eustace would be in the garden-house, waiting, wondering why she did not come. But she repressed her impatience as she felt her husband's eyes upon her face, gravely searching.

"Had you any important engagement for this evening?" he asked.

She felt a slight tremor: there was something new in his tone. Did he, after all, suspect? Certainly his manner was not as usual.

"Nothing," she answered. "Nothing—at this hour! But—I have a slight head-ache—I was going to bed early—."

"I will try not to keep you long."

She forced a smile.

"Is it something important that you have to tell me?"

"Very."

"Well, I am here," she said.

"You will be seated?"

She sat down at last.

He crossed to the French windows, closed them, and drew back the dark hangings across. The stars—the stars that glimmered down on the garden-house where Eustace Tracey was to wait for her—were shut out.

She tapped her foot impatiently on the parquet, her irritation growing, and with it a faint sense of uneasiness.

If he knew—if he had been told—But his manner was calm, sedate: it might have been thought affectionate. He was changed from his usual self: but she could hardly tell in what the change consisted.

He came back towards her, and sat down, in a chair facing her, by the Indian table. She leaned her elbow on the table, her cheek on her hand, keeping her face in shadow. Opposite her, across the great room, the colours of the peacock-feather screen glowed and gleamed.

"I have much to say to you, Myra," Sir Paul said, gravely, "I hope I shall not tire you. I do not often take up your time, my dear, and you must forgive me for once."

"I am waiting."

"It is two years since you married me, Myra—a man fifteen years older than yourself, unworthy of you and your great beauty. My only claim was that I loved you—loved you as I verily believe no woman ever was loved before. I loved you so much that I was ready to deceive myself, to believe that you loved me, and when you accepted me, I was the happiest man in the earth. I vowed that I would make you happy—that no thought of self should ever enter my mind—that I would live only for your happiness. It was little enough—when I would willingly have died for it."

He paused for a moment.

"I am tiring you," he said, "But be patient with me, Myra; what I have to say must be said."

She did not answer: she remained without movement. If he chose to talk sentiment, she could not prevent him. She only wished that he would have done.

"When I found that you did not care for me," he resumed, "it was a great blow to me. I do not charge you with deceiving me—I deceived myself. It was my own folly, and my great love for you, that led me into self-deception. For you, my dear, I felt only sorrow. Had it been possible, I would have undone what had been done, for your sake. But that was not possible—and all that I could do, was to let you go your own way, to relieve you of a presence you found irksome, of attentions that bored you, of caresses that you shrank from and detested. That much I could do, and that much I did—and only sorrowed that I could do no more. Was there more that I could have done, Myra?"

She did not speak.

"To me, loving you as I did, loving you as I do, Myra, it was hard . . . hard! Many times I hoped that you would change, that you would turn to me, that you would value my love, as I should have valued yours could I have obtained it. These hopes died away in time—the gulf between us grew deeper and wider with every passing day. I knew that it was for ever: and I was content, so long as what I could give you made you happy. Only one black thought haunted me: that you, so beautiful, made for love as you are; would love some day—you, who had never loved, would some day give your heart, which was never given to me, to another. That possibility, or rather that certainty, was always in my mind: and I had thought out the position, Myra, and decided what I would do if, and when, the time came."

She made a slight movement.

He *knew*!

She knew now that he knew! But she knew, too, that she had nothing to fear, not even a reproach, from this grave, quiet man, who loved her, and to whom she was the beginning and end of all things. Yet she shivered, and drew her furs a little more closely about her.

"I had decided, before it happened," said Sir Paul, in the same quiet, gentle voice, almost affectionate in its tones, "I will tell you what was my decision, Myra. I observed you—while you fancied me buried in my collection,—even when we met but seldom, and after your long absences, I observed you, and when the time came, I knew when your step became lighter, when a new light that I had never seen before dawned in your eyes, Myra—I knew that you loved, and it only remained to learn who had gained your love. If he was worthy of you, Myra, if he was to be trusted with yout happiness, my dear child, the man whom you did not love would not stand in your way. All my plans had been thought out—all was definitely arranged: a mountaineering accident in the Alps was to be the means, and you would be left free to marry the man you loved."

She started violently.

For a moment she looked at him: and then her face was shaded again by her hand.

"When Eustace Tracey came, I knew who the man was," he went on, "My friend, whom I had not seen since my marriage—he was the man. You had met him at a country-house—your heart was his when you returned to me. When he came, I knew, and my heart ached, Myra. Not for myself—for you! For he was not worthy of you—he was unworthy, of you or of any other woman."

She caught her breath.

"I will not say, that only a base man could enter, as a friend, the house of a man he betrayed. For that, you will deem his love an excuse. It was more than that. You knew—you must have heard—that he was long my friend—and you knew that since my marriage I had not seen him. You did not know the cause—that it was his base, heartless betrayal of a woman who trusted him, that turned me from him, that made me erase his name from the list of my friends. But that was the cause, Myra."

She panted.

"It is false—false—When he came, you received him as a friend—he is your friend still—till you found out—."

"Till I found out, Myra?" Sir Paul Trench smiled sadly, "Have I not said that I knew whom you loved, the first time I saw you in Eustace Tracey's presence?"

"If you knew—why—."

"You would not have believed me, Myra, if I had told you that the man you loved was a scoundrel, that he would take all that you had to give, and abandon you as he has abandoned others. That he is a scheming wastrel, who depends on his good looks to marry money. That you were, to him, one more trusting victim in a long list of victims, to be thrown aside as soon as some other fancy seized his mind—and still more certainly, as soon as the opportunity of a wealthy marriage came his way. You would not have believed it, Myra. You do not believe it now."

"Never! Never!" She choked, "It is false—false—it is your jealousy and cruelty that speak. It is false—false! You have brought me here to taunt and torture me because I love him."

He looked at her, and his look was only grave and pitying.

"Have I taunted you, Myra—all this time, when you fancied that I knew nothing, and I knew all? Have I even betrayed my knowledge? Have I not received Eustace Tracey as a friend—have I not hidden the loathing with which he filled me, and allowed him to meet me on the old friendly footing, and for what reason, do you think? I would not shatter your dreams—so long as it would last. That he would be as false to you as to others, I knew—but so long as you believed in him, you were happy. And it was of your happiness I thought. Not till the time came when his falsity must be evident to you, would I have uttered one word."

She gave him a scared look.

"I loved you," said Trench, "I loved you, and I hated him—I hated him so much that my hands ached to be upon his throat. And yet I could meet him with an unmoved face, Myra—so long as it lasted. So long as your happiness was possible, I would not shatter it. So long as it was possible, my dear! I speak now because—."

"Because—?" she whispered.

"Because your belief in him is no longer possible—because he has betrayed you in your turn: because you will not be able to doubt the proof of it."

She shook her head incredulously.

Eustace loved her—loved her! Was he not waiting, at this very moment, in the shadowy garden-house—waiting with his burning kisses to press upon her lips? At the thought, she smiled.

"No!" said Sir Paul. Did he read her thoughts? "No, Myra—he is not there. My dear, you believed I knew nothing of the garden-house—."

She gave a faint cry.

"My dear, the garden-house was so secure a trysting-place, because I had given orders that it should never be approached," said Trench. "So long as your dream could last, my poor darling, I was determined that it should last—that no rude hand should disturb it. But Eustace Tracey will never wait again in the garden-house. I am not keeping you from meeting your lover, my dear—your lover is not there."

She gazed at him in terror.

"You—you knew?"

"I knew."

"My God!"

"He was here this evening," said Sir Paul, "He came to see my collection. I asked him, Myra, because—I knew that the end had come. He has been watched—and I knew. I knew that he would not have the courage to break with you personally—and I knew that in to-morrow's *Morning Post* his engagement to Miss Vanderhagen would be announced. That is why I asked him here."

She choked.

"His—his engagement."

Sir Paul Trench nodded.

"It is false!" she said, in a dry voice.

"It is true, my dear—he has not told you—but it is known to others, and to-morrow the official announcement will be in the papers. You will read it yourself—and then you would have known that he had deserted you, if I had not told you."

Her fingers were tearing at the costly furs of her cloak.

"It is false—false—false! "she repeated.

But she knew that it was true.

"Miss Vanderhagen is rich—a millionaire's daughter," said Sir Paul, "A great match for an almost penniless fortune-hunter. I knew that he would throw you over, if such a chance came his way—It came. It is three days since I knew the certainty:—."

"Three days!" she breathed.

"But I would not speak, till the knowledge could be kept from you no longer. To-morrow all the world will know of the engagement between Eustace Tracey and Miss Vanderhagen. That is why I have told you to-night."

She rose unsteadily from the chair.

She stood, her hand resting on the edge of the Indian table, her face white and strained. The glowing colours of the peacock-feather screen danced before her eyes. The room was swimming.

A strong hand caught her.

She came to herself, and threw Trench's hand aside.

"Do not touch me!"

Her voice was shrill and broken.

"You can spare me that, at least. And I do not believe you—I do not believe—and if it is true, I still love him. I love him—and I shall see him—I shall see him—and then—."

"You shall see him!" said Trench, and his face was strange and sombre. He made a gesture towards the peacock-feather screen.

Her white face grew like marble.

"What—!" Her voice failed.

"You shall see him!" he repeated, and he stepped towards the peacock-feather screen, and laid his hand on it.

"He was here!" she breathed, "He was here—and you—."

"While he loved you, he lived!" said Trench, "So long as he was true to you, Myra—he lived. And now—you shall see him."

With a swing of his arm, he threw the peacock-feather screen aside. The light streamed into the hidden alcove.

It streamed upon a huddled form—a form that did not stir, that never would stir again.

A cry broke the silence: and Sir Paul Trench caught his wife in his arms as she fell fainting.

THE END

TWO SONGS

by Frank Richards, sent to his brother-in-law, Percy Harrison, on the occasion of the Abdication Crisis of 1936

I HAVE A SONG TO SING, OH!

I have a song to sing, oh!
  Sing me your song, oh!
It was sung, poor thing,
By a love-lorn king,
Whose love-affairs went all wrong, oh!
It's the song of a Teddy-man grim and glum,
Whose taste in widders was rather rum,
Who wriggled about under Baldwin's thumb,
  As he sighed for the love of a lady!
Hey, dee, hey, dee, misery me, lackaday dee!
He was rather deaf, but far from dumb,
  As he sighed for the love of a lady!

I have a song to sing, oh!
  What is your song, oh?
It was sung like this
By a Yankee miss
Who was married but not for long, oh,
It's the song of a Simpson, pale and wan,
Who left her Teddy and went to Cannes,
And was photographed with a Brownlow man,
  For she was a flighty lady,
  Hey, dee, hey, dee, misery me, lackaday dee,
She threw glad eyes at the Brownlow man,
  For she was a flighty lady!

WILLOW WILLOW WAILY!

Tell me, Mrs Simpson, prithee tell me true,
    Hey, but I'm doleful, willow-willow-waily,
Have you many husbands, more than one or two?
    Hey, Mrs Simpson, oh!
Tell me, I implore, dear,
Have you three or four dear?
    Hey, Mrs Simpson, oh!

Say, big boy, my heart is frolicsome and gay,
    Hey, but I'm doleful, willow-willow-waily,
I've a coupla husbands in the U.S.A.,
    Hey, Teddy Windsor, oh!
In the U.S.A., bo,
That is quite O.K., bo,
    Hey, Teddy Windsor, oh!

Tell me, Mrs Simpson, will you marry me,
    Hey, but I'm doleful, willow-willow-waily!
I should be delighted to be number three,
    Hey, Mrs Simpson, oh!
Baldwin I will tell, dear,
He can go to ——— well, dear,
    Hey, Mrs Simpson, oh!

Teddy, now you're talking, sure you've spilled a heap!
    Hey, but I'm doleful, willow-willow-waily!
Buddy, you're the husband, that I'm gonna keep.
    Hey, Teddy Windsor, oh!
You are sure the guy, Ted,
Let us be united,
    Hey, Teddy Windsor, oh!

HANDS OFF OUR KING
ABDICATION MEANS REVOLUTION

THE CASE OF THE PERPLEXED PAINTER

A HERLOCK SHOLMES ADVENTURE BY PETER TODD

THE CASE of the Perplexed Painter was one in which were displayed most brilliantly the remarkable mental aberrations of my amazing friend, Mr Herlock Sholmes. We were at lunch in our rooms at Shaker Street when the telephone bell rang, and Sholmes, slipping his fish-sandwich into his pocket, removed his feet from the mantelpiece, and answered the call. His face was very grave when he turned from the instrument.

"A client, Sholmes?" I asked.

"A distinguished one, Jotson," he answered. "No less a person than Mr Scrooluce, the celebrated painter. You have heard of him, of course. His rise to fame has been recent, but his system of painting his pictures with a blacking-brush, and the mystery surrounding their meaning, if any, have made him a great figure in Art circles. No doubt you have heard how he achieved sudden and dazzling success with his picture 'October Moon'."

I shook my head.

"As a medical man, Sholmes, I have to give my attention to more practical matters than Art," I replied.

"True, my dear doctor. But the story is an interesting one," said Sholmes. "Scrooluce, as a young painter, had no success. He painted ships that looked like ships, cornfields that looked like cornfields, clouds that looked like clouds: and but for a happy accident, might have gone on doing so till this day. But it chanced that, having painted one of his usual landscapes, he inadvertently leaned against the canvas while the paint was still wet: after which it resembled nothing in the earth or in the waters under the earth. A great Art critic came into the studio, while he was cleaning his coat: and, seeing the picture, was overcome with admiration. He hailed it as a work of undoubted genius: and Scrooluce, who had thought of cleaning the canvas for future use, wisely decided to leave it as it was. He was undecided whether to call it 'Venus Rising from the Waves' or 'The Battle of Lepanto', but finally decided on 'October Moon'. From that time, he never looked back. However," added Sholmes, briskly, "we must not waste time. Mr Scrooluce is in great trouble, and requires my professional assistance."

"What is the nature of the trouble, Sholmes?"

"It seems that some disaster has occurred, while he was away on holiday, in connection with a portrait he has painted of Lord Popcorn, and another picture called 'Sunset on the Apennines'. He tells me that his lordship was painted with his favourite collie dog, Rover, at his feet, and that he is calling this very afternoon to see the finished picture. He was so very agitated that it is not easy to deduce what has really happened: but he is anxious for me to go round at once, before Lord Popcorn arrives. So come, my dear Jotson: we must not lose a moment."

"But, my dear Sholmes—"

"This is no time for butting, Jotson," said Herlock Sholmes, severely.

"But," I persisted. "I have several patients to see this afternoon— I really must call on my patients, Sholmes—"

"Not at all," answered Sholmes. "Let live, my dear fellow. Come!"

And without waiting for a reply, my amazing friend hurried me out into Shaker Street and into a taxi.

We found Mr Scrooluce pacing his studio in a state of wild agitation when we were shown in. Two large canvases stood leaning against the wall: and from moment to moment, the painter paused, and stared at one or the other of them, and shook his head despairingly. What was the matter was not clear: but it was evident that something was very much the matter.

"Which?" the painter was exclaiming. "His lordship will be here in a quarter of an hour—he must see the picture. But which—which—which?"

The painter was obviously in a state of utter perplexity: from what cause I could not fathom. Indeed I doubt whether Herlock Sholmes himself was much wiser than I for the moment. Both of us, however, were deeply moved by the agitation and distress of the artist.

As our names were announced, Mr Scrooluce turned from the pictures, and rushed across to meet us, in his excitement catching my amazing friend by the arm.

"Mr Sholmes! Can you help me?" he panted.

"Quite!" said Herlock Sholmes, calmly. "If you will give me a few details—you may speak quite freely before my friend Dr Jotson—"

"But this is no ordinary case," said Mr Scrooluce, hoarsely. "I am aware of your great reputation, Mr Sholmes—I know how successfully you investigated the case of the missing marksman at Bisley—how you traced Lord Stoney de Broke's watch when it mysteriously disappeared after a visit to his uncle—how you, and you alone, tracked down the Lost Chord. But this case, I fear, must be beyond even your powers. Help me if you can—before Lord Popcorn arrives."

He led us towards the two pictures leaning on the wall. He pointed to them with a trembling finger.

We looked at them. What either was intended to represent, if indeed anything, was a secret known only to the painter. They were, I gathered, painted in his later, or blacking-brush, style: but beyond that I could guess nothing.

"I will tell you the dreadful disaster that has occurred, Mr Sholmes," went on Mr Scrooluce, huskily. "I painted these two pictures before going on a week-end trip. One of them is the portrait of Lord Popcorn with his dog at his feet. The other is 'Sunset on the Apennines'. Before leaving, I gave strict instructions that nothing in the studio was to be meddled with. Nevertheless, an unthinking housemaid tidied up during my absence. On my return to-day, I found that the pictures had been moved, and, worse than that, that the labels attached to them had disappeared. Lord Popcorn is calling this afternoon for his portrait, Mr Sholmes, to take it away with him in his car. He will be here in a matter of minutes now. His portrait is here—it is one of these two pictures. But which is it, Mr Sholmes?"

Mr Scrooluce paused, and wiped the perspiration from his brow.

Herlock Sholmes nodded, slowly. We now had an inkling of the cause of the painter's perplexity and distress.

"Which?" said Mr Scrooluce, despair-"Which is which? One of these two pictures is the portrait of his lordship—the other is 'Sunset on the Apennines'. But which, Mr Sholmes, is which? Is that a problem beyond even your powers, Mr Sholmes?"

Gazing at the two pictures, I could well understand the painter's perplexity. There was absolutely nothing in either to give a clue. Either might have been the portrait of Lord Popcorn, or a sunset scene in the Italian mountains: or indeed, anything else. There was not the ghost of a clue.

"His lordship may be here any moment," muttered Mr Scrooluce. "Every moment I expect to hear his car. He must take away his picture, Mr Sholmes. But which is his portrait? Which? Can you help me?"

"I can!" said Herlock Sholmes.

"Bless you for those words," said Mr Scrooluce, brokenly.

"Lord Popcorn was painted with his dog Rover?" asked Herlock Sholmes.

"He was! He and his dog are inseparable."

"Then Rover will be with him when he calls this afternoon?"

"Undoubtedly."

"Then all is simple," drawled Herlock Sholmes. "You may rely upon the sagacity of the faithful hound, Mr Scrooluce, to pick out his master's portrait."

"Do you think so?"

"I am sure of it. Hark! I hear a cry!" said Sholmes. "Go down and meet his lordship, please, and make sure that his dog accompanies him into the studio. I answer for the rest."

"If you are right—!" gasped Mr Scrooluce.

"There is no 'if' about it," said Herlock Sholmes, coldly. "My friend Jotson could tell you that. Please go down—"

"You assure me—?"

"I do!"

"I will trust you!" breathed Mr Scrooluce, and he hurried out of the studio. Alone with Sholmes, I gazed at him. To my surprise, he drew from his pocket the unfinished fish-sandwich which was a part of his interrupted lunch.

"Sholmes!" I exclaimed, "this no time for finishing your lunch—"

"I am not thinking of finishing my lunch, Jotson."

"Then what—"

I broke off, in astonishment, as Herlock Sholmes stepped up to the nearest of the two canvases, and proceeded to rub the fish-sandwich on it. I gazed at him almost open-mouthed. Well as I knew my amazing friend's remarkable methods, I could understand nothing of this.

He stepped back, and replaced the remains of the fish-sandwich in his pocket. There was an inscrutable smile on his face.

"My dear Sholmes—!" I gasped. "What—?"

"Wait and see, my dear Jotson," he replied.

I had not long to wait. The door opened, and Mr Scrooluce ushered Lord Popcorn into the studio. A collie dog was prancing round their legs.

But the next moment, the dog ceased to prance, made a rush at the canvas on which Sholmes had rubbed the fish-sandwich, and began to lick it with every sign of pleasure.

Mr Scrooluce stared, evidently amazed by this prompt verification of the assurance Herlock Sholmes had given him. Lord Popcorn smiled genially.

"Rover knows his master!" he remarked. "What?"

"Oh! Yes! He—he—he does!" stammered Mr Scrooluce. "Undoubtedly! Good dog—good dog!"

"But—!" I remarked later, when we were back in our rooms at Shaker Street.

"But what, Jotson?" drawled Herlock Sholmes. "My client is satisfied. His client is satisfied. So what?"

"But Lord Popcorn's portrait, which his lordship took away in his car, may after all be the 'Sunset on the Apennines', Sholmes."

"Quite possible, Jotson. But as no one could ever know, that is quite irrelevant. You may add to your memoirs, as one more of my astounding successes—The Case of the Perplexed Painter."

THE END

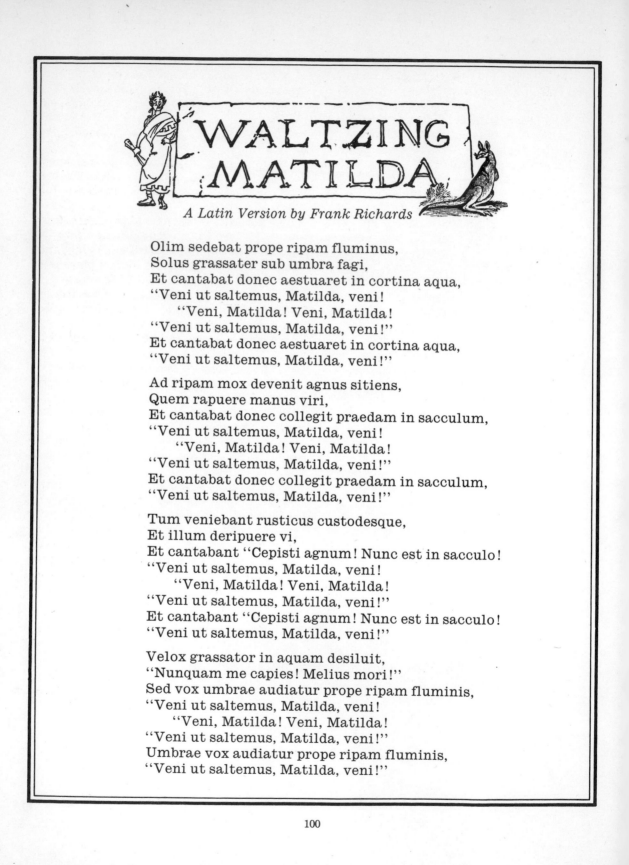

WALTZING MATILDA

A Latin Version by Frank Richards

Olim sedebat prope ripam fluminus,
Solus grassater sub umbra fagi,
Et cantabat donec aestuaret in cortina aqua,
"Veni ut saltemus, Matilda, veni!
   "Veni, Matilda! Veni, Matilda!
"Veni ut saltemus, Matilda, veni!"
Et cantabat donec aestuaret in cortina aqua,
"Veni ut saltemus, Matilda, veni!"

Ad ripam mox devenit agnus sitiens,
Quem rapuere manus viri,
Et cantabat donec collegit praedam in sacculum,
"Veni ut saltemus, Matilda, veni!
   "Veni, Matilda! Veni, Matilda!
"Veni ut saltemus, Matilda, veni!"
Et cantabat donec collegit praedam in sacculum,
"Veni ut saltemus, Matilda, veni!"

Tum veniebant rusticus custodesque,
Et illum deripuere vi,
Et cantabant "Cepisti agnum! Nunc est in sacculo!
"Veni ut saltemus, Matilda, veni!
   "Veni, Matilda! Veni, Matilda!
"Veni ut saltemus, Matilda, veni!"
Et cantabant "Cepisti agnum! Nunc est in sacculo!
"Veni ut saltemus, Matilda, veni!"

Velox grassator in aquam desiluit,
"Nunquam me capies! Melius mori!"
Sed vox umbrae audiatur prope ripam fluminis,
"Veni ut saltemus, Matilda, veni!
   "Veni, Matilda! Veni, Matilda!
"Veni ut saltemus, Matilda, veni!"
Umbrae vox audiatur prope ripam fluminis,
"Veni ut saltemus, Matilda, veni!"

Babe Bunter

Bunter the Toddler

Bunter the Adolescent

Bunter the Future Prime Minister

THE FORBEARS OF WILLIAM GEORGE BUNTER

GRANNY BUNTER c. 1915

HECTOR HORATIO BUNTER ~ c. 1423

SIR RUPERT DE BUNTER c. 1679

REMBRANDT BUNTER c. 1650

SCENE ONE

The form-room at Greyfriars: Mr Quelch and the Remove.

BUNTER. (*Snore!*)

WHARTON (*whispering*). That fat ass Bunter has fallen asleep.

CHERRY (*whispering*). Nodded off, by gum!

NUGENT (*whispering*). Quelch will wake him up.

BUNTER. (*Snore!*).

QUELCH (*sharply*). Bunter!

BUNTER. (*Snore!*).

QUELCH. Upon my word! Has that boy fallen asleep in class? BUNTER!

BUNTER. (*Snore!*).

QUELCH. He is asleep! Actually asleep, in class! Wharton.

WHARTON. Yes, sir!

QUELCH. Wake Bunter up at once, Wharton.

WHARTON. Oh, certainly, sir. I'll give him a shake, sir!

BUNTER. (*Snore!*).

WHARTON. Wake up, Bunter.

BUNTER. Ow! Leggo! Tain't rising-bell! Leave off shaking me, you beast!

Laughter in the class.

WHARTON. Bunter, you ass, wake up—.

BUNTER. Shan't! Beast! Leggo! I was just dreaming of a lovely spread in Smithy's study, and now you go and wake me up. I can't hear the rising-bell if you can.

WHARTON. Do you think you're in bed, fathead?

Wake up! You're in form, you ass, and Quelch is looking at you.

BUNTER. Oh, crikey! Oh, crumbs! Did—did I nod off? It's so jolly warm this afternoon. Oh, scissors!

QUELCH. Bunter!

BUNTER. Oh! Yes, sir! I wasn't asleep sir! I—I—I listen better with my eyes shut, sir, that's all.

QUELCH. You were fast asleep, Bunter.

BUNTER. Oh, no, sir! I never closed my eyes, sir, and I only closed them because I listen better—.

QUELCH. You are an idle, inattentive boy, Bunter.

BUNTER. Oh, really, sir! I heard every word you were saying, sir!

QUELCH. You heard every word I was saying, Bunter!

BUNTER. Oh yes, sir! I'm keen on history, sir, especially Roman history. I—I wouldn't miss a word.

QUELCH (*in a grinding voice*). Very well, Bunter. If you heard every word I was saying—.

BUNTER. Oh, yes, sir!

QUELCH. Then you will be able to answer my questions on the lesson, Bunter.

BUNTER. Oh, lor'!

QUELCH. Now answer this question, Bunter. What was it Julius Caesar said when Brutus struck him with his dagger in the Senate-House.

BUNTER. Oh, crikey!

QUELCH. What?

BUNTER. Oh! I—I didn't mean that Julius Caesar said, 'Oh crikey', sir! Not at all, sir! I—I meant—.

QUELCH. Tell me at once, Bunter, what Julius Caesar said on that occasion.

BUNTER. He—he—he said, "Kiss me, Hardy!'

QUELCH. Upon my word!

BUNTER. I—I—I mean, he said, 'Take away that bauble!' sir.

QUELCH. Bunter!

BUNTER. And—and—and he never smiled again, sir.

QUELCH. Bunter, how dare you make such an answer? When Brutus struck him in the Senate-House, Bunter, Caesar said, '*Et tu, Brute!*'

BUNTER. Ate two? Ate two what, sir? I didn't know he ate anything.

QUELCH. You absurd boy, Caesar was speaking in Latin. '*Et tu, Brute*', means "And thou, Brutus!"

BUNTER. Oh! Does it, sir? I—I mean, that's just what I was going to say, sir.

QUELCH. After this class, Bunter, you will write out 'Julius Caesar said, "*Et tu Brute!*" ' fifty times.

BUNTER. Oh, really, sir, he couldn't have—.

QUELCH. What?

BUNTER. Well, I don't see why he should, sir. But—but if you say so, sir I—I suppose you know best.

QUELCH. I should imagine so, Bunter. You will bring me your imposition after tea.

BUNTER. Oh! Yes, sir!

QUELCH. And now Bunter, if you do not give attention to the lesson, I shall cane you.

BUNTER. Oh, lor' I—I mean, yes, sir! Oh yes sir.

SCENE TWO

Harry Wharton's study. WHARTON, CHERRY *and* NUGENT *at tea. Enter* BUNTER.

CHERRY. Hallo, hallo, hallo! Here's Bunter! How did Bunter know we had a cake for tea!

BUNTER. Oh, really, Cherry—.

NUGENT. Bunter has a wonderful nose for a cake.

BUNTER. Oh, really Nugent—.

WHARTON. Shut the door after you, Bunter.

BUNTER. Certainly, old chap.

Door is heard to shut.

BUNTER. Now, I say, you fellows—.

WHARTON. I meant, get on the other side of it first.

BUNTER. Oh, really, Wharton—.

ALL: Scat!

BUNTER. I say, you fellows, I never knew you had a cake, of course. I didn't see you getting it at the tuck-shop. I was looking the other way when I saw you,—I mean, when I didn't saw you—.

ALL: Ha, ha, ha!

BUNTER. I mean when I didn't see you. Still, as you've got a cake, I'll have a slice, if you don't mind. I hope you're not going to be mean about a slice of cake.

NUGENT. Cut yourself a slice and travel.

BUNTER. Thanks, old chap! Hand me that knife! Good!

Sound of munching.

I say this is a decent cake. Not like the cakes I get from Bunter Court, of course. But not bad.

CHERRY. Oh, my hat! Which is the slice, and which is the cake?

BUNTER. (*his voice muffled by cake*). Oh, really, Cherry—.

CHERRY. Better lose no time with that cake, you fellows. If Bunter takes another slice like that, there will be only the plate left.

BUNTER. I say, you fellows, you know I've got an impot to do for Quelch. Do you remember what it was that beast Caesar said to the other beast when he poked him with his dagger?

WHARTON. '*Et tu, Brute*', fathead.

BUNTER. I don't think that's right! Quelch never said anything about him calling Brutus a fathead.

ALL. Ha, ha, ha!

BUNTER. Blessed if I see anything to cackle at. I jolly well know that Quelch never said so.

WHARTON. You fat ass, I didn't mean that Caesar called Brutus a fathead! I was calling you a fathead!

BUNTER. Oh, really, Wharton—.

WHARTON. What Caesar said was, '*Et tu, Brute!*'

BUNTER. Quelch said it meant something, I forget what.

WHARTON. It means, 'And thou, Brutus!" Or you could translate it 'Thou too, Brutus!'

BUNTER. Well, I don't care what it means, anyway. I've only got to write the words for Quelch, and never mind what they mean, if they mean anything. I say, I thought Quelch would be shirty about a fellow nodding off in class! He looked it! Pretty decent of him to give me only one line, wasn't it?

WHARTON. Only one line?

BUNTER. Yes. He generally makes it twenty at least. He let me off very light with only one line to write.

CHERRY. You've got fifty lines to write.

BUNTER. Fifty! Wharrer you mean?

NUGENT. Aren't you going to do fifty lines for Quelch?

BUNTER. No jolly fear! Didn't you hear what Quelch said in the form-room? He said I was to write out Julius Caeser said, '*Et tu, Brute!*' fifty times. Not that I believe he did, you know.

ALL: Wha-a-a-at?

BUNTER. I mean to say, people do repeat themselves sometimes: Quelch often does in the form-room. But fifty times! That's altogether too thick, you know. As if he would!

CHERRY. Oh, scissors!

BUNTER. I mean, why should he? He just wouldn't, in my opinion. Quelch makes out that I'm dense, but I'm not dense enough to believe that Julius Caesar said the same thing over and over again fifty times. He wouldn't have had the breath for one thing, when they'd all been poking him with their daggers.

NUGENT. Oh, help!

BUNTER. Well, look at it! Why should Caesar, or anybody else, say it fifty times over, as Quelch said he did?

CHERRY. Fan me, somebody!

BUNTER. The truth is that Quelch has got it wrong. You can't argue with a beak, but I jolly well know he had it wrong. Quelch don't know so much as he makes out! Lots of beaks don't! School-masters are a dense lot, if you ask me! Not that it matters really. I've only got to write out what Quelch said. But mind you, I don't believe a word of it!

CHERRY (*shouting*). You fat ass, Quelch gave you fifty lines to write.

BUNTER. Eh? What makes you think that, Bob Cherry?

WHARTON. He said so, fathead. He said you were to write 'Caesar said Et tu, Brute' fifty times.

BUNTER. Yes, that's what I'm going to do, though I don't believe he said it fifty times or anything like it.

CHERRY. He said it once, but you've got to write it out fifty times. Do you mean to say you're going to write only one line for Quelch?

BUNTER. Of course! That's what he told me to do, isn't it?

NUGENT. He meant fifty lines—.

BUNTER. That's rot! He meant what he said,—Quelch always does.

WHARTON. Yes, and he said—.

BUNTER. I know what he said. Mind, I don't believe what he said, but I remember it all right. You can't pull my leg, Wharton.

WHARTON. What?

BUNTER. Pretty ass I should look, taking Quelch fifty lines, when he told me to write it out only once.

WHARTON (*shouting*). I tell you he meant—.

BUNTER. Chuck it, old chap, you can't stuff me. I'm too wide for that. I say, you fellows, is there any more cake?

NUGENT. Not a crumb!

BUNTER. Well, I may as well get my impot done, then. It won't take me long—just one line! Lend me a spot of paper and a pen, and I'll do it here. Oh! How do you spell Caesar, Wharton? Are there two Z's in it or only one?

WHARTON. None at all, ass.

BUNTER. Well, there must be one at least, I think. Isn't it spelt S-E-E-Z-E-R?

ALL. Ha-ha-ha!

BUNTER. I wish you wouldn't cackle every time a fellow opens his mouth. Look here, how do you think Caesar is spelt, Wharton?

WHARTON. C-A-E-S-A-R.

BUNTER. That doesn't sound right to me.

WHARTON (*laughing*). It will sound all right to Quelch.

BUNTER. Well, I'll take your word for it, but if I get into a row over the spelling, it will be your fault.

WHARTON. You won't get into a row over the spelling, old fat man, but you will if you take Quelch only one line when he said fifty.

BUNTER. Oh, pack that up, old chap—don't I keep on telling you that you can't pull my leg? Well, here goes!

Scratching of a pen is heard.

There,—that's soon done. Jolly decent of Quelch to let me off with one line,—after a fellow nodded off in form, you know.

Bell is heard.

Hallo! There goes six! I'd better take this down to Quelch.

CHERRY. You can't take that to Quelch, Bunter.

BUNTER. Why can't I? I've written just what he told me to write—here it is—look! 'Julius Caesar said "*Et tu Brute*" fifty times.' That's right, isn't it?

ALL (*shouting*). Quelch meant fifty lines—.

BUNTER. He, he, he! You can't stuff me!

Bunter is heard going. Door closes.

CHERRY. Oh, suffering cats and crocodiles! If he takes that to Quelch—!

ALL. Ha, ha, ha!

SCENE THREE
Mr Quelch's study. A tap is heard at the door.

QUELCH. Come in!

Door opens.

Oh! Bunter!

BUNTER. Yes, sir!

QUELCH. Have you brought me your imposition, Bunter?

BUNTER. Yes, sir: I've done it, sir.

QUELCH. I am glad that, for once, Bunter, you are handing in an imposition punctually.

BUNTER. Oh, yes, sir! It didn't take me long to write, sir. I—I mean, I always try to be punctual, sir. I always remember the proverb, sir, that punctuality is the procrastination of princes.

QUELCH. The what, Bunter?

BUNTER. The procrastination of princes, sir.

QUELCH. Punctuality is the politeness of princes, Bunter.

BUNTER. Is it, sir? I thought it was procrastination—.

QUELCH. You are an absurd boy, Bunter. However, I am glad that you have been punctual for once, and I trust that your imposition has been carefully written. You may hand it to me.

BUNTER. Here it is, sir. I hope the spelling's all right, sir. Oh! I—is—is anything the matter, sir?

QUELCH. Why—what—what—what is this? Bunter, what does this mean?

BUNTER (*anxiously*). Ain't the spelling right, sir? I—I knew there ought to be a 'Z' in 'Caesar', but I asked a chap, and he said there wasn't, and I—I took his word for it, sir—.

QUELCH. Bunter! Explain yourself! You have written a single line—.

BUNTER. Yes, sir! You told me—.

QUELCH. Making the ridiculous statement, Bunter, that Julius Caesar said '*Et tu Brute*' fifty times!

BUNTER. Yes, sir, that's right.

QUELCH (*thundering*). Right?

BUNTER. I mean, sir, that's what you told me, though it did seem to me queer that Julius Caesar said it fifty times, sir.

QUELCH. How dare you write such nonsense, Bunter, and bring it to me?

BUNTER. I had to do what you told me, sir. Don't you remember, sir, in the form-room,—you told me to write 'Julius Caesar said "*Et tu Brute*" fifty times'?

QUELCH. I gave you fifty lines, Bunter.

BUNTER. Oh, no, sir! All the fellows heard you, sir. You said—.

QUELCH. Upon my word! You have written this—this—this absurdity, and have ventured to bring it to me, your form-master. I shall double your imposition, Bunter,

BUNTER. Do you mean two lines, sir, instead of one?

QUELCH. I mean a hundred lines, Bunter.

BUNTER. Oh, crikey!

QUELCH. Let there be no mistake this time, Bunter. You will write, 'Caesar said "*Et tu Brute*".' You will write that sentence one hundred times. Is that clear to you, you stupid boy?

BUNTER. Oh! Yes, sir! But—.

QUELCH. You may go, Bunter.

BUNTER. But, sir, as I wrote exactly what you told me in the form-room—.

QUELCH. Grant me patience! Bunter, if you utter another word, I shall cane you. Leave my study this instant, or—.

Door is heard to close hurriedly.

SCENE FOUR
In the Rag. WHARTON, NUGENT, CHERRY, *others.*
Enter BUNTER.

BUNTER. I say, you fellows—.

CHERRY. How did you get on with Quelch?

NUGENT. Did he like your impot, Bunter?

WHARTON. Whopped?

BUNTER. Well, Quelch is a beast, but he ain't such a beast as to whop a chap for doing exactly what he was told. But he's given me a hundred lines. I don't know why but he has.

WHARTON. You don't know why?

BUNTER. He made out that my impot wasn't right. You fellows know that I wrote exactly what he told me—.

ALL. Ha, ha, ha!

BUNTER. Well you can cackle: but what's a fellow to do, except what his beak tells him? Now I've got a hundred lines, for nothing at all. That's the sort of justice we get here.

ALL. Ha, ha, ha!

BUNTER. Oh, cackle! Jolly funny for a fellow to get a hundred lines for nothing at all, ain't it? Well, I'm not taking it lying down, I can tell you. I'm going to make Quelch sit up. And I jolly well know how. He won't think it so jolly funny when a booby-trap falls on his head.

WHARTON. What?

CHERRY. You potty porpoise, what have you got in your noddle now?

NUGENT. Forget it, fathead.

BUNTER. Think I'm going to have a hundred lines for nothing? I'll watch it! Quelch has got it coming, I can jolly well tell you. I'm going to fix up a booby-trap in his study! I'll show him!

NUGENT. With Quelch sitting there watching you?

BUNTER. Quelch won't be there. I just saw him taking a deck-chair out into the quad. He won't be back in his study yet awhile, as he's sitting out in the quad in that deck-chair with a book. See? Easy as winking to get into his study without being seen.

CHERRY. Better keep out of it, all the same.

BUNTER. I'll watch it!

WHARTON. Look here, you fat duffer—.

BUNTER. Oh, really, Wharton—.

NUGENT. You'll get into a fearful row, if you set up a booby-trap for Quelch!

BUNTER. He, he, he! He won't know a thing! How's he to know? It's jolly easy, really. Now he's out, I can walk into his study, can't I? Well, I'm going to stack a pile of books on top of his study door, a few inches open, you know—.

CHERRY. Oh, my hat!

BUNTER. He won't see them from outside, of course, when he comes back to the study. He will just push the door open and walk in! Then down comes the lot on his nut, see? He, he, he!

CHERRY. Are you going to stay and wait for him to get it?

BUNTER. No jolly fear!

CHERRY. Well, how will you get out, after fixing the booby-trap over the door?

BUNTER. That's easy, too. Of course I shan't be able to get out at the door, as it will be only a few inches ajar. But what about the window? It's an easy drop to the ground from Quelch's study window.

CHERRY. By gum! It might work! Much safer to leave Quelch alone, though, and go and do your hundred lines, old fat man.

BUNTER. I'll show him! But I say, you fellows, don't get saying anything about it: I don't want Quelch to know it was me. That's important. Quelch simply must not know that it was me did it.

NUGENT (laughing). Do you mean, Quelch must not know that it was I did it?

BUNTER. Eh? How could Quelch know it was you, when it was me. You won't have anything to do with it, Nugent.

ALL. Ha, ha, ha!

BUNTER. Blessed if I see anything to cackle at. Quelch couldn't know it was you, Nugent, when it was me. How could he? Wharrer you mean?

NUGENT. Only that there's such a thing as grammar, old fat man. You can't say 'Quelch mustn't know it was me'—.

BUNTER. You can't teach me grammar, Frank Nugent.

NUGENT. No: even Quelch can't.

BUNTER. Quelch won't know it was me, so that's all right. But I say, you fellows, will you come along and lend me a hand fixing up the booby-trap for Quelch?

WHARTON. Time we got out, you men.

BUNTER. But I say—.

ALL. Cheerio, Bunter.

Departing footsteps.

BUNTER. I say, you fellows, don't walk away while a fellow's talking to you. I say—Beasts! Yah! Well, I'm going to Quelch's study to fix up that booby-trap. Quelch won't know it was me, and if Nugent thinks he might think it was him, that's his lookout. Quelch has got it coming,—right on the nut! He, he, he!

SCENE FIVE
Mr Quelch's study. BUNTER *enters.*

BUNTER. O.K. Nobody here, and nobody about! Quelch won't be coming back to this study yet. Safe as houses. I shall want a chair to stand on.

Sound of chair being moved.

Now, I'd better set the door five or six inches ajar—not more than that, or Quelch might spot what's on it. I'll get a specially big book to stick across from the top of the door to the lintel over the doorway—and pile the rest on it! He, he, he! Quelch won't know a thing, till he pushes the door open, and they come down—wallop! He, he, he!

Sounds of rummaging in a bookcase.

That big Latin dictionary—that's all right to start with. Now, then, to heave it up to the top of the door.

BUNTER *is heard getting on the chair, panting and grunting.*

That's right—safe till the door's pushed open from outside,—he, he, he! Let's see—the *Works of Josephus*—they go up next! They look jolly heavy! The *Works of Josephus* on top of the Latin dictionary, and the *Odes of Horace* on top of the *Works of Josephus*, and *Cicero's Letters* on top of the *Odes of Horace,*—he, he, he! May as well shove up *Pliny* and *Virgil*, too! He, he, he! Will Quelch jump, when he gets that stack of books on his napper? He, he, he! I'll show him! Giving a fellow a hundred lines for doing exactly what he was told! Yah!

BUNTER *is heard to step off the chair, and replace it against the wall.*

Now all I've got to do is to clear off by the window. All ready for Quelch, now: but the sooner I get out the better. Better take a squint round and see if there's anybody about, though. Only Wharton and Nugent and Cherry over there by the elms—they're staring at this window, but they don't matter. Well, here goes—it's an easy jump!

BUNTER *is heard to clamber into the window and jump out.*

SCENE SIX

In the Quad. WHARTON, NUGENT, CHERRY.

CHERRY. Hallo, hallo, hallo!
WHARTON. What—?
CHERRY. Look!
NUGENT. Look at what?

CHERRY. Quelch!
NUGENT. Eh? Where's Quelch?
CHERRY. Sitting in his deck-chair—under his study window!
WHARTON. Under his study window!
CHERRY. Well, look!
WHARTON. So he is! Oh, my hat!
NUGENT. Great pip! If that benighted ass Bunter jumps out, as he said he was going to do—!
CHERRY. He will land on Quelch, if he does!
WHARTON. Phew! There he is at the window! Too late to warn him . . . he's fixed up that booby-trap—.
NUGENT. If the fat ass doesn't spot Quelch sitting there under the window—.
CHERRY. He's squinting round—but he's not looking down! The window-sill's in the way—he can't see Quelch unless he leans out. Oh, holy smoke! He's going to jump—.
NUGENT. If he jumps on Quelch—.
CHERRY. No 'if' about it! He's jumping!
WHARTON. Oh, scissors! There he goes!

A terrific crash is heard, as Billy Bunter, jumping down from the window, crashes on MR QUELCH, *and the deckchair folds up.*

QUELCH. Why—what—help! Is the House collapsing! What—what—what is that? Something has fallen on me—something very heavy—.
BUNTER. Yarooooh!
CHERRY. He's done it now.
WHARTON. Never thought I should ever see Quelch on his back, and Bunter sprawling over him.
NUGENT. Does Quelch look shirty?
ALL. Ha, ha, ha!
QUELCH (*thundering*). Who—what—who is that? Is—is—is that Bunter?
BUNTER. Yow-ow-ow! I'm hurt!
QUELCH. Bunter!!
BUNTER. Oh, jiminy! Oh! No, sir! 'Tain't me, sir.
QUELCH. What?
BUNTER. I—I—I mean—.
QUELCH. Bunter, you have been in my study—you have jumped from the window—jumped on me, Bunter! You have knocked me over Bunter! Bunter, are you out of your senses? Why have you done this, Bunter?
BUNTER. I—I haven't, sir—.
QUELCH. What?
BUNTER. I—I—I mean, I haven't done anything in your study, sir—.
QUELCH. In my study!

BUNTER. Yes, sir! No, sir! I haven't fixed up a booby-trap, or—or anything—.

QUELCH. A booby-trap—in my study!

BUNTER. Oh! Yes! No! Nothing of the kind sir! If—if there's a stack of books on top of your study door, sir, I don't know anything about it.

QUELCH. Bless my soul!

BUNTER. I—I never, sir! I—I wasn't wild because you gave me a hundred lines for doing what you told me in the form-room, sir! I—I never said anything about fixing up a booby-trap for you, sir,—you can ask Wharton and Nugent and Cherry, sir—they heard me—.

QUELCH. Upon my word! Bunter! Come with me. The severest chastisement—the very severest chastisement—.

QUELCH'S *voice fades out.*

SCENE SEVEN
In the Rag. BUNTER.

BUNTER. Ow! wow! wow!

Enter WHARTON, NIGENT, CHERRY.

WHARTON. Had it bad, old fat man?

BUNTER. Ow! wow!wow!

CHERRY. Did Quelch lay it on?

BUNTER. Ow! wow! wow!

NUGENT. Thinking out another booby-trap for Quelch, Bunter!

BUNTER. Ow! wow! wow! Wow! Ow! wow! wow!

THE END

113

W.G.B. as William Shakespeare

W.G.B. as Hamlet

W.G.B. as Shylock

W.G.B. as Malvolio

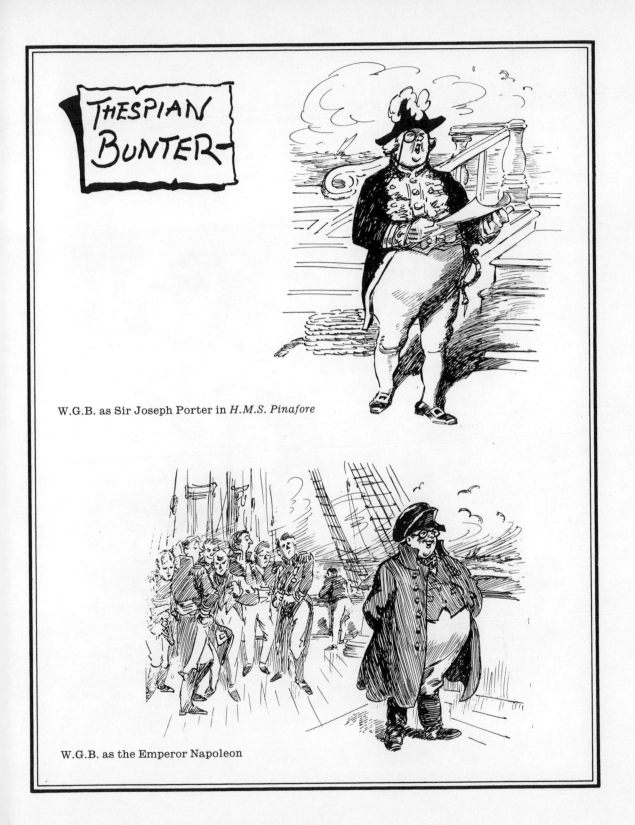

THESPIAN BUNTER

W.G.B. as Sir Joseph Porter in *H.M.S. Pinafore*

W.G.B. as the Emperor Napoleon

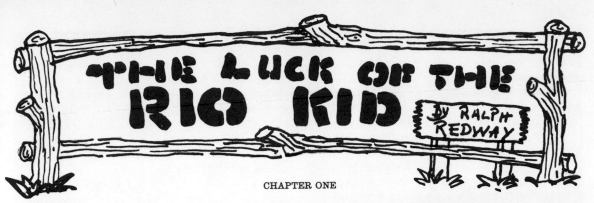

THE LUCK OF THE RIO KID
By Ralph Redway

CHAPTER ONE

"PUT 'em up, Kid!"

The Rio Kid opened his eyes, startled. Seldom, if ever, was the Rio Kid, the boy outlaw of the Rio Grande, caught napping.

But as his eyes opened, under the shady branches of the ceiba trees, and he looked into the muzzle of a levelled Colt, and at the hard, grim face that stared over it, he knew that it had happened for once.

If the Kid had been dreaming, as he lay in slumber in the timber-island, lonely amid the wide Texas grass-lands, he had not been dreaming of danger. He knew that the sheriff of Frio and his posse were hunting him: but he had ridden fast and far that day, till even the black-muzzled mustang showed signs of fatigue. And then the rain had come on: drenching rain that turned every hollow in the prairie into a lake, washing out every sign of his trail. The Kid had reckoned that he was through with the sheriff and his posse, and he had gladly pushed into the shelter of the clump of ceibas, and camped down there. It was dry, under the thick massive branches: and there he had bedded down the mustang, and rolled himself in his blanket for a much-needed rest. And now—!

The walnut-butted guns, in their low-slung holsters, were close to his hands. But he did not touch them. The Kid knew when he had a chance, and when he had none. And he had none now, with a .45 looking him full in the face, at a distance of six feet, with a finger on the trigger, and Jake Watson's grim bearded face staring over it. The sheriff wanted to take the Kid alive, and ride him back to Frio a prisoner: but at the first move towards a gun he would have pulled trigger without hesitation. And the Kid was not looking for sudden death. His eyes blazed, for a second: but there was a faint smile on his sunburnt face, as he sat up, with his hands lifted over his head.

"Your game, sheriff!" he said, lightly.

"Keep 'em up!" grunted Jake Watson. He was watching the Kid like a cat. Only too well he knew how elusive the boy outlaw could be. He was not giving him the ghost of a chance.

"Feller," said the Kid, "I was brought up too careful, to argue with the guy holding the gun! It's your say-so."

"Get on your feet."

The Kid stood up, dropping the blanket into the grass. A grey mustang with a black muzzle stirred in the thicket, and there was a low whinny from Side-Kicker. The Kid glanced, for a moment, towards his horse. But the Frio sheriff's glinting eyes remained fixed on the Kid. He could not have watched a panther, about to spring, more warily.

He stepped closer, and the muzzle of his Colt almost touched the Kid, as with his left hand he detached the boy outlaw's gun-belt. The Kid breathed very hard. But he made no move. He had to take this, and he took it with his accustomed careless coolness.

Sheriff Watson breathed more freely, as he tossed the Kid's gun-belt, with the two walnut-butted guns, behind him. The Kid was disarmed now. But the sheriff did not holster his own gun. He was wary of a sudden spring.

But the hard grimness in his bearded face relaxed a little.

"I sure got you, this time, Kid!" he said.

The Rio Kid nodded.

"You said it, feller!" he assented, "You sure got me by the short hairs. But it's a long ride to Frio, sheriff: and you sure ain't got me packed in the calaboose yet."

"I guess I'll get you there, dead or alive!" said the sheriff, "You've ridden a long trail, Kid, and snapped your fingers at all the sheriffs and town marshals in Texas: but it's the end of your trail this time."

"Mebbe!" said the Kid, with a shrug of his slim shoulders. "How'd you run into my camp, sheriff? You sure never picked up my trail in all that rain."

"Nope! I guess we scattered to look for sign," said the sheriff, "But we sure never found any." He grinned, for a moment. "It was jest luck, Kid, and I don't mind letting you know. I guess I'd had enough of the rain, and I pushed in here for shelter—and lighted on you in your blankets. Jest luck!"

The Kid set his lips. They had hunted him long and hard, and he knew that he had eluded them and left no sign. Sheer chance had delivered him into the hands of the law. Jake Watson was alone—his men scattered far and wide on the prairie looking for sign. And he had pushed into the timber-island for shelter from the drenching rain, just as the Kid himself had done. It was a cruel turn of fortune's wheel.

"But I got you." Jake Watson's look was almost gloating. "By the great horned toad, I guess there will be hats waved in Frio when I ride you in, Kid—roped in at last! No more hold-ups for you, Kid—no more cattle-rustling on the ranches."

The Kid's lip curled.

"You dog-goned geck," he said, "It's no good telling you that I never held up any galoot, and never rustled a cow in my life: you couldn't get it into your bone head."

"Not so's you'd notice it!" said Jake Watson, sarcastically. "Keep them paws up, or you get yours sudden."

"You're the doctor!" drawled the Kid.

The sheriff, still watching him like a cat, backed to his horse, standing a few yards away under the trees. From a saddle-bag he drew a rawhide rope: thin, flexible, but almost as strong as a steel chain. The Kid smiled sardonically. The sheriff would have had little chance of roping him up in that rawhide, if he had not been taken off his guard. But the cards had gone against him: and he had to take it.

With the rawhide, already noosed, in his hand, the sheriff came back to him. Again the muzzle of his Colt almost touched the Kid.

"Put your hands down behind you, Kid, and turn your back."

For a second the Kid hesitated.

His hands were to be roped behind him. After that, what chance remained? None at all, so far as the Kid could see: and for a moment he was tempted to make a desperate spring, like a cornered panther. The sheriff read the desperate thought, in his eyes, and his face set like iron.

But it was only for a moment. Hope lasted as long as life—and the Kid was not going to ask for it. He lowered his hands behind him, and turned his back to the sheriff, as bidden. With his left, Jake Watson noosed the slim wrists in the rawhide, and drew the noose tight, pinning the wrists together. He twisted the rope, till the bite of it on his wrists almost caused the Kid to utter a cry of pain. But he set his teeth and endured in silence. Holstering his gun at last, the sheriff put both hands to the rope, knotting it, and knotting it again, and yet again. Evidently he was taking no chances with so elusive a prisoner as the boy outlaw of the Rio Grande.

"I guess that fixes you!" he said at last.

"You said it, Jake! You ain't a guy to take chances: but I'll mention that that gol-darned rope sure is hurting my wrists a few," drawled the Kid. "Mebbe you'd let it a piece looser."

"Forget it!" said the sheriff, briefly. "You ain't getting a paw loose this side of Frio, Kid."

He turned to the mustang. Side-Kicker watched him with gleaming eyes, and bared his teeth. But a word from the Kid quieted the mustang: and he allowed the sheriff to saddle and bridle him.

"Get on that cayuse Kid! I guess I'll help you up."

The bound Kid was helped into the saddle.

118

Taking the Kid's own lasso, the sheriff looped it round him, knotted it, and fastened the other end to the saddle of his own horse. Then he slung the Kid's gun-belt to his own saddle-bow. Then, at last, he mounted.

"Us for Frio!" he said.

"Ain't you waiting till the rain stops, sheriff?" drawled the Kid.

"Nix!"

The sheriff of Frio set his horse in motion. He rode out of the trees, the led mustang following, the Kid a helpless prisoner on the back of his own horse. Outside the shelter of the thick-branched ceibas, the rain was coming down in torrents. It was no weather for riding the open plains. But Jake Watson was too anxious to get his prisoner into the calaboose at Frio, to care a red cent for a drenching on the way. Heedless of the downpour, he pushed out into the open, the black-muzzled mustang following: and rode through the pouring rain, splashing through pools in the rugged ground. It was many a long mile to Frio, and the going was slow in the rain and the mud: but Jake Watson pushed on without a pause, and the mustang followed at the end of the riata, and the Rio Kid, as the rain soaked him to the very skin, wondered whether this, at last, was the end of his long wild trail.

CHAPTER TWO

THE Rio Kid set his lips hard.

It was a long ride. Hours, long hours, were likely to elapse, before the sheriff and his prisoner sighted Frio. The rain poured and poured. The prairie was a sea of mud and wet grass.

The Kid rode awkwardly, with his hands bound behind his back, and every now and then a jerk from the lasso that held him to the sheriff's horse: hardly able to save himself from a fall, when his mustang stumbled in a muddy rut, or in a flooded gopher-hole. But worst of all was the pain in his wrists from the grip of the knotted rawhide. Jake Watson did not mean to be brutal: but he was rough and ready in his methods, and grimly determined that his prisoner should have no chance of escape.

The Kid wrenched, and twisted, at the knotted rawhide, in the faint hope of getting his hands loose as he rode. But that hope soon died out. He could not loosen the knots by a fraction of an inch, and he soon gave up the attempt. And as the pain intensified in his wrists, he almost felt that he would be glad to reach Frio, and his lodging in the calaboose of the cow-town. But many long miles lay ahead of him yet: and at length he called to the sheriff.

"Say, Jake!"

Jake Watson glanced round, in the streaming rain.

"You sure got me dead to rights, Jake!" said the Kid, "I guess you could go a piece easier with this gol-darned rope, old timer."

"Forget it!" said the sheriff, briefly.

"I'm telling you, it's hurting me some."

"Mebbe!"

With that the sheriff pushed on through the rain.

The Kid breathed hard.

He would have given much, just then, to have had one hand free, with a gun in it. But he was helpless, and could only set his lips hard and take what had come to him. Jake did not even look round again: with his head bent to the wind and the rain, he pushed doggedly on, the black-muzzled mustang trotting in his wake with the bound Kid in the saddle.

The rain showed no sign of easing. Hard and fast it poured down on the two riders: harder and faster. The Kid's face was streaming wet: his chaps dripping water, and water soaked his skin and ran into his boots. He cared little for that: but the bitter ache in his bound wrists was growing to be a torture, and Frio was still miles distant.

The usually care-free face of the boy outlaw was dark and gloomy. He was cinched: fortune had played him low down, and he was a prisoner—riding into Frio, to be barred in the calaboose, and as likely as not dragged out by a lynch-mob when the news spread that the outlaw of the Rio Grande was taken at last. He was not what men believed him to be—he had hardly heard of half the hold-ups that were put down to his account: it was by no will of his own that he rode the outlaw trail. But that would not help him—there was a thousand dollars on his head, and a rope and a branch ready for him when he was roped in. And Jake Watson had roped him in. He had been caught napping, like a tenderfoot from Tendertown, as he told himself bitterly: and his one chance was to get loose before the sheriff rode him into the cow-town on the banks of the Rio Frio. And there was no chance of that.

But was there not?

Suddenly, a gleam came into his eyes. He caught his breath. For as he moved his aching wrists, to ease the pain, he felt a faint, slight, almost imperceptible "give" in the knotted rawhide that fastened them together.

For a moment, he could not understand it. Then it flashed into his mind. It was the rain. The rain that drenched him to the skin, that ran down over his shoulders, and down his arms, had soaked the rawhide binding his wrists, as it soaked every other rag on him. And it is in the nature of rawhide to stretch when thoroughly wet.

The Kid had not thought of it: the sheriff had never dreamed of it. But it was borne into the Kid's mind now.

His heart beat fast.

Far in the distance, through the mists of the heavy rain, there was a blur of smoke against the grey sky. It told where the cow-town of Frio lay. A mile or two more, and the bars of the calaboose would close on him. But there was hope in his heart now.

Carefully, cautiously, wary not to attract a glance from the sheriff who rode ahead of him, the Kid tested the rawhide, striving to draw his bound wrists apart. The pain of the effort caused the sweat to break out on his face. But the pain, bitter as it was, was as nothing, to the delight of feeling the rawhide give. It gave, and gave further.

The knots were as fast as ever: indeed, the silent, steady wrenching, made them all the faster. But the rawhide, where it circled his slim wrists, was giving, enlarging into a loop almost like elastic. It was slow, hard, and heavy work: only by a fraction of an inch at a time, did the rawhide stretch. But it was stretching.

The sheriff looked round: and the Kid, for a moment, ceased his effort. They had left the rugged prairie for a well-marked trail: a trail that ran direct into Main Street at Frio.

"I guess we're soon in, Kid," called out Jake Watson. "I'll say I'll be glad to pull out of this dog-goned rain, and you too, I guess."

"Oh, sure!" answered the Kid.

"I'll sure get that rope off'n you, the minute we pull in, Kid!" added the sheriff. "I got to keep you safe: you sure are too slippery a cuss for a guy to take chances. Jest you wait till we ride in."

The Kid laughed.

"Feller," he answered, "you've ridden me hard but I ain't got no kick coming: and mebbe I won't make it last sickness for you, next time I get you under a gun."

"I'll tell a man, that'll be a long time, Kid," said the sheriff, with a dry chuckle: and he rode on, his head down to the rain.

The Kid, heedless of pain, put a steady pressure on his wrists. The rawhide gave more and more. They were little more than half-a-mile out of the cow-town now, and minutes were precious. If only he could get his hands free before they hit Frio—!

He set his teeth, to keep back an exclamation of delight, as, at length, one of his hands slipped through the yielding rawhide. He drew it free, and the rawhide dropped from the other, into the wet grass.

He drew a deep, deep breath.

His wrists and his hands were numbed, from the grip of the bonds, and the cold of the rain. He kept them behind him, as if they were still bound, in case the watchful eye of Jake Watson should turn on him. Well he knew that the sheriff's gun would be out, in the twinkling of an eye, if he divined what was happening.

Keeping his hands behind him, he chafed the aching wrists and the numbed fingers, till they were in a state of action. Seconds were precious now, with the cow-town in sight across the weeping prairie.

A pressure of his knees was enough for his mustang: Side-Kicker was accustomed to obeying the slightest sign. The black-muzzled mustang put on speed, and the Kid rode close beside the sheriff. Jake stared at him. To his eyes, the Kid was still bound and helpless.

"Say, feller," said the Kid, softly, "You don't feel like letting that rope loose a piece, seeing as it hurts a guy more than a few."

"Aw, can it, Kid," snapped the sheriff, "You gotta wait till I got you safe in the calaboose. I guess—Thunder!" The sheriff broke off, with a startled yell, as one of the hands, that he had believed to be bound behind the Kid, flashed round and a clenched fist drove into his face like the kick of a mule.

Jake Watson went out of the saddle as if he had been shot. He crashed headlong into wet grass. The Kid was on the ground the next second, bending over him: two riderless horses at a halt. Before the half-stunned sheriff could begin to realise things, the Kid had gripped the gun from his holster: and as Jake Watson sat up dazedly, the muzzle of his own Colt was jammed into his face, with the Kid's finger on the trigger.

"Put 'em up, sheriff!" grinned the Rio Kid.

The sheriff stared at him: dazedly, almost unbelievingly. He was utterly confused and confounded by that sudden turning of the tables. Blindly he groped at his holster for the gun that was no longer there—the gun that was looking him in the face. He panted.

"You gol-darned, dog-goned, pesky scallywag—."

"I guess I ain't asking you to chew the rag, Jake Watson—I'm telling you to put up your hands, or—!" The Kid's eyes flashed over the Colt.

And Sheriff Watson, panting with rage, lifted his hands above his head, as he sat in the wet grass in the falling rain. The tables had been turned, how the sheriff could hardly guess, and it was now the Rio Kid who held the upper hand—and the gun!

CHAPTER THREE

THE Rio Kid laughed.

He laughed loud and long.

Only half-a-mile away, the smoke of the cow-town blurred the rainy sky. In Frio, a hundred guns would have leaped from their holsters, at a word that the Rio Kid was around. But nowhere at hand was there help for the sheriff of Frio: he was utterly at the mercy of the boy outlaw of the Rio Grande: and as he stared at the levelled Colt, and the handsome, rain-wet face behind it, he did not expect mercy.

"You dog-goned young lobo-wolf—!" he muttered. He glared in rage at the Kid's laughing face. "How'd you get loose? I guess I had you hog-tied okay. Dog-gone you—."

"Can it, Jake!" grinned the Kid. "This is my sayso. You rode me hard, Jake, when you had me cinched, and I guess I'd be a dog-goned bonehead not to let daylight through you, now I got the gun."

The sheriff's face set savagely.

"Shoot and be durned!" he snarled.

The Kid laughed again.

"I ain't going to spill your juice, Jake, not if you behave!" he grinned. "Keep them paws up, if you don't want to get yours sudden. Don't you give jest one kick, feller, or Frio will want a new sheriff. I'd jest as soon leave you here for the buzzards as not, you ornery piecan—you jest behave, Jake, or you get yours from your own gun."

The sheriff of Frio writhed with rage. But he kept his hands up, and made no attempt at resistance. He had come out at the little end of the horn: and it was for the Kid to dictate.

The Kid reached for his gun-belt, which the sheriff had slung over his saddle. He hooked it away, laughing. Then he made a motion with the Colt.

"Get on your legs, Jake!"

The sheriff struggled to his feet. He was shaken and bruised by his fall, and a black bruise was forming on his rugged face where the Kid's knuckles had struck. The Kid kept him covered, while he gathered up the lasso by which he had been led a prisoner. He threw the noose over the sheriff's head, and drew it tight, pinning his arms to his sides. The sheriff watched him with silent rage, as he knotted the rope. It was the sheriff of Frio who was a bound prisoner now, and the Kid, with a laugh, shoved the Colt back into Jake's holster: the sheriff could not move a hand to touch it. He buckled on his own gun-belt; the walnut-butted guns were ready to his hand now, if he wanted them. But the Kid had no need of a gun now. He had the sheriff of Frio where he wanted him.

"You're going back to Frio, Jake!" he said, laughing. "You ain't riding the Rio Kid in, not by long chalks you ain't! You sure are not going to have all the guys in Frio rubbering at the Rio Kid! But I guess they'll be rubbering a few, when they see you ride in. Get on your cayuse, Jake—face to the tail!"

The sheriff panted with fury.

"I guess—!"

"Can it, and do like you're told!" interrupted the Kid. "You're getting off easy, sheriff—you was riding me to a rope and a branch, and I guess I'm a bonehead not to blow your caboza into little pieces: but I always was an easy-going guy. But if you don't do like you're told, you geck, you get yours, and I'll mention that I ain't waiting."

The Kid's had dropped to a walnut-butt.

White with fury, the sheriff of Frio did as he was bidden. With the Kid's help, he clambered clumsily on his horse, and sat with his face to the tail, his eyes burning at the boy outlaw. With a length of the lasso, the Kid tied his feet under the horse.

"Okay, sheriff!" he asked, banteringly.

The sheriff choked with rage.

"You sending me into Frio like this?" he breathed.

"Surest thing you know!" grinned the Kid. "Your cayuse will find his way in, sheriff, and I guess the rain won't keep the Frio guys indoors, when their sheriff's seen riding into town that-a-way! What you figure?"

"By the great horned toad, Kid, I'll get you for this—I—I—I'll—." Fury choked the sheriff of Frio.

The Kid laughed, and started the sheriff's horse with a smart smack. The animal broke into a trot: and the sheriff, backwards in the saddle, stared back at the boy outlaw as he went, his face a mask of fury.

The Kid waved a hand in mocking farewell.

"Adios!" he called out.

And he mounted the black-muzzled mustang and rode away into the rain. And Jake Watson, with feelings that could not have been expressed in words though Jake knew many expressive ones, rode backwards into Frio at a trot, while the Rio Kid vanished over the rainy prairie at a gallop.

THE Kid had said that the rain would not keep the guys at Frio indoors when their sheriff rode in, tied on his horse with his face to the tail: and he was right. As that remarkable horseman appeared on Main Street, he was greeted by a roar of surprise and merriment: and all the cow-town turned to stare. When at length a friendly hand released him, Jake Watson was glad to hide his furious face behind the closed door of his office. The next day, the sheriff and his men were riding hard in search of the Rio Kid. But they did not find him. Jake was not likely to catch him napping a second time. They hunted him long, and they hunted him hard: but the luck of the Rio Kid held good: and when weary horseman at last rode back to Frio, the boy outlaw was still riding the prairies of Texas, free and care-free.

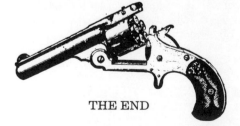

THE END

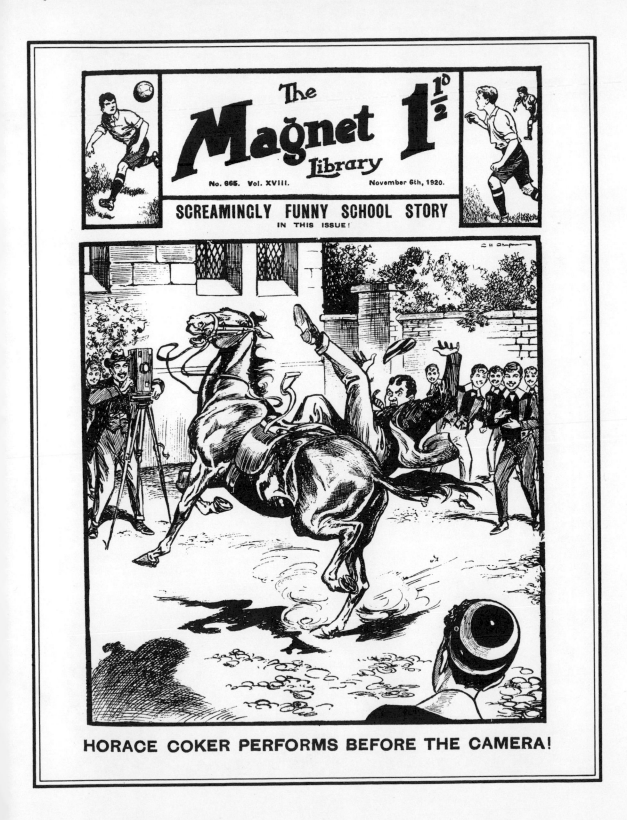

The **Magnet** Library 1½d

No. 665. Vol. XVIII.   November 6th, 1920.

SCREAMINGLY FUNNY SCHOOL STORY
IN THIS ISSUE!

HORACE COKER PERFORMS BEFORE THE CAMERA!

IMPERIAL HERITAGE
by *Frank Richards*

As one of an Imperial race,
  My heart swells high with pride.
My vast imperial heritage
  Stretches far and wide.
Three hundred million dusky men
  In dusky tropic lands,
Must yield obedience, more or less,
  If I should give commands.

Each morn I jump into the Tube
  And to the City hie,
For thirty-five and six a week—
  Not much—but what care I?
As one of an Imperial race,
  A despot from my birth,
Strap-hanging in a stuffy Tube,
  I govern half the earth!

If I should chance to lose my job
  And lose my weekly screw,
I'll have my Indian Empire left,
  If that White-Paper crew
Don't hand it over to the folks
  To whom it did belong.
Ye gods! It makes my blood to boil,
  To think of such a wrong!

But stay—but stay—if I should lose
　　My thirty-five and six,
If bailiffs came and cleared me out
　　And sold up all my sticks,
If meals grew smaller by degrees
　　And then, at last, they ceased—
How much then could I raise upon
　　My empire in the East?

As one of an Imperial race,
　　Whose high and potent sway,
Extends from Quetta to Ceylon,
　　From Goa to Bombay,
It seems more than a little odd,
　　That I should starve and freeze
While my Imperial standard flies
　　O'er countless lands and seas.

Those dusky millions whom I rule,
　　What are they worth to me?
Not all those subject dusky men
　　Would stand me one rupee.
Between me and the Union
　　Stands but my weekly screw,
So on the whole, I won't get mad
　　With that White-Paper crew.

In fact, if I should have to choose,
　　Between my weekly dough,
And my Imperial heritage,
　　I'd let my Empire go!
For thirty-five and six a week
　　Seems to be more to me,
Than holding with Imperial hand
　　The gorgeous East in fee!

THE NEW MASTER

BY FRANK DRAKE

"HOW dare you, sir?"

"I don't think I understand you, Doctor Tasker. How dare I?"

"Don't seek to evade me in casuistry, sir. I said how dare you, and I mean how dare you."

Mr Paget, the Fourth Form master, could not repress a shade of annoyance passing over his face.

"You have been taking sustenance to a boy who is under my displeasure, and have wilfully broken the rules of the school, and my express wishes in this matter are deliberately set aside . . ."

"If you mean that I have taken some food to a little lad whom you are treating brutally, I assure you I shall know how to reply to you," said Mr Paget, unable to restrain himself any longer. "I am not aware it is the rule at St Mary's to starve boys—."

"Do you mean then to add impertinence and insolence to your already unpardonable conduct? Then hear me. You can go at once, sir. Leave the college!" roared the angry pedagogue.

"As you will, Doctor Tasker," returned the master with a slight inclination of the head. "You have made yourself as unpleasant as possible to me for some time now because I could not help but take the part of the boy, Harold Lonsdale—."

"Enough of this, sir," thundered the angry Head. "I warn you to be gone lest I forget myself!"

"I will go with pleasure, Doctor Tasker. But you must hear what I have to say first."

"I will not."

"You will."

The Head strode to the bell to give the alarm. Like a flash Paget was in front of him.

"Do you mean to persist in this folly then, Mr Paget," hissed the angry man, almost white with rage. "Am I to use force to you, sir?"

"Whatever you do, I am determined that you shall hear me. It is strange to hear the headmaster of St Mary's talking of using force, but I can only remind you that I am a strange man, Doctor Tasker—and I could use force too, when it is necessary—."

"Have done with your absurd prating, sir—."

"Certainly, sir. Then you will listen?"

The pedagogue did not reply.

With chest heaving, face pale as death, he stood clenching his hands like a wild animal at bay.

"I took a little food to Harold Lonsdale," said Mr Paget, quietly. "Because I have reason to believe that it is the first meal he has had to-day."

Doctor Tasker started.

"How do you know?" he snarled. "But what am I thinking of?" he laughed scornfully, making for the bell rope again. "I'll soon see who's master here, you upstart with a pedigree—."

"If you make another step, I'll knock you down!" said Mr Paget, in a quick tone like a rifle shot.

His warning had its effect on the elder man. Gritting his teeth he went back to his old position.

"Now," said George Paget. "You must listen. I am going away from here. I would have given the place up long ago if it hadn't been for that boy, and, Doctor Tasker, have a care what you're about. If that boy is hurt after I go, be assured you will hear about it, and be made to smart for it. I am quite aware who has put him under your care, and I think I know the person's object, so take my advice in the spirit I give and be more kindly towards him."

A contemptuous smile flitted over the headmaster's face.

"I shall inform the police about you, sir," he began.

"I have a remedy for that Doctor Tasker, and I advise you not to attempt anything of the kind. The police have a way of inquiring into these things, and they may not be so kind to you as I am."

Doctor Tasker sneered.

"Your language is grotesquely inflated, Mr Paget," he said. "You have evidently been listening to gossip and you wish to frighten me."

"Gossip or not, I know that Lord Revelle, failing this boy, is heir to the Lonsdale estates."

"And—what of that, pray, Mr Paget," said the schoolmaster, who almost tottered.

"Only that the authorities would not like you to feed so distinguished a pupil as Harold Lonsdale on bread and water—."

"Sir!"

"To thrash him for every trifling offence."

"I'll stand no more of this," roared Doctor Tasker, this time reaching the bell rope. "Will you desist, sir, or am I to ring?"

"And confine him to the punishment room until the lad is quite ill," pursued George Paget relentlessly.

The infuriated man gave the bell-rope such a tug that the lever gave way and the thing fell clattering to the floor.

"I give you five minutes to get out of St Mary's," he hissed. "Jarvis will be here in a moment and I shall send him for assistance."

"It may interest you to know that Jarvis has been gone to the village this half-hour."

"You cur!"

"Take care, Doctor Tasker."

"You—."

But the gleam in George Paget's eyes effectually restrained the head of St Mary's.

Flinging a look of mortal hatred at his enemy, he banged the door open with his clenched fist.

"You shall repent this," he said.

And without another word he strode off to his study.

George Paget soon completed his packing, and when the Head came up to his room he was in the act of leaving it.

"Here you are, my men," said Doctor Tasker to the returned Jarvis, and the gardener who accompanied him. "You will see this person off the premises. There's your wages in place of the usual notice," he continued to Paget, as he tendered a cheque.

"Will you carry my bag as far as the gates, Jarvis, please?"

The headmaster fumed at this use of the house-porter, and the polite tone of the Fourth Form master stung him to the quick.

"Hang him!" he muttered under his breath, as he regained his study. "The presuming puppy to lecture me in my own place. But I'll—I'll—."

And resolving to act, Doctor Tasker sat down to write to the Agency for another master, complaining at the same time of the conduct of Mr George Paget. "I shall have to take the Fourth myself to-morrow," he mused as he finished the letter.

In due course the new master arrived.

The irascible headmaster was also informed by the agency that they were inquiring into the case of Mr George Paget.

"I hope our relations will be happier, Mr McDermott," said the Head after he had given the new man an idea of what qualities he most disliked in a Fourth-Form master.

"I hope so sir," replied the keen-looking man who sat opposite him in his study. "Are there any juniors whose conduct requires—?"

"Excuse me," interrupted Doctor Tasker, "I think I can anticipate you. There are several who require to be well-watched."

And the tormentor of Harold Lonsdale went on to explain his treatment of several youths among whom Harold was mentioned.

But McDermott, with the sharpness of his race, easily discerned that the impression desired was that Harold Lonsdale was really the person to be watched.

"By the way. Have you met Mr Paget?" queried the Head, as he rose to terminate the interview.

"I have met him, sir," returned the other in a very non-committal tone.

"Just so. Well I wish you better success, Mr McDermott."

"Thank you sir."

And the Irishman bowed himself out.

There was a curious glitter in his eye as he went to his room, and it being too late in the day to begin his tutorial duties he went out to make an inspection of the school.

He was interested in many things, but strangely enough he seemed to want to linger in the vicinity of the punishment room.

The juniors were bitterly disappointed at losing Mr Paget.

But though the new master was at first taken very cautiously, before the day was over the boys realised that he was a "good sort" too.

But their hopes were dashed to the ground when after a week it could not be denied that he, too, was interested in the case of Harold Lonsdale.

"He'll not last long," they said. "And it's a jolly shame."

Doctor Tasker, however, had somewhat profited by George Paget's lecture.

His thrashings of Lonsdale had almost ceased, or were really very light since the old Fourth Form master left.

"And that's something anyhow," said Berry Fay, the leader of the Fourth. "I say. I think what I heard Jarvis say one day, must be true, chaps."

"Then Paget laid it down to him before he went?" said several youths.

"Yes."

"Hope so," rejoined the lads, heartily. "The leathering of Lonsdale has gone on quite long enough."

But the new form master had been seen talking with Lonsdale.

"This must be stopped at once," said the Head to himself as he saw them together. "They are far too intimate for pupil and master."

Precisely how he should do it, Doctor Tasker had not yet decided.

His experience with George Paget had not improved his confidence in being able to do what he liked with his assistants. "I must think out something crushing," he thought.

"We will talk of this again, Lonsdale," Mr McDermott was saying, meanwhile, in the quadrangle.

"Yes, sir. And thank you so very much. But I hope you will excuse me saying that the last master of our form lost his position through taking so much notice of me, sir."

"That is all right, Lonsdale, thank you," returned the sharp looking man. "I shall not lose my place. We will have another talk after tea to-day if you will come to my study."

"I shall be delighted, sir."

"Very good. You may go."

"Thank you, sir."

But Harold Lonsdale did not keep his appointment.

Early in the afternoon he was told to present himself in the Head's study, and he did not appear in class again that day.

Nor on inquiry by the new master, had any of the juniors seen him at tea.

"Aha!" said McDermott, as a short time afterwards he found the door of the passage that led to the punishment room locked. "So that is your little game, Doctor Tasker, is it?"

And taking a key from his pocket he noiselessly entered the passage.

Half a minute sufficed for him to get to the punishment room, and entering that in turn he found Harold Lonsdale groaning on the floor.

"Mr McDermott!"

"Do not be surprised or alarmed, my lad," said the Irishman quietly. "Now tell me what is the meaning of this. What have you done?"

"Nothing, sir."

The form master seemed not unprepared for the reply. "Well tell me what happened, Lonsdale."

The poor lad with a great effort pulled himself together. "You saw how I was sent for of course, sir?" he began.

McDermott nodded.

"Well, sir. As soon as he saw me—oh, I beg you will not say anything, sir. I really meant to say the Head. The Head told me to go before him to the punishment room, and after he had locked the door he flogged me till he was breathless."

"And you are to be kept here with only that bread and water to eat till to-morrow morning, I suppose?"

"Yes, sir. He said he had warned me times without number and—."

"That will do, Lonsdale. I think I know the rest. I'm afraid I cannot get you some tea without it's causing suspicion, but I'll see that you have your proper bed to-night. And a proper meal, too."

"Oh sir! You'll lose your—."

"Make the best you can of the German, Lonsdale. I know you are only just beginning the study of that language. But it's as well not to give the Head any further cause for thrashing you, and leave—the rest to me," said Mr McDermott quickly rising.

"Certainly, sir."

And late that night Harold Lonsdale was spirited to his bed and he sank into a troubled sleep as he thought that there were some good masters in St Mary's after all.

To say that Doctor Tasker was surprised to see Harold Lonsdale in class next morning, would be mild.

"Come here, sir," he roared as he caught sight of his victim.

"Stop where you are, Lonsdale."

As Harold Lonsdale hesitated a silence as of death fell on the whole school.

"Mr McDermott!" expostulated the schoolmaster when he had gained control of himself. "What can you be thinking of? Lonsdale, come here at once!"

Force of habit made the junior move forward a step or two, when the quick dry voice of the Form Master rapped out once more. "Stay where you are, my lad."

For a moment the infuriated headmaster was speechless with amazement.

"I have had quite enough of interference from under-masters in the past, Mr McDermott," he said through his clenched teeth, picking up his cane as he strode towards the trembling lad. "But I will show you both who is master here!"

And without more ado the angry man lifted his cane to strike McDermott.

Quick as lightening the new master dodged the blow and seizing Doctor Tasker's wrists his disengaged hand flashed to and from his hip pocket.

There was a sharp click and the school was electrified to see that the cad was securely handcuffed.

"What is the meaning of this tom-foolery, sir?" bellowed the pedagogue. "Release me at once, I say. Mr Stretton! Mr Beasely! Assist me, if you please!"

"If they can," returned McDermott complacently.

"You can go, sir," went on the Head.

"And I'll take you with me."

All at once the truth dawned on the schoolmaster and he sank into a chair, with an ashen face. "What am I arrested for?" he said endeavouring to preserve as much dignity as he could.

"For cruelty and persecution to this boy. Your accomplice, Lord Revelle, has been watched by us as well and—."

"You really are the—?"

"New master—from Scotland Yard," said Detective Officer McDermott bowing.

And a few minutes later Doctor Tasker was conducted out of his own school for good—the "new master," on one side and a police officer on the other.

THE END

Gerald Campion as Billy Bunter in the
BBC television series that was launched
in 1952 and ran, off and on, for ten years

Ron Moody as Hurree Singh, Barry
Macregor as Johnny Bull, Michael
Danvers-Walker as Frank Nugent,
Gerald Campion as Billy Bunter, Harry
Searle as Harry Wharton and Brian
Smith as Bob Cherry in a 1954 episode of
the BBC TV Bunter series

BUNTER THE HYPNOTIST

A TELEVISION PLAY BY FRANK RICHARDS

A landing.

BUNTER *is sprawling on a settee by the bannisters, reading a book. He is deeply engrossed in it.*

CHERRY'S VOICE *(calling from below).* Bunter!

Bunter does not heed.

CHERRY'S VOICE. Hallo, hallo, hallo! Bunter!

Bunter makes an irritated movement, but takes no other notice.

WHARTON'S VOICE. Fetch him down, Bob.

Footsteps on stairs. Bunter, heedless, mumbles aloud over his book.

CLOSE UP: *Book, showing title:* 'HOW TO HYPNOTIZE! One shilling.'

BUNTER *(mumbling to himself).* Looks easy enough. You simply have to learn the passes, from these diagrams, and once you've got 'em perfect, you can put the 'fluence on.

He puts down the book on his knees and makes a few passes in the air with his hands.

I shall want some practise, of course. But it will come all right! And then, won't I make 'em hop.

He picks up the book again, and reads aloud.

A hypnotist requires a strong personality and an iron will! *(He nods.)* Well that's me all over! I fancy I shall get it all right!

CHERRY *enters.*

CHERRY. Hallo, hallo, hallo! Here you are, you fat ass.

Bunter hastily closes the book and puts it under his arm.

CHERRY. Deaf, old fat man? I've been calling you.
BUNTER *(irritably).* Well, don't.
CHERRY. Wharton's sent me up to fetch you.

BUNTER. Bother Wharton!
CHERRY. Can't bother your form-captain. Come on.
BUNTER. Oh, do go away.
CHERRY. You're due for games practice, fathead. Come down and squeeze into your flannels.
BUNTER. I've no time for that. Go away.
CHERRY. What?
BUNTER. You're interrupting me.
CHERRY. That's what I've come up for, ass. Games practice . . .
BUNTER. Blow games practice.
CHERRY. Every man in the Remove has to turn up.
BUNTER. I don't need so much practice as you fellows do. I can *play* cricket! Anyhow I'm too busy now . . . I'm studying this book . . .
CHERRY. Blessed if I ever saw you swotting before. Mugging up Latin for Quelch?
BUNTER. Oh, don't be an ass! Think it's a school book?
CHERRY. Well, I suppose it wouldn't be, as you're reading it! But chuck it now, whatever it is . . .
BUNTER. Shan't!
WHARTON'S VOICE. Are you coming, Bob? Roll that fat slacker down.
CHERRY. Coming! Now, then, Bunter . . .
BUNTER. Do shut up! I tell you I've got to study this. Ow! Leggo!

CHERRY *takes him by the collar.*

BUNTER. Beast! Leggo!

BUNTER *struggles, and the book falls from under his arm.*
CHERRY *stoops to pick it up, and* BUNTER *dives for it at the same moment. Their heads meet with a crack.*

CHERRY *(staggering).* Oh!
BUNTER. Yarooooh!
CHERRY. You clumsy fat ass, you've jolly nearly cracked my nut. *(He rubs his head).*
BUNTER *(also rubbing his head).* Ow! Oh! Ow! Wow!

CHERRY *picks up book, and holds it out to Bunter.*

CHERRY. Here you are! Now . . .

BUNTER (*yelling*). Gimme my book! Don't you jolly well look at that book!

He jumps at CHERRY, *snatching the book from his hand.*

CHERRY (*staring*). You potty porpoise. Think I want to look at your book, whatever it is. Look here, come on and get changed. Here . . . hallo, hallo, hallo . . . Stop!

BUNTER. Beast!

He crams the book into an inside pocket, dodges CHERRY, *and bolts across the landing.*

CHERRY (*shouting*). Stop!

Enter SKINNER *and* SNOOP, *coming across landing towards stairs.* BUNTER *in full flight, crashes into them.* SKINNER *totters on one side* SNOOP *on the other.* BUNTER *sits down between them gasping for breath.*

SKINNER. Why, you mad ass . . . !

SNOOP. You dithering rhinoceros . . . !

BUNTER. Oooooooooh!

CHERRY *grasps him by the back of the collar and heaves him to his feet.*

CHERRY. Now come on, fathead.

BUNTER (*yelling*). Leggo!

CHERRY. This way!

CHERRY *propels* BUNTER *towards the stairs.* SKINNER *shakes fist after him.* BUNTER *resists. Enter* WHARTON, NUGENT, BULL *and* HURREE SINGH *from stairs, all in flannels.* WHARTON *has bat under his arm.*

WHARTON. Bring that fat slacker along.

BUNTER. I say, you fellows, I just can't go down to games practice this afternoon. I've got to bot over a swook . . .

WHARTON. What?

BUNTER. I mean swot over a book.

WHARTON. Catch you swotting, you fat slacker.

BUNTER. I . . . I mean, I've got a pain in my leg . . .

WHARTON. Not much difference between swotting over a book, and a pain in the leg!

ALL. Ha, ha, ha!

BUNTER. It's an awful pain . . . like burning daggers . . .

BULL. Which leg?

BUNTER. I forget . . . I . . . I . . . I mean, the right leg. A pain like red-hot needles. I just can't go down to cricket.

NUGENT. Gammon!

SINGH. The gammonfulness is terrific, my esteemed fat Bunter.

CHERRY. Come on!

BUNTER. I . . . I . . . kik-kik-can't! I couldn't hold a bat with this awful pain in my back . . .

BULL. In your back?

BUNTER. I . . . I mean in my arm . . . that is my leg. I . . . I mean in my back as well. I . . . I've got a pain all over.

CHERRY. Nothing to worry about, if it's all over.

ALL. Ha, ha, ha!

BUNTER. Oh really, Cherry! I didn't mean it's all over . . . I mean it's all over . . .

ALL. Ha, ha, ha!

BUNTER. Blessed if I see anything to cackle at, in a fellow having a fearful pain in his neck . . . I mean his back . . . that is, his leg . . . I just can't walk!

WHARTON. Sure you can't walk?

He slips his bat down from under his arm into his hand.

BUNTER. Quite sure, old chap.

WHARTON. Think you could run?

BUNTER. Of course I couldn't.

WHARTON. Well I'm going to prod you with this bat till you get a move on. I fancy you will be able to run.

He prods BUNTER.

BUNTER. Yaroooh! Keep off! Keep that bat away! I'm coming, aren't I? Wow!

Exit BUNTER, *running for the stairs, followed by* HARRY WHARTON *and Co. laughing.*

Remove Study.

BUNTER *alone. His is standing before a looking glass, waving his hands at his reflection. He takes a book from his pocket, and scans it anxiously, his brows wrinkled over his spectacles.*

BUNTER. It's coming! It's coming all right! I've only got to practise the passes, and it will be O.K. And I won't jolly well make those fellows hop when I can put the 'fluence on! He, he, he!

He puts the book back into his pocket and resumes passes before glass.

BUNTER. I get better every time! Once I get it right, catch old Quelch ragging me in the form-room any more! Why, I could make him cane himself with his own cane, once I get going as a hypnotist.

Hypnotism is a wonderful thing . . . puts tremendous power in a fellow's hands. Lucky I've got a strong personality and an iron will, that's what's wanted!

He continues to make weird passes before the glass. CHERRY *looks in at door and stares blankly at* BUNTER.

CHERRY. Bunter! What the dickens . . .

BUNTER *turns round angrily.*

BUNTER. Oh, get out!
CHERRY. But what . . . ?
BUNTER. I said get out!
CHERRY. That a new thing in physical jerks?
BUNTER. Buzz off!

He slams the door angrily and resumes passes before glass.

I can do it! Why, it's easy! When I've had a bit more practice, I'll put the 'fluence on the lot of them! I'll make them sack Wharton and elect me form captain! I'll make Mauly ask me home for the holidays at Mauleverer Towers. I'll make Nugent write my lines for me. I'll make Quelch kow-tow to me in the form-room, by gum! He, he, he! I've got the power!

More passes. Door opens and MR QUELCH *looks in.* BUNTER *spins round angrily*

BUNTER. Is that you again, you silly idiot? Keep your ugly mug out of this study . . . Oh! I . . . I . . . I . . . I didn't know it was you, sir!

He blinks in dismay at MR QUELCH.

QUELCH. What did you say, Bunter.
BUNTER. I . . I thought it was Cherry, sir! I . . . I didn't mean to call you a silly idiot, sir! I . . . I didn't know it was you. I . . . I thought it was another silly idiot, sir . . .
QUELCH. Bunter, what were you doing when I looked in? Why were you standing and waving you hands about in that extraordinary manner? What is the meaning of these absurd antics, Bunter?
BUNTER. Oh! Nothing, sir, I . . . I . . . I wasn't practising anything . . .
QUELCH. Practising!
BUNTER. Oh! No, sir! Nothing of the kind. I . . I . . . I was just exercising my muscles, sir. I . . . I'm a bit stiff after the cricket, sir. My . . . my elbow's very stiff, sir. I . . . I think it may be a touch of pneumonia . . .

QUELCH. Pneunomia . . . in your elbow, Bunter?
BUNTER. Ye-e-es, sir! It . . . it runs in the family, sir! My . . . my grandfather was lame with it.
QUELCH. You utterly absurd boy . . .
BUNTER. Oh, really, sir . . .
QUELCH. Have you written your lines, Bunter? You have not brought them to me.
BUNTER. Oh! Yes, sir! I . . . I mean no sir! I mean, I was going to. I had to go down to the cricket, sir . . . I'm awfully keen on games, sir . . . I couldn't cut the cricket . . .
QUELCH. You have had ample time to write your lines, Bunter.
BUNTER. Yes, sir, but I was practising . . .
QUELCH. Practising what?
BUNTER. Oh! Nothing, sir! I . . . I . . . I . . .
QUELCH. I will hear no excuses, Bunter. You have not written your lines, and your imposition is doubled.
BUNTER. Oh, lor'.
QUELCH. (*sternly*). You will write two hundred lines of Virgil, Bunter, instead of one hundred . . . two hundred lines from the Second Book of the *Aeneid*, from *"conticuere omnes"* to *"improvida pectora turbat"*.
BUNTER. Oh, crikey!
QUELCH. You will bring me the completed imposition in the form-room tomorrow morning. If you fail to do so, Bunter, I shall cane you.
BUNTER. Oh scissors!
QUELCH. That is all. You are an incorrigibly idle boy, Bunter, and you will be caned if your lines are not handed to me tomorrow morning.

Exit QUELCH. BUNTER *shakes his fist at the door after it is closed.*

BUNTER. Beast! You wait! You just wait till I get going with hypnotism and then won't I jolly well make you cringe. You just wait till I get the 'fluence on you! Yah!

Turns back to the glass and resumes practising hypnotic passes.

LORD MAULEVERER *stretched lazily in an armchair at the fireside : alone in the room. He glances round as the door opens and* BILLY BUNTER *enters.*

BUNTER (*coming across*). Oh here you are, Mauly.
MAULY. Yaas.
BUNTER. I've been looking for you, Mauly.
MAULY. Now be a good chap, Bunter, and go and look for somebody else.
BUNTER. Oh, really, Mauleverer . . .

135

MAULY (*making a motion to rise*). I think I'll be pushing off . . .

BUNTER (*sharply*). Sit where you are!

LORD MAULEVERER *stares at him in astonishment.* BUNTER *stands in front of him, waving fat hands in the air.* MAULY *squeezes further back into the armchair, in surprise and alarm.*

MAULY. What on earth's that game, Bunter?

BUNTER. That's telling.

MAULY. Gone crackers?

BUNTER. (*sternly*). Don't you be cheeky, Mauleverer. You may be asking for what you don't want. It isn't safe to cheek a fellow with tremendous and irresistible power in his hands.

MAULY. Wha-a-a-t?

BUNTER. How would you like me to make you put the coal-scuttle on your head, and walk out into the quad with it?

MAULY. Eh?

BUNTER. I could if I liked.

MAULY (*faintly*). Oh gad! Could you?

BUNTER. Easily, now I've had some practice. Easy enough to a fellow with a strong personality and an iron will. The book says . . .

MAULY. The book? What book?

BUNTER. That's telling! I'm not going to tell you anything about the book, Mauly. But it says that weak-minded people are the easiest subjects. That's why I'm trying it on you first, Mauly.

MAULY. Trying it on? What are you trying on?

BUNTER. Never mind that! I'm not giving away the secret of my tremendous powers, Mauly.

MAULY. Your what?

BUNTER. My tremendous powers. Now, look at this!

BUNTER *picks up the poker from the fender. He holds it up, and* MAULY *in alarm pushes the armchair back on its castors.* BUNTER *closes in following the armchair as it backs away.*

MAULY. Bunter! Put down that poker, for goodness sake.

BUNTER. It isn't a poker, Mauly.

MAULY. What?

BUNTER. It's a stick of toffee!

MAULY. Oh, help!

BUNTER. What I mean is, that now you're completely under the influence of my iron will, I can make you believe it's a stick of toffee, see?

MAULY. If you've gone crackers, Bunter, for goodness sake put down that poker.

BUNTER (*commandingly*). It's a stick of toffee, Mauly! I order you to believe it's a stick of toffee. Now, what is it?

MAULY. Have it your own way, Bunter! It's a stick of toffee, if you like. Keep it away from me.

BUNTER (*chuckling*). I knew it would work! I've got it all right now! Quelch is going to get a surprise before long, I can tell you. But never mind Quelch now! Don't try to resist my iron will, Mauly. I've got you just where I want you. You're the slave of my will.

MAULY. Oh, scissors! Am I?

BUNTER. Exactly! You have to do just what I order you. Why, I could make you chew that poker, if I liked, thinking it was toffee.

MAULY. Oh dear! I wish somebody would come in!

BUNTER. But I won't, old fellow. We're pals, ain't we? We're going to fix up the hols together, old chap.

MAULY. Are we?

BUNTER. That's it, Mauly. That's really what I want to talk to you about. Let's talk it over.

MAULY. Will you put down that poker?

BUNTER. Oh, all right! Now, about the holidays at Mauleverer Towers . . . here . . I say . . . where are you going, Mauly?

As BUNTER *turns to replace the poker in the fender,* LORD MAULEVERER *bounds out of the armchair and bolts for the door.* BILLY BUNTER *stares after him blankly.*

BUNTER (*shouting*). I say, Mauly! Come back old chap!

The door bangs shut after LORD MAULEVERER.

BUNTER (*perplexed*). What on earth's the matter with him? I had him right under the 'fluence—and then he suddenly bolts like that? I . . . I wonder if I got the passes quite right! (*Takes out book from his pocket*). Perhaps I need a bit more practice. Maybe Mauly wasn't quite under the 'fluence after all. But it only needs practice . . . the book says so!

A Remove Study.

FRANK NUGENT *sitting at the table pen in hand. The door opens and* BILLY BUNTER *enters.*

NUGENT. Buzz off, bunter.

BUNTER. Oh really, Nugent . . .

NUGENT. Shut the door after you. I'm busy.

BUNTER. I've come here . . .

NUGENT. I can see that! I'm waiting for you to go away again.

BUNTER (*darkly*). Better be civil, Nugent! I'm not going to bully fellows, or anything like that, now that I've got tremendous power in my hands. But you'd better be civil all the same.

NUGENT (*staring*). What does that mean, if it means anything?

BUNTER. Never mind that. Sit still.

He stands facing NUGENT *across the table, making hypnotic passes at him.*

What are you busy about, Nugent?

NUGENT. I've got a translation to do for Monsieur Charpentier. No time to waste. Go away.

BUNTER. I've got two hundred lines to do for Quelch. He says that they're to be handed in tomorrow morning, or it will be whops.

NUGENT. Better cut off and write them, then.

BUNTER. I've no time for it. I've got more important things to think about, I can tell you. You'd be surprised, if you knew.

NUGENT. If I knew what?

BUNTER. Oh nothing, I'm not going to tell you, or anybody else. I'm simply going to do what I jolly well like, in the future, and all the fellows will have to toe the line, like it or lump it. You see, I've got the power.

NUGENT. Wandering in your mind, old fat man?

BUNTER. You're going to do my lines, Nugent.

NUGENT (*laughing*). Am I?

BUNTER. You could make your writing like mine, near enough for Quelch.

NUGENT. Easily! I should only have to make it look as if a spider had swum in the inkpot and crawled over the paper. Nothing doing, all the same. Now go away and let me get on with my translation for Mossoo. What on earth are you up to, Bunter?

BUNTER, *without replying, speeds up his hypnotic passes.* NUGENT *stares at him across the table.*

BUNTER. Now, do you feel it coming on?

NUGENT. Feel what coming on?

BUNTER. Sort of drowsy feeling. That's how it comes on. Feel drowsy?

NUGENT. No, I don't.

BUNTER. Oh, you're a rotten subject. You ought to be drowsy by this time. You go all drowsy and dreamy, and become the slave of my iron will.

NUGENT. Oh, crikey!

BUNTER *continues making passes :* NUGENT *in astonishment and alarm sits staring at him across the table.*

BUNTER. That's better! I can see you're getting it now! Now, Nugent, you've got to write my lines! I order you!

NUGENT. Oh crumbs!

BUNTER. Two hundred from the second book of Virgil, beginning with What-do-you-call it and ending at Thingummy-bob. Mind you make your writing like mine, so that Quelch won't smell a rat. Not that I care a lot for Quelch, you know. I shall soon be giving him orders.

NUGENT (*gasping*). Giving Quelch orders!

BUNTER. Certainly. It may not be quite so easy with Quelch as with a weak-minded fellow like you for instance . . .

NUGENT. Eh!

BUNTER. But I shall manage it all right! I fancy later I'll jolly well make Quelch walk round the form room with the waste-paper basket on his head!

NUGENT. Wha-a-a-t?

BUNTER. I could do it, I can tell you. How would you like to see Quelch caning himself with his own cane?

NUGENT. Oh, jiminy!

BUNTER. He couldn't resist me. Still, I'm leaving Quelch till later. Must be a bit careful with Quelch! Now, you're going to do my lines, Nugent. I command you!

BUNTER *leans over the table, making hypnotic passes right in* NUGENT'S *face.*

NUGENT (*in a yell of alarm*). Keep off!

He jumps up, grasping the edge of the table and up-ends it towards BUNTER. *Books, papers, inkpot, land on* BUNTER *as he staggers back. He sits down, and the table rests on his legs.*

BUNTER. Yarooooh!

NUGENT *dodges out of the study.*

Oh crikey! Ow! Wow! Beast! Oh crumbs! I'm all inky! Ow! Oooooooh!

He is left scrambling up.

Remove passage, outside study door.

HARRY WHARTON, NUGENT, CHERRY, BULL, HURREE SINGH, LORD MAULEVERER, SKINNER AND SNOOP.

WHARTON. Poor old Bunter!

SINGH. The poorfulness of old Bunter is terrific.

CHERRY. He will have to be looked after.

137

BULL. Better take him to Quelch. Quelch will know what to do.

NUGENT. He's quite crackers! He said he could make Quelch cane himself with his own cane.

MAULY. Yaas. And he got hold of a poker. I can tell you fellows it gave me a scare.

SINGH. The scarefulness must have been preposterous.

CHERRY. It certainly looks as if he's gone off his rocker.

SKINNER. He hadn't far to go.

WHARTON. He's seemed rather queer lately . . . always with his nose in a book! He never was a fellow for reading!

CHERRY. And he won't let anybody see the book, whatever it is.

BULL. He's got to be taken care of before he gets worse.

MAULY. Yaas. Getting hold of a poker, you know . . .

CHERRY. Give him a look in, anyway.

WHARTON. Yes, but keep quiet! Mustn't excite the poor chap. It would be bad for him, in that state.

CHERRY *opens the study door softly. They all look in.*

Interior of study

BUNTER *at the looking glass making passes at his reflection. Doorway crowded with staring faces.*

BUNTER (*grinning into the glass*). All right at last, I fancy. But I've got to make absolutely sure before I try it on Quelch, or it would be too risky. He, he, he! Fancy making the old bean walk round the form room with the waste-paper basket on his head! He, he, he!

WHARTON (*whispering*). That does it! Mad as a hatter.

He steps into the study.

Here, Bunter old chap.

BUNTER *blinks round, and waves an impatient hand at the boys.*

BUNTER. Go away! I'm busy! Bunk.

WHARTON. We've come here to look after you, Bunter.

BUNTER. Eh? Who wants looking after?

NUGENT. You jolly well do.

CHERRY. Come down with us, Bunter, and see Quelch.

BUNTER (*staring*). I don't want to see Quelch. What do you fancy I want to see Quelch for?

BULL. You'll have to see a doctor. Quelch will ring up the school doctor for you.

BUNTER. Wharrer you mean! I'm not ill, am I?

WHARTON. Yes, you are, old fellow, though you don't know it. You've got to come down to Quelch. He will know what to do.

BUNTER. Look here, you get out, when a fellow's busy. I've got to be ready for Quelch in the form room tomorrow morning. He said he'd cane me if I didn't take in my lines.

SKINNER. You're not doing your lines.

BUNTER. I'm jolly well not going to. I know how to handle Quelch, I can tell you, now I've had some practice. You fellows may get a surprise in the form room tomorrow. Like to see Quelch stand on his head?

SNOOP. Oh, crikey!

BUNTER. I could make him do it.

SKINNER. Quite crackers!

SINGH. The crackerfulness is terrific.

WHARTON. That does it! He's simply got to be taken care of. Now, be a good chap, Bunter, and come quietly.

BUNTER. Shan't!

WHARTON. I'll take one of his arms, and you take the other, Bob, and we'll walk him down.

They advance on BUNTER, *who jumps back.*

BUNTER. I say, you fellows, stop larking. Just clear off. I keep on telling you I'm busy.

MAULY (*anxiously*). Mind he doesn't get hold of a poker.

WHARTON *takes* BUNTER *by one arm*, CHERRY *by the other.* BUNTER *struggles.*

BUNTER (*yelling*). Beasts! Leggo! I'm not going to Quelch. Wharrer you want me to go to Quelch for?

SNOOP. Hold him! He's not safe!

CHERRY. Shut up. The poor chap can't help it. Now Bunter old fellow, you're not going to be hurt . . . you're only going to be looked after for your own good.

BUNTER (*yelling*). Leggo.

WHARTON. Walk him along!

BUNTER (*struggling*). Beasts! If you don't jolly well let go, I'll put the 'fluence on the lot of you and make you punch your own heads!

SKINNER. He's getting dangerous.

SNOOP. For goodness sake, keep tight hold of him.

MAULY. Keep hold of his fins. Don't let him near the poker.

Right
Gerald Campion as Billy Bunter on BBC TV in 1961

Below right
Kynaston Reeves as Mr Quelch and Gerald Campion as Bunter on BBC TV in 1954

Below left
Cavan Kendall as Bob Cherry, Richard Palmer as Harry Wharton and Gerald Campion as Bunter on BBC TV in 1959

CHERRY. Come on quietly, Bunter, old boy.

BUNTER (*frantically*). Shan't! Leggo! Beasts!

BUNTER *wrenches loose and makes a rush for the door.* SKINNER *grabs at him and* BUNTER *hits out.* SKINNER *staggers, clasping his nose with both hands.*

SKINNER. Ow! Oh! Wow!

CHERRY. Collar him!

BULL. Get hold of him!

SKINNER. Ow! Ow! Ow! I'll smash him! I'll . . .

WHARTON *and* CHERRY *grasp* BUNTER'S *arms again.* SKINNER, *clasping his nose with his left hand, brandishes his right fist.*

CHERRY. Don't you touch him, Skinner! The poor chap can't help being in this state.

BULL. Keep off, Skinner.

SKINNER *is hustled back.*

MAULY. Go easy with the poor chap, but for goodness sake don't let him loose again. If he got hold of a poker . . .

CHERRY. We've got him all right!

BUNTER (*yelling*). Will you leggo? Wharrer you collaring a chap like this for?

SKINNER. Because you're crackers, you fat lunatic! Ow! My nose! Ow!

BUNTER (*raving*). I'm not crackers! What have I done?

CHERRY. Well, when a chap waves his hands about in the air, and makes faces at himself in the glass . . .

BUNTER. Oh, you chump! Oh, you ass! Oh, you cuckoo! I was just practising . . .

BULL. Practising what?

BUNTER. I'm not going to tell you. I'm not going to tell anybody how I got my wonderful power.

WHARTON. Wandering in his mind, poor fellow. Walk him along to Quelch.

CHERRY. Come on, Bunter.

They walk him to the door.

BUNTER (*yelling*). Leggo! Look here, you leggo, and I'll tell you! There!

WHARTON. You'll tell us what?

BUNTER. I was practising hypnotism. Now you know!

CHERRY. Hypnotism!

NUGENT. What on earth do you mean?

BUNTER. Don't you know what hypnotism is? You put the influence on a fellow, and make him do anything you like. He hasn't any will of his own! I'm really a born hypnotist, having a strong personality and an iron will!

WHARTON. My hat!

CHERRY. Whow!

NUGENT. Holy smoke!

BUNTER. Now you know, you silly asses! Mind you keep it dark! I don't want Quelch to know, or I mightn't be able to hypnotize him. I might not pull it off.

SINGH. The mightfulness is terrific.

ALL. Ha, ha, ha!

BUNTER. Blessed if I see anything to cackle at. I'm learning it from this book. Look! (*Takes book from pocket*). Look at that! *How to Hypnotize!* Now you know! I wasn't going to tell you, but it's all right, if Quelch doesn't know! Now you leggo!

They release BUNTER.

CHERRY. You fat, footling, frowsy fathead . . .

BUNTER. Oh really, Cherry . . .

CHERRY. You fancy you can hypnotize! Oh, my only hat! Ha, ha, ha!

ALL. Ha, ha, ha!

MAULY. Oh gad! He fancies . . . ha, ha!

BUNTER. I can jolly well do it, too. You fellows look out! But old Quelch is my game. I'm going to put the 'fluence on him when he asks for my lines tomorrow.

CHERRY. Oh help!

BUNTER. I've got to be careful with Quelch, of course. He won't be so easy as Mauly was, when I made him believe that the poker was a stick of toffee . . .

MAULY. Oh gad!

ALL. Ha, ha, ha!

BUNTER. I'm getting on all right! I'm a pretty good hypnotist already! But I may need some more practise before I start on Quelch.

WHARTON (*laughing*). I fancy you may.

NUGENT. Quite a lot, in fact.

ALL. Ha, ha, ha!

BUNTER. And I may need one of you chaps to practice on. Just to make quite sure the 'fluence is working you know. I don't want to risk it until I'm sure. Quelch has such a beastly temper you know, and he might think I was trying to make an ass of him.

CHERRY. He might!

BUNTER. Well, who's going to be the subject. How about you Cherry?

CHERRY. Nothing doing old fat man.

BUNTER. Beast! Wharton, you'd make a good subject.

WHARTON. No thanks! Come on you men. Bunter is no more crackers than usual. Only learning to be a hypnotist! Ha, ha!

ALL. Ha, ha, ha!

BUNTER. Beasts!

They crowd out of the study laughing, SKINNER *rubbing his nose.* BUNTER *frowns after them, kicks the door shut and resumes practising passes.*

Passage.

SKINNER *and* SNOOP *stop as the others go off.* SKINNER *winks at* SNOOP.

SKINNER. That blithering ass really thinks he can work it. If he got away with it just once, he would try it on Quelch.

SNOOP. But he couldn't get away with it once. He can't hypnotize.

SKINNER. I know that! But it's easy enough to pull his silly leg.

SNOOP. What?

SKINNER. I'll let him hypnotize me.

SNOOP. But he can't . . .

SKINNER. He'll think he can! I've got a pain in my nose where he punched it. Bunter will have a pain or two if he tries hypnotizing Quelch.

He winks at SNOOP *again and opens the study door.*

Study.

BUNTER *is still doing hypnotic practice.* SKINNER *enters.*

BUNTER. Oh get out, Skinner.

SKINNER. How are you getting on with the hypnotism Bunter? I'm awfully interested. It's so jolly clever of you, you know.

BUNTER. Oh! The fact is, Skinner, I'm rather a clever chap! I don't brag of it, you know. It just happens. Some fellows have brains, and some haven't. I have, that's all there is to it.

SKINNER. Oh! Ah! Yes! Quite!

BUNTER. I'm getting on fine. I fancy I've got it all right now!

SKINNER. I wonder if you could hypnotize me.

BUNTER. I've no doubt I could. The book says that weak-minded chaps are the easiest subjects.

SKINNER. Thanks!

BUNTER. You see, when I fix my eyes on you, and make the hypnotic passes, my powerful will overcomes your weak will, and you go right under the 'fluence. I give you orders, and you jump to them, without even knowing what you are doing! You become the slave of my will. That's how it works. It's quite simple, really! I shall have Quelch

in the hollow of my hand, once I get the 'fluence on him! But I shan't try it on till I've hypnotized a Remove man first. So come on Skinner, old chap, I'll try on you.

SKINNER. Will it hurt?

BUNTER. Not in the least! I simply put you into the hypnotic trance. You get sort of dreamy and drowsy, and then go under the 'fluence. I wake you up again as soon as I like. It's perfectly simple.

SKINNER. All right, then.

SKINNER *sits down.*

BUNTER. Now fix your eyes on mine. Look me right in the eye, Skinner! That's right! Now I'm going to make the passes and send you to sleep . . . just as I shall with Quelch tomorrow if this works all right! What are you grinning at Skinner?

SKINNER. Oh! Nothing! Carry on.

BUNTER. Here goes, then.

He makes hypnotic passes at SKINNER *who assumes a dreamy look.*

BUNTER. How do you feel now, Skinner?

SKINNER. Just the same.

BUNTER (*anxiously*). Don't you feel a sort of drowsy, dreamy feeling coming on?

SKINNER. Oh yes! Now you mention it, I feel sort of . . . of drowsy and dreamy . . .

BUNTER (*delighted*). That's right! That's how it works! I've got it all right now! Sort of floating away feeling . . . is that it, Skinner?

SKINNER. It's just that!

BUNTER. I knew I could do it! I hadn't had enough practice when I tried it on Mauly and Nugent, that's all. It's all right now. You're entirely under the influence of my iron will now, Skinner. Got that?

SKINNER (*dreamily*). Yes Bunter.

BUNTER. Now you're the slave of my will, you have to do everything I tell you. Close your eyes.

SKINNER *closes his eyes*

Now open them again.

SKINNER *reopens his eyes.*

That's right! Now stand up.

SKINNER *stands up.*

Take that waste-paper basket out from under the table.

SKINNER *takes out basket*

Now put it on your head!

SKINNER *puts it on his head.*

He, he, he! Now, that isn't a wastepaper basket, Skinner. It's a top-hat. Now, what's that on your head, Skinner.

SKINNER. It's a top-hat!

BUNTER. Fine! Now, your name's not Skinner, Skinner. Your name's John James Joseph Brown. Now, what's your name, Skinner?

SKINNER. John James Joseph Brown.

BUNTER. He, he, he! I've got you under the 'fluence all right! I could make you believe that you were Julius Caesar or Winston Churchill, if I liked! He, he, he! I could make you walk down to Quelch's study with that waste-paper basket on your head! By gum, that's what I'm going to do to Quelch tomorrow, now that I know it's all right! He, he, he!

SKINNER *gives an explosive chuckle.*

Now I'm going to wake you up. I have to make backward passes to wake you up. Stand still!

BUNTER *waves his hands about.*

Now, wake up, Skinner!

SKINNER *gives a dramatic start.*

SKINNER. Where am I? What has happened? Have I been asleep!

BUNTER. He, he, he! You've been under the 'fluence, old chap! You won't remember a thing of it.

SKINNER. What's this on my head? Why, it's a waste-paper basket! How did it get there?

BUNTER. I made you believe it was a top-hat!

SKINNER. Oh! Did you?

BUNTER. I jolly well did! You were the slave of my will, Skinner, while you were under the 'fluence. I made you believe that your name was John James Joseph Brown.

SKINNER. It's wonderful! You've got tremendous power in your hands, Bunter.

BUNTER. I have . . . I have . . . Just wait till I get going on Quelch. When he asks me for my lines tomorrow, I shall simply put the 'fluence on him! It won't be whops for me. I shall make Quelch whop himself!

SKINNER. Oh, holy smoke!

BUNTER. He, he, he! It will be funny, what?

SKINNER. Funniest thing ever! Ha, ha, ha!

SKINNER *leaves the study.* BUNTER *takes "How to Hypnotize" from his pocket and throws it carelessly on the table.*

BUNTER. I shan't want that any more! I've got it perfect now! Won't I jolly well make Quelch sit up tomorrow! He, he, he!

Form room.

Crowd of juniors, but BUNTER *not present.*

WHARTON. Bunter will be late.

CHERRY. Quelch will be here in a minute. The fat ass must have heard the bell.

BULL. Perhaps he's busy practising hypnotic passes.

ALL. Ha, ha, ha!

CHERRY. Hallo, hallo, hallo! Here he comes.

BUNTER *strolls in, in a leisurely way, hands in pockets.*

BUNTER. I say, you fellows, isn't Quelch here yet?

WHARTON. Here any minute now. The bell's stopped. Have you got your lines for him?

BUNTER (*contemptuously*). No fear!

NUGENT. Then you'll be whopped.

BUNTER. Forget it! Quelch won't whop me! I'd like to see him do it!

CHERRY. You fat ass! Didn't he tell you . . .

BUNTER. What do I care what he told me? Think I care a button for Quelch? Pah! Quelch will soon find out who's master here!

ALL. What?

SKINNER. Bunter's master here, now that he can hypnotize fellows. Aren't you, Bunter?

BUNTER. Just that!

CHERRY. You fat ass, you couldn't hypnotize a dead donkey.

WHARTON. Look here, you fat chump . . .

BUNTER. You'll jolly well see! I'll jolly well let Quelch know where he gets off!

MAULY. For goodness sake, Bunter, don't try anything with Quelch.

BUNTER. Yah! I'll soon have him feeding from my hand.

CHERRY. Hallo, hallo, hallo, here's Quelch.

MR QUELCH *comes in to the form-room.* BUNTER *with a careless air lingers behind as the Remove go to their places.*

QUELCH. Bunter!

BUNTER (*casually*). Hallo!

QUELCH *gives a little jump.*

QUELCH. What? What did you say, Bunter?

BUNTER. I said hallo!

QUELCH. Is that the way to answer your form-master, Bunter?

BUNTER. Why not?

QUELCH. Upon my word! I shall deal with you for this impertinence, Bunter. Go to your place immediately.

BUNTER. What's the hurry?

QUELCH. Bless my soul! Do I hear aright?

He stares blankly at BUNTER, *who strolls carelessly past him, hands in pockets.* QUELCH *looks at him, frowning.*

QUELCH *goes to his desk and picks up a cane.*

Bunter! Stand out before the form.

BUNTER (*drawling*). Any old thing.

He strolls out before the form. THE REMOVE *exchanges glances and whispers.* QUELCH *gazes at* BUNTER, *dumbfounded.*

WHARTON (*whispering*). Is he really crackers after all?

NUGENT. Must be, to carry on like that.

CHERRY. He's asking for it!

BULL. Quelch will skin him!

SKINNER (*chuckling*). Oh, he's going to put the 'fluence on Quelch!

SNOOP. Ha, ha!

QUELCH (*finding his voice*). Silence in the form! Silence, I say! Now Bunter . . .

BUNTER (*carelessly*). Carry on!

QUELCH. Bless my soul! First of all Bunter, have you written your lines!

BUNTER (*in the same careless tone*). Oh, no. Haven't had time!

QUELCH. I warned you, Bunter, that you would be caned if your lines were not handed in this morning. I shall cane you, Bunter.

BUNTER. Sez you!

QUELCH. What? What? Is this boy in his senses? What do you mean by this unparalleled impertinence?

BUNTER. Oh come off it, Quelch.

QUELCH. My ears must be deceiving me.

CHERRY (*in a loud whisper*). Bunter, you awful ass, shut up.

BUNTER. Yah!

QUELCH *gazes at* BUNTER, *who whips round to face him and makes hypnotic passes at him.* QUELCH *backs away a pace.* THE REMOVE *look on breathlessly.*

QUELCH (*faintly*). Bunter! What is the matter with you? What is the meaning of these extraordinary antics? Bless my soul, is the boy wandering in his mind?

BUNTER. That will do! Keep quiet!

QUELCH. Wha-a-t?

BUNTER. Don't jaw, Quelch.

QUELCH. I am dreaming this!

He stands rooted, gazing at BUNTER.

BUNTER (*still making passes*). That does it! Keep quiet, Quelch, when I tell you! I've got you under the 'fluence now! I'm giving orders here.

QUELCH (*faintly*). Wha-a-a-t?

BUNTER. You're the slave of my will. I've got you where I want you now. Put down that cane!

QUELCH (*dazed*). Put down this cane?

BUNTER. Yes, and sharp! Sharp's the word, or I'll make you cane yourself with it.

QUELCH. The boy must be insane.

BUNTER. No cheek now! Pick up that waste-paper basket!

QUELCH. Eh?

BUNTER. And put it on your head!

QUELCH. On—on—on my head?

BUNTER. Yes, and walk round the form-room with it on your silly old nut! I say you fellows, you watch Quelch, he, he, he!

QUELCH. Either this boy is out of his senses, or this is the most amazing, the most unheard of impertinence! Bunter! I . . .

BUNTER. That will do! I'm master here, Quelch, and when I say jump, you jolly well jump! You're under the 'fluence now . . . right under.

QUELCH. The 'fluence! What do you mean, Bunter?

BUNTER. You're hypnotized!

QUELCH. Hypnotized!

BUNTER. Just that! I've put the 'fluence on, and you're the slave of my will. Put that waste-paper basket on your head! At once! Do you hear?

QUELCH. Bless my soul!

BUNTER. Jump to it, I tell you.

QUELCH. Bunter! Are you in your senses? Do you imagine, for one moment, that you are able to hypnotize . . . and have you the impertinence, the unheard of audacity, to dream of hypnotizing your form-master? Bless my soul! I shall cane you with the utmost severity for this, Bunter. I shall make an example of you! Bend over and touch your toes, Bunter!

He makes a stride at BUNTER, *flourishing the cane.* BUNTER *starts back in alarm.*

BUNTER. Oh, crikey! I . . . I say, ain't you under the 'fluence after all? Oh jiminy! It worked all right with Skinner! Oh crumbs!

QUELCH (*thundering*). Bend over, Bunter!

BUNTER. Oh, lor! I . . . I . . . I say, sir . . .

QUELCH. *Bend over!*

BUNTER *still backs away.* QUELCH *grasps him by the collar, and bends him over. The cane descends.*

BUNTER. Yarooooh!

ALL. Ha, ha, ha!

BUNTER. Whoop! Oh, crikey! Ow! Stoppit! I never . . . I didn't . . . I wasn't . . . yow-ow-ow-ow!

THE END

144

Gerald Campion as Billy Bunter in 1961

The first appearance of Billy Bunter on television. Gerald Campion as Bunter and Kynaston Reeves as Mr Quelch on BBC TV in February 1952

A SCHOOLBOY'S LOVE-LETTER
by Frank Richards.

Stebbings' House,
Barcroft.

Dearest Loo,

I'm sitting down to write to you, just as I said I would as soon as I got
back. At least almost as soon, because there are some things that a
fellow can't dodge. First of all I had to see old Moon—you remember I
told you Moon was my beak. There was a spot of bother owing to my
losing my medical certificate, through that goat Carter assing about on
the train down. Of course it's all rot: they don't really look at it, but if
you haven't got it there's a row. Luckily I thought of telling Moon that
I'd slipped it into one of my books for safety. That's all right with Moon,
because he never remembers anything the next day. Still it was
annoying at the time, because he kept me a good five minutes, and
Parkinson was waiting in the passage to speak to me, and when I came
out at last he'd gone off with Ling.

My study's in a pretty state, as you may guess on the first day of
term. Everything at sixes and sevens. The table's loaded like a bargain
counter, and I've hardly room to write this letter. There's my bag, and
my football boots, and most of a cake I've just unpacked, and a lot of my
books, as well as heaps of Sutton's things. Sutton is the chap I mess with
here, I think I told you about him. Not a bad chap in his own way, but
frightfully untidy. His slippers are on the table this very minute.

I'd rather have had Parkinson really, we get on together splendidly.
But Sutton seemed to take it for granted that we should be together this
term the same at last, and a chap can't very well let a chap down.
Besides you have to be jolly careful about this, as it's all settled on the
first day. If you're too slow you might get left without anybody, and
then the mob would think nobody wanted you, and it would be against
you all the term.

I got left like that my first term in the Fifth, and had to put up with
Pug Smith in the end, and was really lucky to get even him at the last
minute, but it was rotten all round. This term I hoped to get old
Parkinson. I thought of getting Sutton to go in with Brown major, who,
as I know, would be glad to have him, because nobody wants to mess with
Brown, whose people are rather so-so. His father came down last term in
elastic-sided boots, and after that the fags used to squeak when Brown
passed them, which put him into a terrific bait.

But I should have had to fix it with Sutton before speaking to
Parkinson, and then it might have turned out that old Parky was
snapped up already, he being the most popular man in the House. I
noticed that he seemed rather thick with Potter in the train, and I jolly

well know that that greasy smug Walker meant to bag him if he could. There's hardly a man in the Fifth who wouldn't be glad to have Parkinson: even Bowes-Fletcher, I think. Well, I might have got left, and have had to put up with some nobody like Pug Smith again, so now I'm fixed with Sutton as before, and perhaps it's all for the best for he certainly does get very good hampers. Only I wish he wouldn't leave his slippers on the table, or plug in his smokes among my instruments. Of course, he has to keep them out of sight.

I shall never forget that last evening, Loo. It's just like a dream. What you could see in me I don't know, because I'm not worthy of you in any way I can think of. I'm going to try hard to be, and this term I've made up my mind to have nothing whatever to do with Chowne and his set. I shall bar them utterly. I told Sutton so, and he said I'd better mind my step, because Chowne being a prefect, and in the Sixth, he could make it pretty tough, for a Fifth-Form man who set out to bar him. I said I don't care, and I don't either. I can tell you that I started before we'd been back at Barcroft ten minutes. Chowne was in the quad, and he called out, "Hullo old thing!" and I just walked on with my bag pretending to think that he was speaking to somebody else. Of course with a pre. you have to be a bit tactful.

When I think of that last evening with you, Loo, it seems to bring back something in Tennyson, or perhaps Browning, though I can't remember it just at this minute. Ever since meeting you I seem to see a lot more in poetry than I used to do. I shall go strong on English Literature this term. This will give me a leg-up with Moon, too, for he actually likes it himself, and likes fellows who make out that they do too. You'd never dream how easy it is to pull his leg in English Literature. Old Parkinson is very clever at it. He knows how to get Moon spouting, so that we get through perhaps half the hour practically doing nothing.

But I shall take it very seriously this term, because I am convinced that it is not by any means the tosh I always thought it. I have recently found that I like poetry, and have little doubt that there is a lot in it I never thought of before. Of course, a fellow gets a bit fogged with poetry, because so often it doesn't seem to have any sense in it. But I realize now that football isn't everything: though of course I would not like to say so in the day-room.

Speaking of football, there's practically no doubt that I shall play for School. This may sound like swank, but I assure you that it is not. Parkinson thinks so, which I think as good as settles it. Sutton says that what Parkinson thinks to-day, Barcroft thinks to-morrow: a very neat way of putting it, I thought. Sutton's no fool.

Luttrell—I've told you about our skipper—well, Luttrell nodded to me on the landing when I came up. He didn't speak, but he distinctly nodded, I'm absolutely certain of that. Luttrell, of course, won't be thinking of much beside football this term. He can't very well, in his position. And I think the way he nodded, which I'm quite sure he did, looks as if he has his eyes on me.

I don't mind telling you about this, Loo, because I know you don't look at games in the silly way girls so often do. The first time it came to me that I cared for you so much, was that evening in the hotel garden, on that seat you remember, when I was telling you about the Tatcham match, and you sat listening with your eyes closed, and never interrupted me once. It seemed so splendid to be talking to a girl who really understood. I can tell you that any of my sisters would have shut me up before I'd said a dozen words about Soccer. A fellow's sisters never understand him, as I've noticed. I've got four, and all of them would have said, "Oh, chuck it, Aubrey," if I'd started on Soccer. I was so glad you were interested because it really was a great match. In my opinion Barcroft only pulled it off by a combination of luck and sheer good play. At half-time almost anybody would have said that it was Tatcham's game. In fact right up to ten minutes from the finish the outlook was pretty grim. But after Luttrell equalized, we let them have it—how I wish you'd been there!

It was just luck that I was in the team, being only in the Second eleven at the time, through a man getting crocked at the last minute. Luttrell had to shove in somebody, and he shoved me in. I think the result justified it. I couldn't expect goals, against men like Tatcham: but several fellows said afterwards that my passing was as good as any on the field, and nobody can deny that it was from a pass I gave him that Ling scored the winning goal, though he was rather stand-offish about it when I mentioned it afterwards. But facts are facts, whether Billy Ling likes them or not. To my mind, Ling isn't a First eleven man at all, being altogether too sketchy in his style, though I admit he has luck. If I were in Luttrell's place, I should certainly not play him against a team like Tatcham. I should think it too risky.

Luttrell noticed my play that time. Several fellows said so. I wonder whether he remembers that pass I gave Ling. It looks like it, nodding to me as he did.

That last evening at Vevey was the happiest day of my life, Loo. It seems like a glorious dream when I look back at it now. I was so jolly glad to get away from the hotel crowd and get a spot of quiet, in the garden, with you. How lovely the moonlight looked on the lake. And that jolly little seat under the tree where we sat. I was feeling awfully sorry about catching my foot in your dress in the dance. I know I'm a rotten dancer, but I shall try to improve. Do you know, I thought just for a second that you were stuffy with me when we heard it tear. But the next minute I knew it was all right, you had such a lovely smile. But I was glad you owned up that you were tired of dancing, and said what about sitting it out. I mean to say I was sorry you were tired, but glad to get out into the garden and the moonlight, with you, Loo. I'd wondered and wondered whether I should have a chance of speaking to you before we left, and it made me very miserable to think of that early train in the morning, and going without seeing you again. I'd even thought of coming round very early, before my people had to start for the station, on the off chance that you might be up. But it was all right as it happened.

Will you ever forget that evening, Loo? I never shall, not if I live to be sixty or seventy. Wasn't it jolly luck that my people took me to Vevey for the hols., while you were there at the same time? This was one of those wonderful coincidences that do happen sometimes. But for that I might never have met you. We came near to going to Scotland instead, only the pater thought on the whole Switzerland would be cheaper, also there was the food. A poet whose name I forget said what great events from little causes spring. We had it in English Literature with Moon last term. I think more and more that poets very often hit the right nail on the head, and that there is much more in it than fellows think.

About you being a trifle older I don't think that matters a bit, as I told you. Men really are older than women, even if younger by a year or two, being so much more practical and having so much more knowledge of the world. I feel that I could protect you, and that is what I want to do all my life. That was how I felt that day we had the trip on the lake steamer to Montreux. Looking after a woman, and taking care of her, is a man's job in my opinion. I was so sorry I left your parasol on the steamer, it was a bit of luck that that American chap brought it off and gave it to you. Wasn't that a lovely afternoon at Montreux? Do you remember how we lost our way because I thought it was a turning to the right, and you thought it was to the left, and it turned out to be the left after all? And how jolly nearly we lost the boat back, because it left at 5.30 and not six as I thought.

There's an awful din going on in the passage outside my study. Of course there's always a lot of noise first day of term. I can hear that goat Carter giving one of his imitations of Moon, and all the fellows laughing. Carter's a very funny ass, and I wish you could hear him doing old Moon, saying "Now, now, that's quite enough, we must remember that we are here to work."—he gets his wheezy voice to a T. You might think it was old Moon speaking, and it certainly is very funny and entertaining. It's not much use trying to write a letter with all that row going on, so I may as well go along, and I will close now with dearest love from your own.

XXXX x Aubrey Briggs

EXIT BUNTER!

By FRANK RICHARDS

TAP!

"Oh!"

It was a sudden, startled squeak.

Harry Wharton, the captain of the Greyfriars Remove, had tapped at his form-master's door.

If Mr Quelch was there, he expected to hear Quelch say, "Come in". If Mr Quelch had gone out, he did not expect any answer to his tap. Most certainly, he did not expect to hear the fat and unmistakeable squeak of Billy Bunter of the Remove!

But that was what he heard!

Evidently, Quelch was out. Equally evidently, Billy Bunter was in his form-master's study, for some reason of his own, and was startled out of his wits by the tap on the door.

Wharton opened the door and entered.

Then he stared round the Remove master's study. It was or appeared to be—empty!

For a moment or two, the captain of the Remove stared blankly. Had he not heard that startled squeak, he would have supposed the study to be deserted. But he had heard it! Yet there was no one to be seen!

Then he grinned.

From behind Quelch's armchair, which stood by the window, a foot, a length of striped sock, and about six inches of trouser leg, projected.

Bunter had taken cover—leaving that much in view!

Unaware, no doubt, that his startled squeak had been audible outside the study, the fat Owl of the Remove had dived behind the armchair before the door opened: and was now in the happy belief that he was out of sight and perfectly invisible!

"You fat ass!" exclaimed Harry Wharton, "Come out of it."

"Oh!" came a gasp from behind the armchair, "Is that you Wharton! I thought it was some beak coming to see Quelch!"

A fat face, and a big pair of spectacles, rose into view. Billy Bunter blinked at his form-captain through those big spectacles. His fat face registered relief.

"Only you!" he gasped, "Beast! Startling a fellow like that! I thought I was copped here."

"What are you doing in this study?" demanded Wharton.

"Well, what are you doing, if you come to that?" retorted Billy Bunter, "I suppose you knew Quelch had gone out, or you wouldn't be here."

"I've come here to use the telephone, fathead! Look here, what are you up to?" exclaimed Wharton, eyeing the fat Owl of the Remove very suspiciously.

151

If Billy Bunter had been discovered in a Remove study, it would have been unnecessary to inquire what he was up to. He would have been after some fellow's tuck! But Mr Quelch, master of the Greyfriars Remove, was long past the age when tuck had attractions: there was nothing eatable to be found in Quelch's study. In that quarter, Billy Bunter could not be tuck-hunting.

On the other hand, Bunter had been "whopped" in class that morning, having had no time for prep the previous evening. This seemed to Billy Bunter fearfully unjust. A fellow couldn't sit in an armchair and eat butterscotch, and get on with his prep at the same time. No fellow could do two things at once. And Bunter had been busy in the armchair with butterscotch—with painful results in the morning!

"If you're here to play some idiotic trick on Quelch, you fat ass—!" said the captain of the Remove.

"Well, he's gone out!" said Bunter. "He went out after class. How's he to know who put the gum into his inkpot!"

"Oh, you howling ass! Have you been putting gum into Quelch's inkpot?" exclaimed the captain of the Remove.

"Not yet!" admitted Bunter. "You see, I forgot the gum!"

"Ha, ha, ha!"

"Blessed if I see anything to cackle at! I was going to put Toddy's bottle of gum in my pocket, but I must have left it on the table in No. 7—as soon as I got here, I found that I hadn't got it—"

"All the better for you, fathead!" said Harry Wharton, laughing, "Get out."

"Quelch hasn't come in, has he?" asked Billy Bunter, anxiously.

"Not that I know of."

"Then I'm not getting out! It's safe as houses, unless some other beak pokes in to see Quelch. I was looking for some gum, when you knocked at the door, and made me jump! Quelch must have some gum in his study somewhere! What do you think?" asked Bunter, with an inquiring blink through his big spectacles at the captain of the Remove.

"I think you'd better travel!" answered Harry. "I've got to phone to Highcliffe—get out!"

"I say, help me to find some gum first!" urged Bunter, "You know I'm a bit short-sighted! I daresay it's right under your nose, if you looked."

Harry Wharton laughed again. There was a bottle of gum on Mr Quelch's desk: but the fat Owl had not spotted it there. But the captain of the Remove did not point it out.

Gumming a form-master's inkpot was a more serious matter than the fat Owl seemed to comprehend. Japing Quelch was a very dangerous game—much too dangerous a game for Billy Bunter to undertake. Moreover, as Harry Wharton had visited the study, he did not want a trail of gum to be left behind him. He might be suspected of having done the gumming!

"I say, can you see any gum?" asked Bunter, "Do stop cackling, and help a fellow! Suppose Prout or Hacker looked in, and copped us here! You're wasting time."

"Are you getting out, fathead?"

"No!" hooted Bunter, "Not till I've gummed Quelchy's inkpot. You jolly well known that he whopped me in the form-room—."

"You'll get another whopping, if you gum his inkpot, you fat chump! Travel!" exclaimed Wharton, impatiently.

"Well, so would you, if Quelch knew that you were bagging his phone while he was out—."

"I was going to ask him, if he was here—."

"Well, he ain't here, so you can't ask him! I say, can you see any gum—oh, there it is!"

Billy Bunter, blinking round, spotted the gum-bottle—and made a dive for it! Harry Wharton made a dive after Bunter. To Bunter, after a "whopping", it seemed quite a right and natural proceeding to put gum in Quelch's inkpot. To the captain of the Remove it did not! He grasped at the back of Bunter's fat neck, as the fat junior clutched at the gum bottle.

"Oh! Leggo!" howled Bunter.

"Come away, you ass!"

"Beast!" roared Bunter, "Leggo!" As Wharton pulled at his collar, Bunter clutched hold at the desk.

On that desk lay a pile of Form papers, waiting for correction. Billy Bunter's clutch for hold missed the desk, but caught the pile of papers. They scattered over the floor like a snowfall.

"Oh, crikey!" gasped Bunter, "Look what you've done!"

"You blithering owl!" exclaimed Wharton.

"All your fault, you beast! Leggo!"

Harry Wharton did not let go. He yanked Bunter across the study to the door. With his left hand, he reopened the door. With his right, he swung the spluttering fat Owl into the passage.

"Now cut!" he snapped, "I've got to pick up all those papers, you blitherer! Cut, or—!"

"Beast!"

Thud!

"Ooooogh!" gasped Bunter, as a foot landed on his tight trousers, "Why you beast, you kick me, and I'll—woooooooooh!"

Bunter cut! There was no arguing with a boot at close quarters. One application was enough for Bunter. He travelled!

Harry Wharton shut the door after him. Then he turned to pick up the scattered Form papers.

The whole pile had been scattered, and they lay over Quelch's carpet almost as thick as the autumn leaves in Vallambrosa. There were more than thirty papers: the Greyfriars Remove was a numerous form. Wharton did not feel like leaving them scattered over the floor, to greet Mr Quelch's eyes when he came in—indubitable evidence that his study had been surreptitiously visited in his absence!

Paper after paper was gathered up, and replaced on the desk. But some of them had gone under the table, some behind the armchair, some into corners—and it was quite a little time, before the junior could be sure that he had collected the whole lot.

At length, however, the pile was back in its place: and Harry Wharton turned to the telephone. Had Quelch been there, he would, as he had told Bunter, have asked permission to use the phone, to put through that call to Courtenay of the Fourth Form at Highcliffe School. As Quelch was not there, he couldn't—but this was not the first time that the Remove master's telephone had been borrowed while he was taking a walk abroad!

It was more than ten minutes after Bunter's departure, that Harry Wharton got to the telephone, at last. But he did get to it at last, and picked up the receiver.

MR HACKER frowned.

On that bright June afternoon, most faces were cheery. But frowns came more easily to Mr Hacker than smiles.

The master of the Greyfriars Shell was standing at his study window, looking out into the sunny quad.

There were plenty of fellows to be seen, in the quad, after class. Mr Hacker's eyes fixed on four Remove fellows, talking in a group. Bob Cherry, Frank Nugent, Johnny Bull, and Hurree Jamset Ram Singh.

The fifth member of the famous Co., who was generally with his chums in hours of leisure, was not to be seen—Harry Wharton was not in the quad.

The "Acid Drop" frowned at the Co. He did not like those cheery juniors. He had no doubt that they were hand-in-glove with that young rascal, Wharton, who had given him so much trouble that term. Indeed he wondered, in his acidulated way, whether Wharton was "up" to something in those very moments, and whether that was why he was not with his friends. Whenever Mr Hacker thought of Wharton of the Remove, it was with concentrated suspicion.

A slim and elegant Fifth-form man came sauntering along, and stopped to speak to the group of juniors. It was Hilton of the Fifth: and Hacker heard his drawling voice, as he spoke to the Co.

"Seen Pricey, any of you?"

Hilton, it seemed, was looking for his pal, Price of the Fifth—not that Mr Hacker was in the least interested.

"Blow Pricey!" was Bob Cherry's answer.

Hilton laughed.

"Blow him as much as you like, kid—but have you seen him? He seems to have vanished after class."

"The esteemed and ridiculous Price has gone out of gates!" said Hurree Jamset Ram Singh.

"You saw him go out?" asked Hilton.

"Half-an-hour ago!" grunted Johnny Bull.

"Notice which way he went?"

"No! Just happened to see his ugly mug as he went out, that's all!"

Cedric Hilton laughed again, and sauntered elegantly down to the gates. The Co. resumed their conversation: the murmur of their voices reaching Mr Hacker at his study window. He could not hear what they were saying: but he thought it quite probable that they were discussing the latest trick that had been played on the master of the Shell. Mr Hacker had been given a rather annoying time that term: and everything that happened to him, he set down to Wharton of the Remove, as a matter of course.

As a matter of fact, the chums of the Remove were discussing a visit to Highcliffe, for the following day, which was a half-holiday: and Wharton had gone into the House to get a Highcliffe man on the phone. But Hacker was a suspicious man—he lived, moved, and had his being, in an atmosphere of suspicion.

Buzzzz!

It was the telephone bell, behind him in his study. Mr Hacker gave a grunt, and turned from the window.

He picked up the receiver, and barked.

"Well?"

"Is that old Hacker?" came a voice on the telephone.

Mr Hacker jumped.

"Wh-a-at?" he stuttered.

"Is that the Acid Drop?"

The master of the Shell stood staring at the telephone, as if transfixed. Hacker knew that he was nicknamed the "Acid Drop". It annoyed him extremely. But he had never expected to be addressed personally by that obnoxious nickname.

"Upon my word!" he gasped, "Who—who—who is speaking?"

"Like to know?" came the voice.

"Who is speaking?" hissed Mr Hacker. His bony face was red with wrath, "What impertinent young rascal?"

"I've rung you up to give you a tip, Hacker! We're fed up with your meddling in the Remove."

"What?"

"Keep off the grass! If Quelch wants your help in managing his form, he can ask you! Until then, chuck it. See!"

Hacker gurgled.

This, of course, was some Remove fellow—cheeking him by telephone, safe out of sight! But he strove in vain to identify the voice. Wharton was the name that flashed into his mind. But if it was Wharton speaking over the wires, he was disguising his voice: Hacker could not possibly identify it.

"Stick to the Shell!" went on the voice from the other end, "They have to stand you in the Shell, as you're their beak! But we won't stand you butting into the Remove!"

"Is that Wharton speaking?" hissed Mr Hacker, in helpless fury.

"Find out!"

"You young rascal—!"

"Can it, Hacker! If you fancy that any Remove man cares a boiled bean for you, you're an old ass!"

"I—I—I—."

"We've told you what we think of you, more than once. You've been told to mind your own business! You've had a few messages left in your study to tell you so. Now I'm telling you on the phone. If you don't steer clear of the Remove, you old goat, look out for squalls. Got that?"

Mr Hacker fairly foamed.

He could have given a term's salary to be able to reach along the telephone wire, and grab the cheeky young rascal at the other end.

But that cheeky young rascal was out of reach: and Hacker could not even guess who he was—though, without guessing, he had no doubt that it was Harry Wharton!

"That's all!" added the disguised voice. "Chew it over, Hacker—you'll get toco, if we have any more of your meddling! Put that in your pipe and smoke it!"

Mr Hacker stood trembling with rage.

"Wharton!" he breathed.

He had no doubt of it! This kind of thing had happened before, though not on the telephone. He had never been able to pin that young rascal Wharton down—but he had no doubt of the culprit. He had no doubt now—this was why Wharton was not with his friends after class, as usual: he had gone off somewhere to telephone! Hacker was sure of it. Somewhere out of sight—out of reach—once more he had cheeked the Acid Drop and could not be pinned down!

But could he not!

Hacker's thoughts moved quickly. The young rascal might have gone out of gates to telephone: but it was more likely that he had used one of the school telephones: and his form-master was out—Hacker had seen Quelch walk out with Mr Prout after class.

"Hear me, old pie-face?" The voice was going on. "Take a tip, Acid Drop! We hear altogether too much of you, in the Remove! We're fed up with you, right up to the back teeth! Cheeky old ass!"

Hacker's eyes glinted.

He did not speak: he replaced the receiver quietly, and flew across his study to the door. That young rascal would be still at the phone: and if he was in any study in Masters' Passage using a master's phone, Hacker had him!

Hacker wrenched open his door. He bounded into the passage! He fairly sprinted down the passage to Mr Quelch's study.

He hurled open the door.

Then, at the sight of a Remove junior standing at Quelch's telephone, receiver in hand, he gave a roar!

"Wharton! You young rascal, I have caught you!"

HARRY WHARTON stared round.

He had the receiver in hand, and was about to speak to the exchange, when he was startled by the sudden hurling open of the study door, and the unexpected entrance of the master of the Shell, with flaming face.

He stood and stared.

In using Quelch's telephone, he had to take the chance of another master dropping in, unaware that Quelch was absent. But he certainly had not expected Hacker to drop in: there was a freezing coldness between the masters of the Shell and the Remove, and they never visited one another's studies. But there was Hacker—raging!

"I have caught you!" thundered Mr Hacker, advancing into the study. "You are here."

Harry Wharton breathed rather hard. It was against the rules, of course, for any fellow to use his master's telephone in the master's absence. But it was not a fearfully serious matter: no occasion for all this thunder. And it was not Hacker's business!

"I am here, Mr Hacker!" answered Harry, quietly, "What about it?"

"You young rascal—!"

"Oh, rot!" snapped Wharton, "I was going to use Mr Quelch's telephone. I should have asked leave if he had been in. I shall tell him so. You have no right to interfere, Mr Hacker."

"I knew that I should find you here!" panted Mr Hacker, "You—I know it was you who uttered that string of insults—."

"What do you mean?"

"Do you dare to deny that you have just called me up on the telephone in my study?" roared Mr Hacker.

Wharton blinked at him.

"Certainly I do," he answered, "I have not telephoned at all yet. I'm just going to, though."

"Upon my word!" gasped Mr Hacker, "Such effrontory ... such untruthfulness—such audacity! I have been insulted on the telephone—I find you here, with the receiver in your hand—and you have the audacity to deny—."

"Do you mean that somebody has been phoning you?" asked Wharton, quite bewildered, "It was not I. I have not used the phone yet."

"It is false!" thundered Mr Hacker.

Harry Wharton crimsoned.

"It is not false, and you have no right to say anything of the kind!" he retorted, "Now leave me alone, please."

"Wha-a-t?"

"Leave me alone!" snapped Wharton, "You can report to Mr Quelch, if you like, that you saw me using his phone—I shall tell him myself! If anybody's rung you up, I haven't the faintest idea who it was—I've come here to ring up a Highcliffe chap—!"

That was too much for Mr Hacker! Even a less suspicious man than Hacker, might have believed that he had caught his man, when he found the suspected junior actually standing at the telephone. Mr Hacker gazed round him, and grabbed up Quelch's cane, which lay on the table.

Cane in hand, he made a stride at the captain of the Remove. Quelch was out ... he could not hand over this young rascal to immediate justice: he was going to take the law into his own hands.

Harry Wharton dropped the receiver into place, and jumped away from the telephone as the Acid Drop came at him.

"Hands off!" he roared.

Swipe!

Harry Wharton barely dodged that swipe! It missed him by hardly an inch, as he cut round the study table.

Hacker glared at him across the table.

"Will you have a little sense, Mr Hacker!" shouted the captain of the Remove, "I tell you I have not telephoned to you—."

Hacker, by way of reply, reached across the table, and swiped again with Quelch's cane! Wharton jumped back, out of reach, and the cane landed on the table with a crash.

"You mad old ass!" roared Wharton. He was quite reckless of what he said now. "Will you stop playing the goat?"

Mr Hacker came round the table, with flaming face, and the cane uplifted for another swipe.

Harry Wharton dodged round swiftly, ahead of him. They changed sides of the table, the junior still out of reach.

"Rascal!" gasped Mr Hacker.

He rushed round! Wharton rushed round ahead. Again they changed sides of the study table.

Harry Wharton, certainly, was not going to be caned by the master of the Shell! He could hardly punch Hacker! All he could do was to dodge the infuriated Acid Drop—and that he did! He was a good deal nimbler than Hacker, and he had the best of that game of "Mulberry-bush".

Mr Hacker came to halt, panting for breath, and glaring at the junior across the table.

"You . . . you . . . you young rascal . . . you insolent young scoundrel—!" he panted.

"Oh, chuck it!" snapped Wharton, "I tell you I never phoned you! I know nothing about it! I—keep off, you old ass!"

He circled the table again, as Hacker came barging round. Once more they changed sides, and Hacker halted again, panting for breath.

Then, giving up the chase, he grasped the table, to pull it aside. Once that table was jammed against the wall, Wharton had no more chance of playing mulberry-bush round it!

But, as Hacker heaved at the heavy table, the captain of the Remove shot to the study door, which Hacker had left wide open.

He bounded out of the study: grasping the door-handle as he bounded, and dragging the door shut after him, with a bang.

"Stop!" shrieked Mr Hacker.

He let go the table and jumped at the door. The moment after it had banged, he had hold of the door-handle inside, and was pulling.

But the door did not open. Harry Wharton was holding the handle on the outside! He had no idea of being chased down the passage by a swiping cane! He held on to the door with all his strength.

Inside Hacker pulled and pulled!

"Let go that door!" he roared.

Wharton held on!

In a foaming state, the Acid Drop put his cane under his arm, and grasped the door-handle with both hands. He braced himself for a tug, and put all his beef into it.

That tug was too much for the junior outside! The door began to give! Harry Wharton let go, suddenly!

The door flew open, and Mr Hacker was exerting all his strength in a terrific tug! Hacker was not prepared for that! He went over backwards, letting go the door-handle, and sprawling at full length on Mr Quelch's study carpet. He landed with a terrific crash.

"Oh!" came a roar from Hacker, as he landed, "Oooogh! Oh!"

Harry Wharton did not wait!

He went down the passage, as if it had been the cinder-path. He was out of the House, before Mr Hacker was on his feet. And when he was on his feet, Mr Hacker was not feeling equal to further action. He was a bony gentleman, and his bones had hit Quelch's floor hard—he had an ache in every bone. The Acid Drop was left gurgling, and rubbing aching places, when Harry Wharton, flushed and breathless, joined his friends in the quad.

"HALLO, hallo, hallo! What's up?" exclaimed Bob Cherry.

That something was "up" was very clear to the Co, as the captain of the Remove joined them. They all looked at him inquiringly.

"Hacker!" answered Harry.

"Is the esteemed and absurd Hacker on the war-path again?" asked Hurree Jamset Ram Singh.

"Haven't you phoned to Highcliffe?" asked Nugent.

"No: the Acid Drop butted in! Let's get out."

"It's near tea-time!" said Johnny Bull, "What do you want to go out for?"

Wharton shrugged his shoulders.

"I don't want to have to punch Hacker's nose in the quad!" he answered. "But it may come to that, if he comes after me again."

"Oh my hat! But what—?"

"Let's get out, and give him time to cool!" said Harry. "We can scrounge a tea at the bun-shop on Courtfield."

"Oh, all right."

The Famous Five went out of gates . . . four of them startled and puzzled, and a little alarmed. Trouble between the captain of the Remove, and the master of the Shell, had been incessant, that term: and now, evidently, there was more, and rather more serious. Certainly, it was judicious to keep out of the Acid Drop's way, if the punching of noses was a possibility!

"But what the thump has happened?" asked Bob Cherry, as the juniors left the gates, and walked up the Courtfield road.

Harry Wharton explained.

"It was all that fat ass, Bunter's fault," he concluded. "If I hadn't had to pick up all those papers, I should have been gone, before Hacker butted in. As it was, he caught me just as I was going to phone. He fancied that I had phoned already . . . it seems that somebody had."

"Somebody ragging him over the phone!" said Frank Nugent.

"That's it! Some Remove chap, I suppose . . . the whole form's fed up with Hacker! But I suppose it looked rather suspicious—seeing me standing there at Quelch's phone."

"What made him butt into Quelch's study at all?" asked Bob.

Harry Wharton laughed.

159

"Oh, I expect he thought of me first of all . . . he always does! He must have cut straight to Quelch's study . . . and he found me there! This means a row with Quelch—that ass who ragged Hacker, whoever he was, has landed me in the soup."

"Some japing ass on one of the school telephones, I suppose!" said Bob.

"I suppose so . . . Smithy, perhaps."

"Or perhapsfully not!" remarked Hurree Jamset Ram Singh, shaking his dusky head, "The last time the esteemed Hacker was ragged, we found out that it was the execrable Price of the Fifth—."

"Oh!" exclaimed Harry Wharton. His brow darkened. "I wonder if this is Price at that game again—as likely as not! It wouldn't be the first time that that Fifth-form cad has set Hacker on my track. I wonder—."

"Hallo, hallo, hallo!" ejaculated Bob Cherry, "Talk of rats and you hear them squeak! Here he comes."

From the direction of Courtfield, a cyclist came in sight on the road. It was Stephen Price, of the Fifth Form, riding back to the school.

Harry Wharton fixed his eyes on the bad hat of the Fifth, as he approached. He had not, at first, thought of Price: but as soon as the nabob mentioned the name, he guessed the truth at once.

"It was that cad!" he said, in a low voice, "He was phoning Hacker from the post-office in Courtfield—that's where he's been. Stop him."

"I say, we can't be sure—!" said Nugent.

"I'm sure enough! Get him off that bike."

Price of the Fifth, as he saw the bunch of juniors in the road, started a little. He put on speed, to get past them: perhaps anticipative of trouble. The Famous Five barred the way: and Wharton held up his hand.

"Stop!" he shouted.

Price did not stop: he ground at the pedals, and fairly flew. But he did not get past the juniors.

They parted, as the bike came whizzing out, but as it passed through the group, they grabbed Price on either side.

He was grabbed off the machine, which went curling and clattering over in the road: and Price bumped down in the dust, yelling.

The bicycle crashed by the roadside. Price sat up in the road, smothered with dust, and gasping for breath.

"You young hooligans!" he spluttered, "What do you mean? What—?" He staggered to his feet . . . the Famous Five in a circle round him.

"I called to you to stop!" said Harry, "As you didn't, we've stopped you! Where have you been?"

Price glared at him.

"You cheeky young rascal, what bizney is it of yours?" he snarled.

"Have you been to the post-office?"

"Find out."

"Have you been on the phone to Hacker at the school?"

Price did not answer that. He made a movement to back away towards his bicycle. But the circle of juniors barred him in.

"You're not getting away yet, you cur!" said the captain of the Remove, quietly, "I want my question answered."

"I haven't been to the post-office!" said Price, between his teeth. "Now let me pass, you young ruffians."

"You've landed me in more than one row with Hacker," said Wharton, "You're making use of the suspicious old goat, to pay off your rotten grudges. I licked you in your study for it, last time. Now I want to know if you've been at it again. Hacker had an insulting phone call from somebody, and he's put it down to me ... as usual! Where have you been?"

Price breathed hard.

"I know nothing about it—if you've been playing tricks on Hacker!" he said, "Now let me pass."

"You haven't answered my question."

"You cheeky young cad—."

"Cut that out! Where have you been?"......

BILLY BUNTER
a poem by Frank Richards

I say, you fellows! Now, don't make a noise,
You don't often hear such a musical voice.
I daresay you know
Who is speaking and so
It is needless to say
That it's William George Bunter who's speaking to-day.
The most popular fellow at Greyfriars School,
As everyone knows who is not quite a fool.
It's perfectly easy to prove
That they all love me in the Remove,
The Fourth Form, and Shell,
Other fellows as well
All think that I couldn't improve.

I'm Bunter, Billy Bunter,
They call me grub-hunter,
    And say that I snaffle the tarts,
But it's only their fun,
For the chaps, every one,
    Have taken me right to their hearts.

I say, you fellows! At games we are great,
We play up on every available date,
Billy Bunter's my name,
And footer's my game,
And it's not true at all
That the fellows mistake me, in play, for the ball!
'Tain't true that I stick like a wedge in a groove,
Twixt the posts, keeping goal for the Greyfriars Remove!
A fellow who says I am fat,
Is just talking out of his hat,
And fellows who snigger
At my graceful figure,
Are jealous, that's all: and that's that!

    I'm Bunter, Billy Bunter,
    They call me grub-hunter,
       And make out I snoop all the jam.
    But plenty to eat,
    And most of it sweet,
       Has made me the athlete I am!

I say, you fellows, don't listen to those
Who say that for tuck I've a bloodhound's keen nose.
When feeding in Hall,
I eat hardly at all,
They don't hear me yelping
For a sixth or a seventh or ninth or tenth helping.
I may trickle into the studies to tea,
One after another, perhaps two or three,
But a few eggs on toast,
Nine or ten at the most,
And a few pounds of cake,
Are all I can take,
And then I take leave of my host.

    I'm Bunter, Billy Bunter,
    They call me grub-hunter,
       And I'm delighted to stuff,
    But the truth is, you bet,
    That I'm always sharp set,
       For I never get quite half enough!

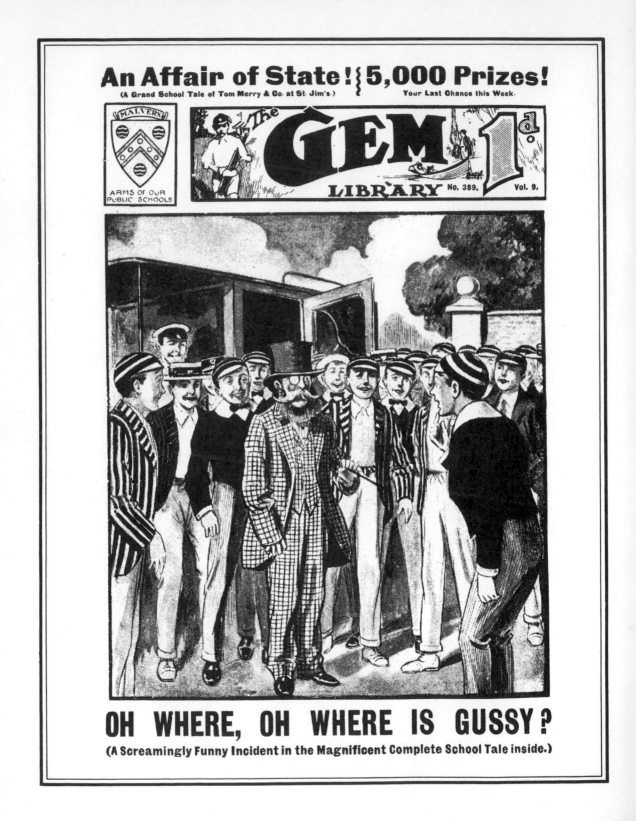

AT THE TOP OF THE TREE FOR BOYS' SCHOOL STORIES!

No. 759. Vol. XXII.

Week ending Aug. 26th, 1922.

The Magnet Library 1½d

WITH WHICH IS INCORPORATED
THE "GREYFRIARS HERALD."

This Week's Story: "THE TERROR TRACKED DOWN!" By Frank Richards.

HARRY WHARTON'S STRUGGLE FOR LIFE!

(A dramatic episode from the long complete school story in this issue.)

BILLY BUNTER'S REFORMATION!

A Grand Long Complete School Tale of Harry Wharton & Co.

The Magnet 1ᵈ Library

No. 460. Vol. 10.

DECEMBER 2nd, 1916.

BRAVO, BUNTER!

(An Amazing Scene in the Grand Long Complete Story in this Issue.)

"BOB CHERRY IN SEARCH OF HIS FATHER."

A Splendid, New, Long, Complete School Tale of the Chums of Greyfriars.

The Magnet 1ª Library

No. 179 | The Complete Story-Book for All. | Vol 5.

HOW BOB CHERRY'S FATHER WAITED FOR THE
JUNIORS OF GREYFRIARS SCHOOL!

In March 1940, in the third issue of Cyril Connolly's monthly 'review of literature and art', *Horizon*, tucked between a poem by W. H. Auden 'In Memory of Sigmund Freud' and an article by Howard Evans on 'the Communist Party and the Intellectuals', was an entertaining essay by George Orwell called 'Boys' Weeklies'. It was a critical survey of the schoolboy papers and comics, old and new, and it concentrated its attack on the ethos and style of *The Magnet* and *The Gem*. Orwell evoked their 'mental world' like this:

'The year is 1910– or 1940, but it is all the same. You are at Greyfriars, a rosy-cheeked boy of fourteen in posh tailor-made clothes, sitting down to tea in your study on the Remove passage after an exciting game of football which was won by an odd goal in the last half-minute. There is a cosy fire in the study, and outside the wind is whistling. The ivy clusters thickly round the old grey stones. The King is on his throne and the pound is worth a pound. Over in Europe the comic foreigners are jabbering and gesticulating, but the grim grey battleships of the British Fleet are steaming up the Channel and at the outposts of Empire the monocled Englishmen are holding the natives at bay. Lord Mauleverer has just got another fiver and we are all settling down to a tremendous tea of sausages, sardines, crumpets, potted meat, jam and doughnuts. After tea we shall sit round the study fire having a good laugh at Billy Bunter and discussing the team for next week's match against Rookwood. Everything is safe, solid and unquestionable. Everything will be the same for ever and ever.'

It was an effective evocation and the essay made some telling points, as well as a few elementary errors of fact. In the May issue of *Horizon*, Frank Richards answered Orwell's attack.

FRANK RICHARDS REPLIES TO GEORGE ORWELL

THE Editor has kindly given me space to reply to Mr Orwell, whose article on Boys' Weeklies appeared in *Horizon* No. 3. Mr Orwell's article is a rather remarkable one to appear in a periodical of this kind. From the fact that *Horizon* contains a picture that does not resemble a picture, a poem that does not resemble poetry, and a story that does not resemble a story, I conclude that it must be a very high-browed paper indeed: and I was agreeably surprised, therefore, to find in it an article written in a lively and entertaining manner, and actually readable. I was still more interested as this article dealt chiefly with my work as an author for boys. Mr Orwell perpetrates so many inaccuracies, however, and flicks off his condemnation with so careless a hand, that I am glad of an opportunity to set him right on a few points. He reads into my very innocent fiction a fell scheme for drugging the minds of the younger proletariat into dull acquiescence in a system of which Mr Orwell does not approve: and of which, in consequence, he cannot imagine anyone else approving except from interested motives. Anyone who disagrees with Mr Orwell is necessarily either an antiquated ass or an exploiter on the make! His most serious charge against my series is that it smacks of the year 1910: a period which Mr Orwell appears to hold in peculiar horror. Probably I am older than Mr Orwell: and I can tell him that the world went very well then. It has not been improved by the Great War, the General Strike, the outbreak of sex-chatter, by make-up or lipstick, by the present discontents, or by Mr Orwell's thoughts upon the present discontents! But Mr Orwell not only reads a diehard dunderheaded Tory into a harmless author for boys:

he accuses him of plagiarism, of snobbishness, of being out of date, even of cleanliness of mind, as if that were a sin also. I propose to take Mr Orwell's indictment charge by charge, rebutting the same one after another, excepting the last, to which I plead guilty. After which I expect to receive from Mr Orwell a telegram worded like that of the invader of Sind.

To begin with the plagiarism. 'Probably', says Mr Orwell '*The Magnet* owes something to Gunby Hadath, Desmond Coke, and the rest.' Frank Richards had never read Desmond Coke till the nineteen-twenties: he had never read Gunby Hadath—whoever Gunby Hadath may be—at all. 'Even the name of the chief comic among the Greyfriars masters, Mr Prout, is taken from Stalky and Co.', declares Mr Orwell. Now, it is true that there is a formmaster at Greyfriars named Prout, and there is a housemaster in Stalky named Prout. It is also true that *The Magnet* author is named Richards: and that there is a Richards in Stalky and Co. But the Fifth-form master at Greyfriars no more derives from the Stalky Prout, than *The Magnet* author from the Stalky Richards. Stalky's Prout is a 'gloomy ass', worried, dubious, easily worked on by others. The Greyfriars Prout is portly, self-satisfied, impervious to the opinions of others. No two characters could be more unlike. Mr Prout of Greyfriars is a very estimable gentleman: and characters in a story, after all, must have names. Every name in existence has been used over and over again in fiction.

The verb 'to jape', says Mr Orwell, is also taken from Stalky. Mr Orwell is so very modern, that I cannot suspect him of having read anything so out of date as Chaucer. But if he will glance into that obsolete author, he will find 'jape' therein, used in precisely the same sense. 'Frabjous' also, it seems, is borrowed from Stalky! Has Mr Orwell never read 'Alice'? 'Frabjous', like 'chortle' and 'burble', derives from Lewis Carroll. Innumerable writers have borrowed 'frabjous' and 'chortle'—I believe Frank Richards was the first to borrow 'burble', but I am not sure of this: such expressions, once in existence, become part of the language and are common property.

'Sex', says Mr Orwell, 'is completely tabu'. Mr Noel Coward, in his autobiography, is equally amused at the absence of the sex-motif in *The Magnet* series.* But what would Mr Orwell have? *The Magnet* is intended chiefly for readers up to sixteen: though I am proud to know that it has readers of sixty! It is read by girls as well as boys. Would it do these children good, or harm, to turn their thoughts to such matters? Sex, certainly, does enter uncomfortably into the experience of the adolescent. But surely the less he thinks about it, at an early age, the better. I am aware that, in these 'modern' days, there are people who think that children should be told things which in my own childhood no small person was ever allowed to hear. I disagree with this entirely. My own opinion is that such people generally suffer from disordered digestions, which cause their minds to take a nasty turn. They fancy they are 'realists', when they are only obscene. They go grubbing in the sewers for their realism, and refuse to believe in the grass and flowers above ground—which, nevertheless, are equally real! Moreover, this 'motif' does not play so stupendous a part in real life, among healthy and wholesome people, as these 'realists' imagine. If Mr Orwell supposes that the average Sixth-form boy cuddles a parlour-maid as often as he handles a cricket-bat, Mr Orwell is in error.

Drinking and smoking and betting, says Mr Orwell, are represented as 'shady', but at the same time 'irresistibly fascinating'. If Mr Orwell will do me the honour of looking over a few numbers of *The Magnet*, he will find that such ways are invariably described as 'dingy'—even the 'bad hats' are a little ashamed of them: even Billy Bunter, though he will smoke a cigarette if he can get one for nothing, is described as being, though an ass, not ass enough to spend his money on such things. I submit that the adjective 'dingy' is not equivalent to the adjective 'fascinating'.

Mr Orwell finds it difficult to believe that a series running for thirty years can possibly have been written by one and the same person. In the presence of such authority, I speak with diffidence: and can only say that, to the best of my knowledge and belief, I am only one person, and have never been two or three.

'Consequently,' says Mr Orwell, cheerfully proceeding from erroneous premises to a still more erroneous conclusion, 'they must be written in a style that is easily imitated.' On this point, I may say that I could hardly count the number of authors who have striven to imitate Frank Richards, not one of whom

---

* 'They were awfully manly, decent fellows, Harry Wharton and Co, and no suggestion of sex, even in its lighter forms, ever sullied their conversation. Considering their ages, their healthy-mindedness was almost frightening.' Noel Coward in *Present Indicative*, 1937.

has been successful. The style, whatever its merits or demerits, is my own, and—if I may say it with due modesty—inimitable. Nobody has ever written like it before, and nobody will ever write like it again. Many have tried; but as Dryden—an obsolete poet, Mr Orwell—has remarked:

The builders were with want of genius curst,
The second building was not like the first.

Mr Orwell mentions a number of other papers, which—egregiously—he classes with *The Magnet*. These papers, with the exception of *The Gem*, are not in the same class. They are not in the same street. They are hardly in the same universe. With *The Magnet*, it is not a case of *primus inter pares*: it is a case of the Eclipse first and the rest nowhere. Mr Orwell in effect admits this. He tells us, quite correctly, that Billy Bunter is a 'real creation': that he is a 'first-rate character': that he is 'one of the best-known in English fiction'. He tells us that in *The Magnet* the 'characters are so carefully graded, as to give every type of reader a character he can identify himself with'. I suggest that an author who can do this is not easily imitated. It is not so easy as Mr Orwell supposes. It cannot be acquired: only the born story-teller can do it. Shakespeare could do it as no man ever did it before or since. Dickens could do it. Thackeray could not do it. Scott, with all his genius, could only give us historical suits of clothes with names attached. Can Bernard Shaw make a character live? Could Ibsen or Tchekov? To the highbrow, I know, a writer need only have a foreign name, to be a genius: and the more unpronounceable the name, the greater the genius. These duds—yes, Mr Orwell, Frank Richards really regards Shaw, Ibsen, and Tchekov, as duds—these duds would disdain to draw a schoolboy. Billy Bunter, let us admit, is not so dignified a character as an imbecile Russian, or a nerve-racked Norwegian. But, as a nineteenth-century writer, whom Mr Orwell would not deign to quote, remarked, 'I would rather have a Dutch peasant by Teniers that His Majesty's head on a signpost'.

Mr Orwell accuses Frank Richards of snobbishness: apparently because he makes an aristocratic character act as an aristocrat should. Now, although Mr Orwell may not suspect it, the word 'aristocrat' has not wholly lost its original Greek meaning. It is an actual fact that, in this country at least, noblemen generally are better fellows than commoners. My own acquaintance with titled Nobs is strictly limited; but it is my experience, and I believe everybody's, that—excepting the peasant-on-the-land class, which is the salt of the earth—the higher up you go in the social scale the better you find the manners, and the more fixed the principles. The fact that old families almost invariably die out in the long run is proof of this: they cannot and will not do the things necessary for survival. All over the country, old estates are passing into new hands. Is this because Sir George up at the Hall is inferior to Mr Thompson from the City—or otherwise? Indeed, Mr Thompson himself is improved by being made a lord. Is it not a fact that, when a title is bestowed on some hard man of business, it has an ameliorating effect on him—that he reacts unconsciously to his new state, and becomes rather less of a Gradgrind, rather more a man with a sense of his social responsibilities? Everyone must have observed this. The founder of a new family follows, at a distance, in the footsteps of the old families; and every day and in every way becomes better and better! It was said of old that the English nation dearly loves a lord. The English nation, in that as in other things, is wiser than its highbrowed instructors. Really, Mr Orwell, is it snobbish to give respect where respect is due: or should an author, because he doesn't happen to be a peer himself, inspire his readers with envy, hatred, malice, and all uncharitableness?

But Mr Orwell goes on to say that the working-classes enter only as comics and semi-villains. This is sheer perversity on Mr Orwell's part. Such misrepresentation would not only be bad manners, but bad business. Every paper desiring a wide circulation must circulate, for the greater part, among the working-classes, for the simple reason that they form nine-tenths of the population. A paper that is so fearfully aristocratic that it is supported only by marquises and men-servants must always go the way of the *Morning Post*. *Horizon*, I do not doubt, has a circle of readers with the loftiest brows; but I do doubt whether Sir John Simon will bother it very much for the sinews of war. Indeed, I have often wondered how so many young men with expansive foreheads and superior smiles contrive to live at all on bad prose and worse poetry. Directors, editors, and authors, must live: and they cannot live by insulting the majority of their public. If Frank Richards were the snob Mr Orwell believes him to be, he would still conceal that weakness very carefully when writing for *The Magnet*. But a man can believe that the 'tenth possessor of a foolish face' has certain qualities lacking in the first possessor of a sly brain, without being a snob. I am very pleased to be an author, and I think I would rather be an author than a nobleman; but I am not fool enough to think that an author is of such national importance as a farmer or a farm labourer. Workmen can, and often do, get on quite well without authors; but no author could continue to exist without the workmen. They are not only the backbone of the nation: they *are* the nation: all other classes being merely trimmings. The best and noblest-minded man I ever knew was a simple wood-cutter. I would like Mr Orwell to indicate a single sentence in which Frank Richards refers disrespect-fully to the people who keep him in comfort. There are three working-class boys in the Greyfriars Remove; Mr Orwell mentions all three by name: each one is represented as being liked and respected by the other boys; each in turn has been selected as the special hero of a series: and Mr Orwell must have used a very powerful microscope to detect anything comic or semi-villainous in them.

It is true that if I introduce a public-house loafer, I do not make him a baronet: and the billiard-marker does not wear an old school tie. But something, surely, is due to reality: especially as Mr Orwell is such a realist. If Mr Orwell has met public-house loafers who are baronets, or billiard-markers wearing the old school tie, I have never had a similar experience.

Of strikes, slumps, unemployment, etc., complains Mr Orwell, there is no mention. But are these really subjects for young people to meditate upon? It is true that we live in an insecure world: but why should not youth feel as secure as possible? It is true that burglars break into houses: but what parent in his senses would tell a child that a masked face may look in at the nursery window! A boy of fifteen or sixteen is on the threshold of life: and life is a tough pro-position; but will he be better prepared for it by telling him how tough it may possibly be? I am sure that the reverse is the case. Gray—another obsolete poet, Mr Orwell!—tells us that sorrows never come too late, and happiness too swiftly flies. Let youth be happy, or as happy as possible. Happiness is the best preparation for misery, if misery must come. At least, the poor kid will have had something! He may, at twenty, be hunting for a job and not finding it—why should his fifteenth year be clouded by worrying about that in advance? He may, at thirty, get the sack—why tell him so at twelve? He may, at forty, be

a wreck on Labour's scrap-heap—but how will it benefit him to know that at fourteen? Even if making miserable children would make happy adults, it would not be justifiable. But the truth is that the adult will be all the more miserable if he was miserable as a child. Every day of happiness, illusory or otherwise—and most happiness is illusory—is so much to the good. It will help to give the boy confidence and hope. Frank Richards tells him that there are some splendid fellows in a world that is, after all, a decent sort of place. He likes to think himself like one of these fellows, and is happy in his day-dreams. Mr Orwell would have him told that he is a shabby little blighter, his father an ill-used serf, his world a dirty, muddled, rotten sort of show. I don't think it would be fair play to take his twopence for telling him that!

Now about patriotism: an affronting word to Mr Orwell. I am aware, of course, that the really 'modern' highbrow is an 'idiot who praises with enthusiastic tone, all centuries but this, and every country but his own'. Why should not a fellow feel proud of things in which a just pride may be taken? I have lived in many countries, and talked in several languages: and found something to esteem in every country I have visited. But I have never seen any nation the equal of my own. Actually, such is my belief, Mr Orwell!

The basic political assumptions, Mr Orwell goes on, are two: that nothing ever changes, and that foreigners are funny. Well, the French have a proverb that the more a thing changes, the more it is just the same. Temporary mutations are mistaken for great changes—as they always were. Decency seems to have gone—but it will come in again, and there will be a new generation of men who do not talk and write muck, and women with clean faces. Progress, I believe, goes on: but it moves to slow time. No real change is perceptible in the course of a single lifetime. But even if changes succeeded one another with kaleidoscopic rapidity, the writer for young people should still endeavour to give his young readers a sense of stability and solid security, because it is good for them, and makes for happiness and peace of mind.

As for foreigners being funny, I must shock Mr Orwell by telling him that foreigners *are* funny. They lack the sense of humour which is the special gift of our own chosen nation: and people without a sense of humour are always unconsciously funny. Take Hitler, for example,—with his swastika, his 'good

German sword', his fortifications named after characters from Wagner, his military coat that he will never take off till he marches home victorious: and the rest of his fripperies out of the property-box. In Germany they lap this up like milk, with the most awful seriousness; in England, the play-acting ass would be laughed out of existence. Take Mussolini—can anyone imagine a fat man in London talking the balderdash that Benito talks in Rome to wildly-cheering audiences without evoking, not wild cheers, but inextinguishable laughter? But is *il Duce* regarded as a mountebank in Italy? Very far from it. I submit to Mr Orwell that people who take their theatricals seriously *are* funny. The fact that Adolf Hitler is deadly dangerous does not make him less comic.

But what I dislike most is Mr Orwell telling me that I am out of date. Human nature, Mr Orwell, is dateless. A character that lives is always up to date. If, as Mr Orwell himself says, a boy in 1940 can identify himself with a boy in *The Magnet*, obviously that boy in *The Magnet* is a boy of 1940.

But it is quite startling to see what Mr Orwell regards as up to date. The one theme that is really new, quoth he, is the scientific one—death-rays, Martian invasions, invisible men, interplanetary rockets, and so on. Oh, my Hat! if Mr Orwell will permit that obsolete expression. This kind of thing was done, and done to death, when I was a small boy; long before *The Magnet* was born or thought of. Before I reached the age of unaided reading, a story was read to me by an elder brother, in which bold travellers hiked off to the moon packed inside a big bullet discharged from a tremendous gun. The greatest of submarine stories—Jules Verne's 20,000 *Leagues*—was published before I was born. The Martians invaded earth, while I was still mewling and puking in the nurse's arms. In the nursery I knew the Invisible Man, though his invisibility was then due to a cloak of darkness. More than twenty years ago I wrote a death-ray story myself: but did not fancy that it was a new idea; even then it had an ancient and fish-like smell. Some of my earliest reading was of flying: there was a strenuous character in those days, who sailed the skies in what he called an 'aeronef'; a direct descendant, I think, of Verne's *Clipper of the Clouds* of twenty years earlier: and Verne, I fancy, had read *Peter Wilkins* of seventy years earlier still; and I believe that the author of *Peter Wilkins* had not disdained to pick up a tip or two from Swift's writings in the eighteenth century. Did not Lucian tell them something about a trip to the moon in the second century? The oldest flying story I have read was written in Greek about three thousand years ago; but I don't suppose it was the earliest: I have no doubt that when they finish sorting over the Babylonian bricks they will find a flying story somewhere among the ruins, and very likely a death-ray and an invisible man keeping it company. If this stuff is new, Mr Orwell, what is old?

To conclude, Mr Orwell hopes that a boys' paper with a Left-wing bias may not be impossible. I hope that it is, and will remain, impossible. Boys' minds ought not to be disturbed and worried by politics. Even if I were a Socialist, or a Communist, I should still consider it the duty of a boys' author to write without reference to such topics: because his business is to entertain his readers, make them as happy as possible, give them a feeling of cheerful security, turn their thoughts to healthy pursuits, and above all to keep them away from unhealthy introspection, which in early youth can do only harm. If there is a Tchekov among my readers, I fervently hope that the effect of *The Magnet* will be to turn him into a Bob Cherry!

A DICTIONARY OF FRANK RICHARDS SCHOOLBOY SLANG

Bags:	Trousers
Beak:	A master
Blubber:	Cry
Bone:	Take without asking
Book:	A punishment involving the copying out of an entire book
Cheese it:	Shut up
Chokey:	Prison
Clobber:	Clothes
Con:	Construe and/or translate
Cuff:	Hit
Dic:	Dictionary
Doorsteps and dish-water:	School tea
Extra:	A punishment involving extra work out of school hours
Fist:	Handwriting
Funky:	Frightened
Gammon:	Nonsense
Impot:	An imposition—a punishment involving the writing out of lines
Jaw:	A telling-off
Jigger:	Bicycle
Jip:	Pain and/or anger and irritation
Lick:	Beat
Lip:	Cheek or impertinence
Napper:	The Headmaster
Oof:	Money
Pre:	Prefect
Prep:	Preparation—set work
Rag:	A practical joke or jape
Rhino:	Money
Sanny:	Sanatorium
Scrap:	Fight
Scrog:	Food
Stickers:	Sweets
Stuff:	Tell a lie
Trans:	Translation
Waxy:	Bad tempered
Whops:	Strokes of the cane

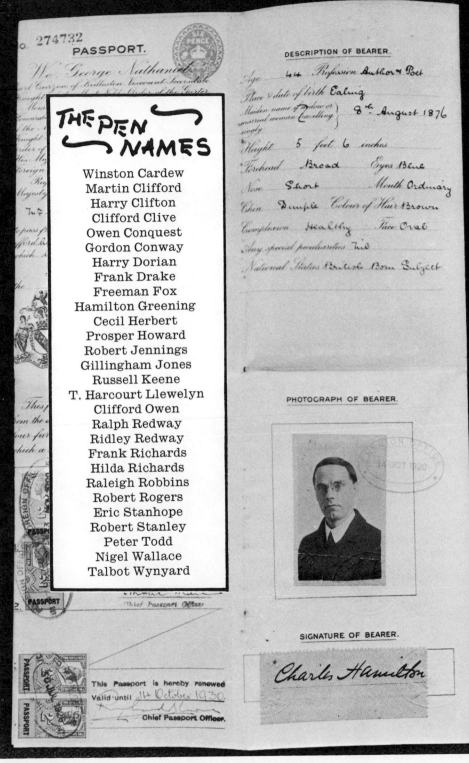

No. 274732

PASSPORT.

We, George Nathaniel...

THE PEN NAMES

Winston Cardew
Martin Clifford
Harry Clifton
Clifford Clive
Owen Conquest
Gordon Conway
Harry Dorian
Frank Drake
Freeman Fox
Hamilton Greening
Cecil Herbert
Prosper Howard
Robert Jennings
Gillingham Jones
Russell Keene
T. Harcourt Llewelyn
Clifford Owen
Ralph Redway
Ridley Redway
Frank Richards
Hilda Richards
Raleigh Robbins
Robert Rogers
Eric Stanhope
Robert Stanley
Peter Todd
Nigel Wallace
Talbot Wynyard

DESCRIPTION OF BEARER.

Age 44 Profession Author & Poet

Place & date of birth Ealing

Maiden name of widow or married woman (travelling singly) 8th August 1876

Height 5 feet 6 inches

Forehead Broad Eyes Blue

Nose Short Mouth Ordinary

Chin Dimple Colour of Hair Brown

Complexion Healthy Face Oval

Any special peculiarities Nil

National Status British Born Subject

PHOTOGRAPH OF BEARER.

SIGNATURE OF BEARER.

Charles Hamilton

This Passport is hereby renewed
Valid until 14 October 1930.
Chief Passport Officer.

ACKNOWLEDGEMENTS

Every one of the pieces in this book, both the published and the unpublished, has been selected from the vast library of material supplied to me by Mrs Una Hamilton Wright, Frank Richards' niece and literary executor. Without her kind cooperation there would have been no book. My debt to her and to her agent, Mrs Hope Leresche, is overwhelming.

Every one of the illustrations in this book, except for the stills from the Billy Bunter television series, and the photographs on pages 86, 94 and 95 has been supplied by the Charles Hamilton Museum in Maidstone. My debt to the Museum, and to its hospitable founder and curator, John Wernham, is equally overwhelming.

I am also enormously grateful to the BBC for permission to reproduce the Bunter TV stills, to IPC for permission to reproduce copyright material, and to John Chandos, Eric Fayne, Philip Ingram and George MacBeth for their generous help. The picture on page 86 is reproduced by kind permission of the Raymond Mander and John Mitchenson Theatre Collection and those on pages 94 and 95 of the Keystone Press Agency and Syndication International.

Of the previously published material, *Hard Lines!*, *Billy Bunter's Boundary* and *Just Like Bessie Bunter* first appeared in editions of *Billy Bunter's Own* published by the Oxonhoath Press in the 1950s. *An Interview with Mr Martin Clifford* and *The Case of the Perplexed Painter* first appeared in *Tom Merry's Annual* and *Tom Merry's Own*, both published by Mandeville Publications in the late 1940s. *The New Master* first appeared in *Picture Fun* in 1911, Frank Richards' reply to George Orwell originally appeared in *Horizon* in 1940, the poem 'Who Would Not Love to Wander' first appeared in *The Autobiography of Frank Richards* (Charles Skilton, 1952) and the song 'On the Ball' was originally published by Stanford & Co. in 1914 and was set to music by Percy Harrison, Mrs Una Hamilton Wright's father.

When dealing with an author as prolific as Frank Richards, whose work was published by scores of publishers over almost seventy years, it is difficult to be certain that owners of copyright have been traced and acknowledged in every case. It is even difficult to be sure that what I have taken to be ur-Richards may not, in some instances, be the work of subtle substitute writers—the hapless 'imposters' Richards so despised. I can only hope that any such errors of omission or commission will be forgiven.

G.B.